Every day, a choice he made when he left for nursing school haunts Peter Gunderson. Now he's leaving his career and returning home to his family's farm.

Home where the girl next door still resides in his heart.

Olivia Olson doesn't let a little thing like being born without a hand slow her down. She's a strong independent woman.

Until she's not.

She can't seem to get her life figured out.

Nothing she chooses seems to be the right fit.

When she and Peter join to search for her bio mom, she discovers both a joy too wonderful to express and a reality too difficult to grasp.

As friendship blossoms into more, they discover the hidden layers and depths of who they are.

Together, Peter and Olivia navigate an adoption journey in which the power of love and miracle of faith promise hope and healing.

I0629359

The Way to My Heart

A FRIENDS TO LOVERS ROMANCE

MERCY
BOOK THREE

JAN JOHNSON

FARMHOUSE
PUBLISHING

What people are saying...

"Your books are darling and I love how you totally paint a picture with details that draw me in."

"Being a retired nurse, I thoroughly enjoyed Jan's books. I loved all the medical humor, it was very realistic as to what we deal with in the hospital. This book had me laughing in one chapter and crying in the next. I would highly recommend it to women of all ages.

I look forward to reading the entire series."

"From the first few paragraphs, the writer's style drew me into this romantic tale. I couldn't put it down. The details, the personality of the main character and the fizzled romance were delicious. The author also led you along, each chapter ending with "will they, or won't they get together again?"

I highly recommend picking up this book, for a romantic escape."

The Way to My Heart

Published 2024

Farmhouse Publications

94436 Mustonen Rd

Brownsmead, Oregon 97103

ISBN: 979-8-9873185-3-9

E-ISBN: 979-8-9873185-2-2

"Before I formed you in the womb I knew you.
Before you were born, I set you apart."
Jeremiah 1:5

Also by Jan Johnson

MEMOIR
   I Will Enter His Gates: A Walk With God

MERCY ROMANCE SERIES
   My Heart's for You
   Windows of My Heart
   The Way to My Heart

HOLIDAY
   Mistletoe @ Christmas Tree Lodge

Chapter One

Peter Gunderson's fingers held the top of his locker door, resting on the cold grey metal, hesitant to let go. His eyes searched the empty space one last time. He removed the Yoda sticker from the door and latched it shut. A grin crept onto his face as *that log had a child* snuck into his mind, and he whistled a few bars.

The *We'll-Miss-You* sign, colored in by Kaitlyn Monroe and Tina Halverson was taped to the wall. Peter's lips formed a sad smile as his eyes slid over the various items he'd become so familiar with over the last three years—stethoscopes, blood pressure cuffs, IV poles, syringes. All symbols of times of caring. Times of pranks. Peter swallowed the lump in his throat.

Daniel Wright pulled him close, his elbow crooked around Peter's neck.

"Stay out of trouble!"

Daniel released him.

Like he was going to get into any trouble now without the Invincibles.

He pulled off his name tag and key card and laid them next to his vocera on his supervisor's desk.

"You know they'll always take you back. You know, like if you change your mind," Kaitlyn said.

Peter's left eyebrow hitched up as he thought back to the many mistakes he had made in the past three years. *Nah, taking him back was never going to happen.*

He shrugged his Carhartt jacket on over his scrubs which were covered in John Deere tractors that Kaitlyn's mom had made for him, and started down the hall.

"Game night at my house Tuesday," Tina called. He turned and gave her a slight nod, knowing that that part of his life was behind him.

OUTSIDE PETER LOOKED up one last time at the lit Mercy Hospital sign, placed his helmet on his head and straddled his motorcycle. He started his old friend and sped away.

He needed to get home to his mom. Her fibromyalgia was preventing her from the passions of her life, and he wasn't going to let anything interfere with his being there for her.

This time.

HE SPED down I-5 thankful that it wasn't raining, and traffic was light. What could he have done for her, really, when their house burned down? He had been finishing his final studies for the NCLEX, at the time and there was no way he could leave. That exam was key to his acceptance as an RN. At least that's what he thought at the time. And it had plagued him ever since.

Well, now he'd make up for it. She'd see.

THE SUMMER SUN had dried the soil around the farm, causing dust to fly as Olivia hopped off her four-wheeler. As she dusted off her jeans, her phone vibrated in her pocket. She glanced at the screen. Peter's goofy face, his bangs falling over his eyes, his crooked smile.

I'm coming home

Huh? He hadn't been home in over a year. More than that, come to think of it. Had she forgotten about some important occasion coming up?

for the weekend?

Nope. For good

is this a surprise?

Kinda

Olivia scanned the five-acre flower field, her pink baseball cap shielding her eyes from the bright sun.

"Evelyn?"

"Over here, Olivia." Peter's mom had blonde hair which was covered with a straw hat, and she held pruners in gloved hands. As Olivia made her way through the tall dahlia stalks, she took in the beauty of the plethora of varieties and colors—dianthus with petals between soft pink and shades of purple, the sweet-spicy smell of pink stock, red peonies, round and full. All soaking up the July sun and waiting to make someone smile.

"I'm so glad you're here. I could use some help. These dahlias need to be deadheaded."

The mixture of fragrances wove an olfactory tapestry. Olivia snagged the pair of pruners from the hip pocket of her overalls and started clipping. The fading pinks and yellows towered above her five-foot five frame. She gazed across the long rows of breathtaking beauty, envious of the skill established in the field. She was okay with digging holes and throwing in some bulbs. But what happened after that was anyone's guess.

Evelyn had such talent with things that grew. And everyone in the valley knew it. They came from miles around for photo shoots and to buy her beautiful blooms and produce. Gunderson Farms had even been listed online as one of the top Oregon growers.

Evelyn's head jerked. "Why are the chickens squawking? Seems like they're all riled up."

Olivia turned to look and saw that the chickens were running and had scattered everywhere. A loose pig ran through them, with their border collie, Zip, on his heels.

"Oh no! I'll take care of it."

Olivia pocketed her clippers and ran toward the wayward animal. She gave a whistle, and Zip crouched low. The pig stopped, put his head down to snuffle in the grass. She walked towards him, one slow, quiet step at a time, but as soon as he saw her, he was off again, followed by the border collie, crouching down to herd the wayward pig.

"Zip, you're worthless when it comes to pigs!"

Jake Miller rounded the corner.

"Hey, what's going on? Here, let me help you!"

Her boyfriend ran towards them and stopped outside the fence. She walked slowly towards the back of the pig hoping he'd stay there a moment longer. The pig snorted as his nose grubbed in the grass. She lunged and grabbed its hind leg, skidding along behind him. Jake strode over, his muscular shoulders taut and ready.

"Here, I've got him," he said.

She gave him a look that would cause a ripe cornstalk to instantly shrivel. It was enough to make him hold up his hands in surrender.

PETER PULLED up and parked in the driveway. He removed his helmet and replaced it with a ball cap. The smell of fresh cut hay caught his attention. In the distance, he could see his father on the

John Deere slowly making his way in circles, the mower leaving cut golden alfalfa laying strewn behind it.

He remembered sitting on that tractor on his dad's lap, learning the ways of the machine.

"You start the engine like this," his dad would say. "Be careful not to—" Peter never noticed the combined smell of motor oil and sweat—it was the essence of his dad.

He was allowed to choose the music in the glassed-in cab—Raffi or sometimes KidSongs. His dad would change the words and sing *Bumping up and down in our big green tractor, til our work is done.* The tractor hummed its way through the fields.

Peter's gaze traveled from the field to the greenhouse next to the cooling room where buckets of flowers were sorted and stored, ready for his mom's stand at the weekly produce market. Peter had been glad there had been a commotion and no one had noticed as he approached. This way he could surprise his mom. He scanned the flower field and saw Evelyn's sunhat. She still had that? He had given it to her for a Mother's Day gift when she had turned forty. That was ten years ago, the fall he had left for college.

It took only a few steps towards the squawks to realize what all the turmoil was about.

Olivia. Right where he would expect her to be—in the middle of some pandemonium. He watched the pig scenario. Zip squatting on the ground, black ears laid back and his eyes eager. Olivia grabbing the pig's hind leg with her good arm as it squealed to high heaven. Jake jumping in to save the damsel. Olivia giving him that look. Jake holding up both hands in surrender, frowning and shaking his head.

He turned back to the flower field. From beneath his baseball cap, Peter looked out over the field. Seeing his mom standing between two rows of red and purple mums, he snuck up behind her and put his arms around her waist. She jumped and turned.

"Peter! What are you doing here?" She grabbed hold of his

forearms. "You have time off? What's the occasion? We haven't seen you since forever!"

"Hi Mama." He grinned. "More than a day off. I quit my job today and am going to stay here and help you and Dad out."

She waved her hand like she was swatting flies.

"You quit your job? Why in the world would you do that? Nursing is a good job!"

"Yeah, I know. But trust me, the patients will be better off without me. I wasn't really cut out for it. I'll be better off being here with you guys taking some of the load off your shoulders."

He moved his hands to her shoulders, holding her eyes.

"And you and I both know that your health isn't that great. I want to be here to help you do as much as you can, so you're not overwhelmed."

"Does Ross know you're here?"

Peter squinched up his nose, making his eyes wrinkle.

"Okay—so obviously you and your dad have been scheming. Well, judging by the sun, it must be getting close to dinner time. Let's go see what we can rustle up."

Chapter Two

"**M**en!" Olivia leaned her hip against the pig pen with her hip and latched the gate.

She did not need to be rescued. She was a strong independent woman. If there's something she couldn't accomplish, she'd ask.

She reached over and scratched the top of the pig's head before it snuffled away. Animals were so much easier to be around than people. They didn't hold expectations. Or jump in to try to *fix* things. She reached out and gently picked up the grey kitty that walked the top of the fence towards her.

"Hello, Miss Molly. What did you think of all that chaos?"

She snugged the soft, thick fur under her neck. Molly purred and her sandpaper tongue licked her chin.

"See, you don't care if I've only got one hand."

Olivia had never known life with two hands. Really never thought about it. That is, unless someone thought she needed them and stepped in to rescue her. Or taunt her.

"I do alright on my own, don't you think? I certainly don't need some guy stepping in thinking they're *all that*. Gotta put you down now sweet kitty."

The cat jumped out of her arms and ran between the hay bales.

Olivia had looked for the rest of the litter when she found the tiny, scraggly kitten taking shelter from the pouring rain under the deck. She never found the rest of the litter or the mama cat. She had put the shaking little thing into a shoebox, lined with an old flannel pillowcase and fed it with the tiniest baby bottle, one droplet at a time until it gained strength.

Olivia settled onto the four-wheeler.

Working at her neighbor's farm had been a godsend. Olivia's last job ended surreptitiously coinciding with Peter's dad, Ross asking her to help Evelyn out at the farm. Saying yes was an easy choice. She wasn't a stranger to this place. After all, she'd spent many hours here hanging out with Peter and his family. And this job gave her the flexibility to study for her accounting courses, which would lead to a job with benefits. A job that should make her parents happy. She had thought of all sorts of jobs she could do —barista, technical support hotline, fitness trainer, marketing specialist. In the end, she chose accounting. It was solid and safe.

She pulled up in front of the home where she grew up. The single-story white house had four pillars framing the entrance. Large picture windows provided a view of the Gunderson farm. Her dad rode the riding lawn mower, earbuds in, presumably listening to one of his favorite podcasts—*Stuff You Should Know* or *This American Life*. He always kept the lawn manicured and the bordering boxwoods, azaleas and hydrangeas trimmed and weed free.

It might be time to start thinking about moving out of her parents' home. She was, after all, turning twenty-nine soon.

And Peter. He was coming home? They were close growing up, but when he left for nursing school, it seemed he had pretty much forgotten about his family. She had relayed his occasional texts or snapchats to Evelyn to keep her in the loop. Why he never texted his mom was a mystery. And why they hadn't really kept in touch was odd, now that she thought about it.

She stepped into the kitchen and walked to the stove where she lifted the lid on the cast iron Dutch oven releasing smells of garlic, beef, and onions. Nicole, her mom, walked in.

"Hey Mom, something smells delicious." Nicole gave her a side hug.

"Thanks. Dad made a big pot. I invited the Gundersons to join us. You know Peter's home, right?"

Nicole side eyed her. She *did* know. And it caused her cheeks to redden and involuntary butterflies to swirl inside her. What would Peter think of Jake?

"Yeah, he texted and said he was coming. Is he here already? I was just over there and didn't see him."

"Today, I guess. Apparently, he quit his job and is sticking around to help Evelyn with the flower business."

Yep, that would be Peter. Always looking out for someone else. But quit his job? It seemed like he loved it there. Then again, thinking back on his posts, maybe he just loved his zany coworkers.

She looked at a large, framed collage that hung on the wall—photos of her coming in first across the 1000-meter finish line in track, her with the swim team wearing a first-place medal for the 800-meter freestyle, and her as team captain of her soccer league. She wasn't sure she would have accomplished any of these if her parents hadn't pushed her. They were under the assumption that a person needn't have all their limbs to succeed in life.

Buck it up, buttercup. You can do this!

"Do you need help with anything?" Olivia took a dishrag and wiped the counter.

"Nah, there's already a fruit salad in the fridge and rolls are in the oven. The potatoes need mashing, but I've got it. They'll be over in about an hour."

Good. Just enough time for her to create a YouTube video. She entered her bedroom and shut the door. She had started a channel talking people through living life with one hand. Some basic how-tos about living life. Like how to put your hair in a ponytail. Or putting toothpaste on your toothbrush. You know, ordinary living. Today she'd share about catching the pig. She sure wished she had some footage of it. A chuckle escaped. The look on Jake's face when she shooed him off. Priceless.

There was a signature knock on the door. That must be Peter. She put her computer to sleep. She checked herself in the mirror. She slipped a hair tie over her fingers, gathered her long hair, and twisted it into a rope and then slid the tie over her hair at the nape of her neck. Not that Peter would care. He was just that way—he simply took her for who she was. She hadn't seen Peter for almost two years. The tingle of excitement surprised her.

"Peter!"

"Olivia! Hey gorgeous!"

He walked up, arms open wide and enveloped her into a warm embrace. She pulled away and placed her hand in front of her like she was going to shake his. Then she glanced at him—a twinkle lit his eyes. He grinned and placed his hands together, palms touching. He slapped the palm of her right hand with his, then the back of her hand and returned to the front. She slapped his hand, below and then above. Together they snapped their fingers twice and both broke into laughter.

Some things you never grew out of. Olivia couldn't remember where they'd learned to do that, but it had been their ritual since grade school.

"What are you doing here? I haven't seen you in a million years!"

Peter glanced behind him toward the sounds in the kitchen where his mom and Nicole were catching up.

"I quit my job." He lowered his voice. "I'm gonna help my mom with the farm. I don't want her to feel like she needs to give up her dreams. I just want to be here for her."

"Well, she'll be glad to have you. You know I've been working at the farm every day, right? Just trying to fill in the gaps."

Peter shook his head. He hadn't known. "Thank you. I'm sure that means a lot to her."

They walked down the hall to the kitchen, where Olivia handed Peter some plates and then grabbed the silverware. A fluid motion—just like old times. Olivia's stomach growled at the mixture of familiar aromas, her dad's signature beef gravy over mashed potatoes, fresh corn from the field and blueberry cobbler. A reminder she had only scarfed down an apple earlier that day.

Brad, Olivia's dad stepped between them and wrapped an arm around each of their shoulders.

"Peter, nice to see you. I hear you'll be around for a while." Peter grinned and nodded.

They sat, blessed the food, and dished up.

Nicole scooped fruit salad onto her plate.

"I'm going to start volunteering at North Peaks Park working on their trails."

"That sounds like fun." Brad reached for a roll. "And probably a lot of work."

"Yeah. I need something to do since I quit my job." Nicole looked at Olivia. "You might want to join me. Some mama-daughter time?"

Olivia shook her head. She had enough on her plate as it was.

"Maybe when my accountant classes are over."

She wouldn't mind volunteering with her mom. It would take away some of the stress of studying. Just not right now.

Evelyn placed her fingers around her glass, her mottled scar showing above her wrist. She took a sip of water.

"I'm glad you're here, Peter—that big flower festival is coming up and I can use all the help I can get." Evelyn smiled at him. "There's a lot to do to get ready, the least of which was to get a handle on those weeds. Olivia, I'll need you to get the bouquet buckets ready. And maybe you could oversee graphics—signs, stickers, postcards, price tags?"

"Yes, of course. I'd totally love that."

Ross and Brad shared a glance.

"What?" Olivia looked from one to the other and took a sip of her iced tea.

Ross shrugged. "It's just nice to see you two. I feel like this is just one big happy family."

Chapter Three

Peter hopped out of bed, yawned, and stretched, his long arms reaching the slant of the dormer. He lifted the window shades, letting the new golden rays slide in and looked out at the farm. The sun was just peeking over the horizon, illuminating the glisten of the dew. A refreshing view after four years of city noises and skyscrapers. Yes, being here was the right decision. He grabbed a t-shirt and yanked it over his head.

He scanned the ceiling till he found the smoke alarm. Pulling a chair under it, he checked the batteries. Still good. He'd make it his first mission to go through the house and check all of them. Better yet, replace them with dual sensor alarms.

Peter followed his nose to the kitchen where his mom had a pan of bacon sizzling and blueberry pancakes on the griddle. She used to make them with smiley faces, blueberries, or chocolate chips for the eyes. He smiled.

"Morning Ma!"

He gave her a hug and kiss on the top of her head. That smile. It was worth coming home for.

"How are you feeling?"

"Morning Peter. Some days better than others. Today I'm good." She scooped a few pancakes onto a plate. "Is that enough?"

"Good for starters." The corner of his mouth turned up and he winked.

Peter couldn't keep his eyes off the burn scar on her arm. The doctors had done a good job of skin grafting, leaving the area a smooth, darker shade of pink. Much nicer than the bubbled, ugly mess it had been. Still, it didn't stop the pain of knowing that in his focused state of getting ready for his final nursing exam and the rushed focus on leaving that he neglected to tell his dad about the frayed wire. The one that would start the fire while he was gone. The one his dad could have taken care of and prevented the disaster. Instead, as usual, Peter's mind was on himself and his own urgent needs.

It was a reminder of when he wasn't there for her. He could have prevented it altogether.

Ross entered the kitchen, gave Evelyn a hug and kiss on top of her head, his muscled arms wrapping lovingly around his wife of thirty years. Peter smiled. Guess it was easy enough to fall into the pattern his dad had modeled for him.

Peter poured homemade blueberry syrup onto his pancakes and dipped his bacon into the excess. Ross patted him on the back.

"Think you could help me get the hay baled today? It should be dry."

"What about the flowers? Don't you need those sorted and ready?"

"Jake is going to help Olivia with that today," Evelyn said. "And let's be honest Peter, you're better at driving a baler than at bouquets." She smirked.

"Yeah, you're probably right."

Jake? Well, he supposed things had to change in the amount of time he had been gone. And let's face it, Peter had always been just a friend. Maybe this Jake guy was who Olivia was supposed to be with. Still, it gave him cause for pause.

Peter loaded his plate into the dishwasher, grabbed one more pancake and some bacon which he rolled into a tidy delicacy and headed out the door. Pita, his black lab, bounded up to him, his tail wagging like there was no tomorrow. Peter hadn't been able to take him when he became a nurse. Having him cooped up in a city apartment would have destroyed him. He needed to be in the country where he could assist with duck and goose hunting. And here is the place that put him in his happy place. Peter reached down and scratched him between the ears.

"Been behaving yourself while I was gone?"

Pita's tale thumped the side of Peter's legs. Ross caught up with him and put his arm around his shoulder.

"It's so good to have you home, son. It was silly of you to go to nursing school anyway. Your place is right here on the family farm." Peter looked away. He had to admit he had his weaknesses at Mercy, but there was this part of him that enjoyed the caregiving. The camaraderie. The learning new things.

"Your mom might not look it, but she gets worn out easily. She usually takes a nap in the early afternoon."

"Just tell me what you need, Dad. I'm all yours. Don't forget I can help with her medications, too."

Ross pulled his arm to his side, looked away and cleared his throat.

OLIVIA BREATHED in the moist fragrance of the greenhouse. She walked to the massive cooler and cleared off the large table. Jake followed her with a cart full of buckets. He filled them with water and set them around the perimeter of the room.

"Peter's back."

Olivia brought out an armload of flowers and set them on the table. "He quit his job and is going to help Evelyn on the farm."

"That's a sacrifice. I mean, nurses get paid a buttload of money, don't they?"

"Yeah. But I'm glad he's back. I've missed him."

Olivia slid a glance at Jake. She sorted the flowers by colors and laid them on the table. She took the stack of paper wrappers and began stamping the farm logo onto them.

Jake side-eyed her and stripped the bottom leaves off each stem.

"I guess I'll have to get to know him. I recognized him from high school, but never was in the same circle."

"Yeah, probably not. You were into basketball and football. But he's fun."

She moved to the other side of the stamped wrappers.

"There was one summer when baling hay was done. His dad and he had stacked the white plastic-covered rounds four high. They looked like stacks of marshmallows for a giant. Peter and I snuck out in the middle of a moonlit night with spray cans and graffitied smiley faces and cows onto them." Olivia giggled. "I'm pretty sure both our parents knew it was us, but they never said a word."

Jake laughed. "You know the Weaver farm down the road? He had a bunch of chickens he wanted to get rid of. So, me and my friends asked if we could take them. We gathered a bunch of dog crates and filled them up with about thirty chickens all squawking and flapping their wings. Then we snuck into the high school on a Sunday morning and released them into different wings. Monday came around and no one could place who could have done it. It was classic!"

"That was you? Huh. I always wondered who did that."

Olivia finished the wrappers, gathered stems from each pile and laid them on the table. She put a rubber band on the table and slipped her fingers through the center, widening the band enough to slip around the stems. Jake finished his batch and began to gather flowers and filler from each pile.

"Let's assembly line this process. You line up the stems and I'll put them in the wrappers."

Olivia hid a smile. He was so organized. They looked up as the greenhouse door slid open.

"Hey Olivia. Jake." Peter nodded. "Dad needs me to run to the feed store. Do you need anything?"

"I think we're good. Give my dad a kiss for me." The corner of Olivia's mouth quirked up.

Peter shook his head, a crooked smile on his lips. When they had been kids playing Truth or Dare, Olivia had dared Peter to kiss her dad. She remembered that?

PETER JUMPED into his dad's old 1980's Ford F-150, the teal paint barely hanging on. Same old cloth bucket seat, nearly thread bare in some places. But when he turned the key, the engine purred to life.

He drove past Jake's jacked up new Toyota Tundra, mud splattered along the sides. Why anyone would want a truck to sit that high was beyond him. Some kind of ego thing?

Peter road down Central Avenue and as he neared the feed store, he passed a sign in front of the fire station.

Today's a good day to become a hero.

It pulled him in like a magnet. He made a turn at the next street and rounded the block to pull into the station.

He was welcomed in with donuts and coffee. The chief was thrilled to take on an RN. Peter filled out a few forms, figured out a schedule that would work and headed to the feed store. He'd had a lot of practice playing the part of the hero at the hospital where so much need and drug abuse abounded. This time, he'd try on a different cape. If a fire broke out again at home, which it shouldn't, considering the precautions he had put in place, he'd be prepared.

Chapter Four

Nicole took a muffin from the table and poured herself a cup of coffee. She glanced at the others in line who had gathered in the meeting room of the North Peaks Park for orientation. Several twenties-somethings laughed and jostled around. A retired couple who looked like they might have been regulars on road scholar trips. She chose a chair on the end where she could gaze out the floor to ceiling window. Magnificent cedars towered and she couldn't wait to get on a trail to smell the mossy undergrowth she knew housed salamanders and banana slugs. This was going to be a fun place to volunteer. Give herself a nature boost. Fresh air, hard work, maybe meet some new friends.

"Hello everyone. Thanks for coming today. My name is Bree Bradley. I've been working here for the past ten years—" Nicole took a bite of her muffin as Bree showed slides of the trails they had created, and some machine safety videos.

Nicole adjusted her *Life is Good* cap and followed Bree and the others down the trail. The clean scent of moss and sorrel invigorated her. They stopped at a shed where Bree handed out leather gloves, loppers, shovels, and some type of tool Nicole had never seen—long poles connected with canvas strips.

"Today we'll be doing some brush maintenance, rock work and drainage."

Bree shoved strands of loose hair out of her face with the back of her hand.

"Notice how the rock has corroded along the trail where the stream overflowed last spring. We'll need to rebuild that."

This was a project Nicole could get into—something attainable. Something that she could admire when it was done and feel like she had accomplished something. Her last volunteer job was at the library. She was tasked with shelving books which soon became monotonous. And quiet. Not particularly fulfilling. She wanted to do something that made a difference.

When Olivia had been young, they had spent hours at story time, watching puppet shows, listening to animated stories, learning fun songs. She had hoped she could bring back some of the same feelings.

Olivia. She and Brad had spent years trying for a baby. They even consulted an infertility specialist who basically told them getting pregnant wasn't in their cards. That's when they had turned to adoption. It had been the best decision they'd ever made.

What was going to happen to Olivia? She and Brad had done all they could to treat her like a full-bodied girl. And she had excelled in everything she touched. But now she was pushing thirty and still living at home. It didn't seem like she was ever going to find herself. Nicole and Brad had had long discussions about if they had been enabling her by letting her live at home. The truth was, they loved having her there.

Nicole worked beside Bree, shoveling an area to begin rebuilding a trail that had slid in the last big storm.

"So, you've worked here eight years?" Nicole asked.

"Yes, I love it. Being outdoors, meeting new people. It's a great job. My husband Phil works here as well. He's in charge of maintenance."

She called the crew to follow her to a spot near the riverbank.

19

"We'll need a mixture of those large flat rocks and round ones."

Bree laid out a net attached to poles and demonstrated how to use their picks to remove the rocks. Next, she showed them how to roll them onto the nets.

"Team up—find a partner. It works way better that way. No one wants to hurt their backs."

Bree directed the volunteers to fill the toter with rocks.

Nicole and Bree heaved a rock from the toter placing it on the ground. Nicole sat on the ground and pushed the rock down the small slope into place with her boots.

"Where do you live?" Bree asked.

"Near Willowbrook in the country. Next door to Gunderson's Flower and Pumpkin Patch."

"Oh, I've been there. I took my kids last fall. They're teens, but they still love to go—get their picture by the scarecrow, do the corn maize thing."

"It's a lot of fun. My daughter Olivia works there."

Maybe not much longer when she gets her accounting degree.

"Really? Maybe we can stop by. I need some flowers for an upcoming event." Bree stood. "This is looking pretty good." She checked the time. "Let's stop for lunch."

Nicole pulled a meatloaf sandwich and bag of chips from her thermal lunch bag. She arranged them on the picnic table beside Bree.

"Well, we're making progress on the trail. How much longer do you think it will take?" Nicole twisted the cap from her bottle.

"If we can keep going, we'll have it open by the end of July for the state hiking event."

"Well, I for one, have been enjoying this. Getting outdoors, doing something useful, making new friends."

She looked at Bree over her sandwich. She seemed to have so much in common with her. It was nice, having a new friend.

"We're having a surprise birthday party for my daughter this weekend. She'll be twenty-nine. I can't believe it. And if she's twenty-nine, what does that make me?" She laughed.

Bree grew quiet and looked past Nicole to the woods.

"You should come. I'd love for you to meet her and my husband, Ross."

Bree gave a slight nod of her head, seeming to shake off her thoughts.

"Uh, yeah. That would be fun. Could I bring my kids? I'm sure Maddie and Matt would love a chance to come to the farm."

"That would be great. We'll see you Saturday around five."

PETER SWUNG up into the tractor cab and adjusted his ball cap. Pita jumped up beside him and settled at his feet. Peter turned the key and stopped to pull out his phone. He tapped his fire safety app, one he'd found out about at the fire station to make sure everything in the house seemed okay. *Just another way to keep Mom safe.*

He headed down the row of mounded hay. The weather had been perfect giving the alfalfa time to dry out before the v-rake twisted and turned the hay preparing it for the hay baler. Why had he thought being a nurse would be such a great thing? Sure, the pay and benefits were great. But when he thought of his anxiety at possibly giving the wrong meds, or naively succumbing to the pleas of IV drug users to allow their friends to visit and finding out they had been supplying them with heroin in the bathroom, well, driving a tractor was a piece of cake. It gave him peace of mind. What was the worst he could do? Run into the barn? Break a machine part? All fixable.

Peter drove his way down the long row, the circular hooks twirling rhythmically, pulling the hay into mounded rows. He rounded the end and headed towards the barn. Olivia and Jake walked hand in hand towards the flower shed. A twinge of jealousy roused creating a souring in his stomach.

21

When Peter moved on to college and then his internship, he'd become a part of a different community. One that had likeminded goals. And thinking about it now, he had put away his old life and all those in it. He had become a part of a community with those incredibly wonderful humans in the world of the Invincibles.

It would only make sense that Olivia had moved on. Not that he and Olivia had ever dated. But he had thought she would always be there if he were ever bold enough to make the move.

He pulled the John Deere up to the barn.

"Jake!"

Jake glanced over his shoulder, set his buckets down and his long legs strode towards Peter.

"Could you help me get the tube wrapper set up?"

"Sure. I'll just let Olivia know."

Peter watched him return to the flower shed where Olivia met him at the entrance. Jake gave her more than a quick kiss and returned to Peter.

Jake hoisted the heavy tubes of thick white plastic to Peter who fed them onto the feeding rods.

"Do you mind if I ask you something?" Jake said.

"Sure."

"You've known Olivia for a long time, right?" Peter nodded and checked the placement.

"Do you think she'd like a surprise party for her birthday?"

Her birthday? Oh man, he was out of touch. He never would have forgotten her birthday in the past.

"Maybe."

That was the type of thing Olivia would do for others. But Peter had never seen her really enjoy a birthday. Would she like a surprise?

"Where should I have it?"

Jake lifted his cap and ran his fingers through his hair.

"We could set up a space in the barn. Mom and Nicole would be happy to bake. And dad's the king of barbecue. I'm sure there's plenty of chicken in the big freezer. They butchered not too long ago."

"You wouldn't mind helping? I mean, I really like this girl and want to do things right."

"No, of course not."

Peter swallowed. For now, it would have to suffice to watch from the sidelines.

Chapter Five

Peter hopped on his motorcycle and revved the engine. He pulled onto the two-lane road, grateful that he wasn't riding in the busy Portland streets. He saw Olivia, out for her morning run, her orange tank top exposing her muscular shoulders and tanned arms. He slowed and pulled over.

"I've got a few errands in town, but how about we go for a hike this afternoon."

Olivia ran in place.

"I've got to study a few more chapters of my homework, but sure, I can do that after my run. That would be fun."

She swept loose hair from her eyes. Peter drank in her smile, one side quirked up causing her eyes to sparkle. He hadn't realized how much he'd missed that.

"Okay, I'll check in with you around two."

Good. Plan one is in place. He passed the wooden sign signaling the entrance to Willowbrook. In high school shop class Olivia had created the design and together they carved into the cedar. Remembering his hand on hers guiding the chisel brought an unexpected warmth to his cheeks.

It was good to be back in a small town. Everyone knew you

and people had your back. Like when their house caught fire. Not only did people help with the cleanup, but someone leant his folks their motorhome until the house was back in shape. When his mom was recuperating from burns, someone filled the freezer with casseroles. He wondered if those same people remembered he hadn't been there for her. It triggered a visceral reaction, and he felt the grief rise to his chest.

He pulled up to Cool Beans Coffee Shop and stepped under the red and white striped awning. A flier on the window reminded him that the County Fair was coming up. Not that he needed the reminder. His dad had been holding 4-H meetings in the barn with the members, showing them how to strengthen the hind legs of their lambs.

"By building a feeder set high enough, your lambs will have to stand on their hind legs to eat. Then when the judges feel their hinds, they'll choose yours. Everyone wants a good leg of lamb to eat."

"You mean they're going to kill our lambs?" A look of horror filled the middle school girl's face.

"Duh! What did you think market lambs meant?"

That from a ten-year-old boy. Oh, the realities of life.

Peter went straight for the dark roast beans, Olivia's favorite. And a bag of chocolate covered beans. He set them on the counter and pulled out his wallet.

"Peter? You here visiting?"

The clerk glanced at him, her perfectly plucked eyebrows raised and she set her hand on the beans.

"Oh, hi."

He had to think a minute to remember her name.

"No, I moved back. Needed to help my mom out."

What was her name? He tapped his credit card on the reader.

"I guess you've seen Olivia. You know she's dating Jake, right?"

Yes, he knew.

"He's an okay guy, I guess," she said, "But he's not you."

She handed him the receipt and leaned over the counter.

"I always thought you guys would end up together. Everyone did."

Phoebe!

"Uh, yeah. Well, I better get going."

He slid a half smile and left, tucking that remark in the recess of his heart.

PETER WALKED behind Olivia as she made her way up the trail. Her jeans perfectly fit her slim figure and her boots left prints in the soft mud from last night's rain.

"How do you think things are with my mom? I feel bad I haven't been here for her more."

"Up and down. She has her good days and bad days."

"I'm really glad you're there to help her." Peter stepped aside, avoiding a yellow spotted banana slug.

"I love your mom. It's been fun. And I've learned a lot about flowers that I never knew."

She stepped down a side trail to view the river. The rain had caused the waters to rise. It tumbled over the rocks and eddied between boulders.

"And you? You actually quit your job?" Olivia turned to look up at him.

"I know, right? Sometimes you gotta do what you gotta do."

He sat down on a log.

"Nursing wasn't really a good fit for me. There was so much crazy stuff going on at the hospital. It just seemed like there was no end—so many things that could be prevented with proper care and nutrition, but people just don't make their health a priority."

"Maybe another medical setting would be better for you."

"Yeah, maybe. But I'm sure I can use my nursing skills here on the farm. And I joined the fire department, so there's that."

Olivia sat down beside him. A breeze floated by, grabbing a

strand of her blonde hair, and moving it over her eyes. Peter moved the back of his fingers to wipe it back into place, gentle as the butterfly flitting from one elderberry bloom to the next.

"And you, Ollie. Are you satisfied with where you're at?" She snorted.

"Not really. I mean, I like working with your mom—working with the flowers. And the pumpkin patch is always fun in the fall. But I don't know, I need a real job. I'm pushing thirty and still living at home."

"And *I've* just moved back home. There's no shame in that."

"I suppose. I've been studying for an accountant degree. Something solid with benefits."

Peter looked at her, eyebrow cocked.

"Accounting? That's not even you."

Olivia shrugged. "I've gotta do something with my life."

She pulled out her phone and snapped a few shots of the river. Then turned it towards them and snapped a selfie. Peter leaned over and looked at the shot.

"Hey, you can do better than that. Look at my hair—it's all goofy."

Olivia reached out and brushed his hair into place. She took another shot.

"Much better."

Phoebe's words echoed in Peter's mind. They did look good together.

ALL WAS quiet when Olivia and Peter returned, except for the sound of the chickens squawking and Pita announcing them. The hike had been refreshing, reminding her of all the times she and Peter would hike to the falls or take long bike rides, sharing their stories. Their lives.

"Let's go look at the kittens. They're in the barn."

Peter followed her. She stopped after she grabbed hold of the metal handle and slid the squeaky barn door open.

"Surprise!"

Friends and family were surrounded by decorated tables, balloons and patio lights strung from the beams. Olivia's mouth formed an O and she started laughing. She caught her mom's eye. Nicole walked over to her, a hand on a woman's shoulder.

"Hey sweetie, happy birthday."

"Mom! What is all this? You didn't have to do this."

"It wasn't me. It was Jake."

She nodded her head towards him.

"I want you to meet my friend Bree. She's the director of the park I've been volunteering at."

"Nice to meet you. Mom is loving volunteering there."

Bree smiled. But her mom was glancing between her and Bree, a wondering frown above her hazel eyes. Why was that? What was going on?

Jake interrupted and planted a kiss on her lips. He took her hand and led her to a table filled with barbecued chicken, potato salad, watermelon, and chips. A mug with an excel logo said *Oh, this calls for a spreadsheet* held a small bouquet of flowers. She glanced at Jake.

"Did you do this?"

He grinned. Olivia shrunk her shoulders. She should be happy that he encouraged her career choice. Why did a little thing like that make her doubt herself? It drew attention to a decision she wasn't totally in love with.

"You didn't have a clue, did you?" Jake asked.

She smiled and shook her head. She squeezed his hand.

"That was sweet. No, I figured Peter just took me for a hike to be nice."

"Yeah, well, he helped me figure out how to pull this off."

Jake held two plates while Olivia filled one for herself.

"You probably won't want anything else. Your mom made your favorite chocolate cake." Jake nodded towards a table.

Her dad sat on a stool playing his guitar into a mic and singing country songs. Her mom joined him, her harmony in perfect tune.

Olivia watched Peter sitting on an upturned bucket playing with a little girl. She held a calico kitten, and he stroked its fur. *He's sweet like that. Tender.*

They finished their lunch and Jake called everyone around the cake. He lit the twenty-nine candles as they sang. Peter took hold of the mic.

"I just want to say, Olivia doesn't look so bad for an old lady." He grinned. "But really, she's been a great friend over the years and I'm glad I'm here to celebrate her. Wishing you a great future, Ollie."

He held his glass in the air, looking around at all those who applauded.

Olivia locked eyes with him, a smile filling her face and warming her heart. It was good to have him home.

Jake put his hand around her waist and pulled her to the open floor space. Brad segued to a slow melody and Jake pulled Olivia close, taking measured steps to the tune. She lay her head on his chest. She had never had a surprise party before. It was endearing that Jake would have thought to make it happen. Still, she couldn't quite put a finger on why she never thought she deserved one or was ever excited about birthdays.

Chapter Six

Olivia sat at the dining room table surrounded by textbooks and her laptop. She leaned back, crossed her arms, and stared at the mound of books. Why had she chosen accounting, of all fields? Besides the classes costing a ton of money, it was boring. She knew she could accomplish the certificate, but what was the point? So that she could look at numbers all day and make sure they came out to the penny?

She'd way rather be outside playing with animals. Which led her thoughts to Peter stroking the kitten's fur at her birthday. And their hike where he said accounting was not her. And the look that reminded her he knew her through and through.

Her mom was rattling around in the kitchen, opening the fridge door, setting something on the counter, pouring water into the espresso machine. The fragrance of freshly ground coffee beans filled the air, bringing a sense of comfort.

Olivia could have been adopted into any family. God must have known which one she needed because she couldn't have a better mom. *Concentrate, Olivia. You've got a test coming up.*

She clicked start on her excel training video.

"Now if I click on E3 I can create a formula by starting with an equal sign—"

The monotone voice droned on and on. Olivia rolled her shoulders.

"Blah blah blah." She sighed.

"Hey honey, I made you a coffee."

Nicole brought in a latte in Olivia's favorite cup, the one that said *If you can dream it, you can do it* and set it beside her. What was her dream, really? She glanced at her books and shook her head. Olivia looked over her shoulder at Nicole, breathed and placed her hand on her mom's.

"Thank you. It smells delicious. You always know what your girl needs." She gave her hand a squeeze.

"How's it going? Your finals must be coming up."

"They are."

"I know how stressed you get."

Nicole started rubbing Olivia's shoulders.

"But you're going to do great. You've been studying so hard and I'm sure you'll whiz through this just like you've done all your life."

Olivia gave her a pained look. She wanted to blurt out that she hated this. That she daydreamed of quitting. But how could she quit? She had no plan B. Or C or D. And she couldn't stand to be a disappointment. Everything her mom did was for her. She only wanted the best.

"Yeah, I feel like I understand most of it. I'm sure this coffee will kick my brain into gear."

A knock on the door and Jake let himself in. Olivia glanced up and gave a half smile.

"Oh good, you're studying. Olivia, you've been spending too much time with the fair stuff. You know this is way more important."

Olivia shrunk in her seat, keeping her eyes on the table. Her face wrinkled.

"I know, Jake. There's kind of a deadline for fair."

"There's a bigger deadline for your exam. Come on. Show me where you're at."

His voice low and guttural. He sat down beside her and looked over her page. His sweaty odor, which she ordinarily liked, almost made her gag. She turned her head away.

"Right here."

He pointed, each syllable clipped and precise.

"This figure isn't right. What's going on Olivia? You know how to do this. I already showed you how."

He shook his head.

"You're wasting your time if you don't take this opportunity seriously."

His jaw jutted forward, and his face flushed.

Olivia was in no mood for this. She couldn't put her finger on why this bothered her so much. Was it his tone of voice? "*Wasting her time?*" What makes him so sure he knows what's best for me. She stood up.

"You need to leave."

"What? I'm trying to help you."

"Just go."

Jake ran his hand through his hair and stood. He shook his head and stomped out the way he came in.

PETER UNLACED his boots and left them side by side on the porch before he entered the house. Something smelled good. Barbecue? Maybe Mom was making pulled pork. The instant pot hissed. He pulled off his cap and hung it on the rack by the door and headed to the kitchen to wash his hands. A pile of dirty dishes littered the sink. Flour was scattered over the counter with a round cookie cutter sitting amid it. A tray of golden-brown biscuits sat on the stove top. This was one of those time-to-help-your-mom-out moments. He pulled open the dishwasher door and unloaded the clean dishes. Pulling dinner together must have wiped her out. How long had her chronic fatigue been going on? He should have been here for her sooner.

He knew what it was like. He'd had his fair share of patients who had suffered with fibromyalgia. It seemed that the families of those afflicted didn't really understand auto immune diseases. They seemed to think that someone could just will themselves out of it, or try to get a better night's sleep. Peter knew it didn't work that way.

He looked out the window as he rinsed and loaded the dishes. He watched his dad who was in the barn spreading hay for the dairy cows. Peter looked forward to the gallon of raw milk, topped with heavy cream that he could whip into a topping. Maybe he could slice some strawberries to go on some of the biscuits for dessert. That would put a smile on Mom's face.

Peter wiped down the counters and went to the living room. His mom was snuggled under a homemade quilt, snoring softly. He stood over her, wanting to reach down and smooth her hair from her face, but didn't want to wake her. The pager on his hip beeped. He hurried out of the room. Time to take off his domestic hat and replace it with the fireman's. He hoped that barbecued pork and biscuits would be waiting for him when he got home.

The roar of Peter's motorcycle came to life, and he sped to the firehouse. He ran into the building. Mac slapped him on the back and nodded to where his turnouts were already laid out. He slipped his feet into his boots, pulled up his pants, slipping his suspenders over his shoulders, pulled the Nomex hood over his head and reached for his jacket. He sat and slipped on his self-contained breathing apparatus, a cylinder, the backpack and the mask over his shoulders and latched the buckles. Last he pulled his gloves over his fingers. He hopped in the passenger side of the engine whose lights and siren were already running. Adrenaline was already pumping. This was his first fire call. He'd been to a few accidents, but he had to admit, this made his insides swirl. What was this going to be like? Could he be relied upon to make rational decisions?

Peter saw the plumes of smoke blocks before they arrived. The radio belted out, "Anderson Creek Road, structure fire of the two-story building."

FLAMES SHOT out the second story windows and a man stood on the lawn holding his cheeks in his hands. Anguish engulfed his features. Mac ran to him. The man pointed to the house screaming for Mac to find his wife. Mac grabbed a wrench and the hose and ran to the hydrant to attach it to the engine. He followed Vinny Carloni through the front door who pulled out his thermal imaging camera. It was up to them to find this man's wife.

Like someone had done for Peter's mom.

As Peter and Vinny entered the first floor, hopeful that the woman could be found soon. Smoke billowed out of the rooms, but flames were not evident. They searched the living room and kitchen. There was no sign of anyone. He ran down the hall, checking the bathroom and bedroom. The nozzle team held a hand line heading upstairs. He took the steps two at a time. The upstairs was an inferno. Peter took a step back and gulped air. His heart pounded in his ears.

He couldn't stop now. This family depended on him. Was this what it was like when his house burned down? Had his mom and dad lived through this fear?

The floor to the back bedroom started collapsing, bringing Peter to his senses. Vinny held the thermal imaging camera. Clarify the use being important to finding her as the nozzle team extinguished flames and motioned for Peter to follow him through the flames into the bedroom. The woman had collapsed on the floor. Peter hoisted her limp body over his shoulder and hastened down the stairs and out to the yard. He gently placed her on the ground.

The man and his daughter ran to her, tears streaming down their faces.

Peter yanked off his helmet and gloves and placed two fingers on her neck to check for pulse. He turned to the medics.

"We need oxygen, quick. She's going to need fluids."

They brought a gurney and carefully hoisted her onto it.

"You and your daughter can hop into the ambulance. You can keep her company." The man nodded to the medic.

Peter watched the ambulance go, taking the wife and mother to safety.

He hadn't been there to see his mom rescued. To feel their same relief of her being found.

A whine took him out of his revery. He frowned, looked around, and started towards the sound. He walked to the back of the remains of the house where embers still flickered. A golden lab pup had its paw caught under a beam. Her tail wagged weakly and sad eyes begged Peter to help.

"What have we got here? Did you get caught? Let's see if I can get you out of here."

Chapter Seven

Peter looked around for something to lift the smoldering beam. A large branch which had fallen in the last storm lay beside him. How he wished that pouring rain hadn't stopped. It would have doused the fire before it had gotten out of control.

"Hey, you need help? Whatcha got there?" Vinny took long strides to Peter.

"There's a little golden lab caught here. Can you help me out?"

Vinny wedged a sturdy branch under the beam and Peter carefully slid the scared little critter out. She licked her dangling front paw.

"Oh boy, we're gonna need to get you some help, little princess. Hold on, you're gonna be okay."

Peter took her to the engine where Vinny pulled out the medical kit.

"Get the self-adhering bandage. Let's see if we can save the paw." Peter stroked the pup's head.

"Are you kidding, dude? It's holding on by a thread. There won't be any saving that paw."

Vinny wasn't convinced, but still took the orange bandage and wrapped it gently around the whimpering pup's paw.

Peter thought back to when he and Daniel had been able to save a man's severed thumb by stitching it back on. Maybe that wasn't a thing with animals, but he could hope.

Back at the station, Peter placed the puppy in an empty box with a clean blanket and then he showered. He let the warm water stream down his face, washing away the soot and grime. His clothes. saturated with the smell of smoke lay in a heap on the floor.

Then he gently wrapped the pup in the blanket and put her into his backpack. He threw his leg over his motorcycle and put the key into the ignition. He couldn't wait to give this puppy to Olivia. To see the look on her face.

Her mouth forming an O.

Her shoulders sinking as she sighed.

Her compassion stirring her to help fix this little piece of adorableness.

WHEN HE ARRIVED HOME, cars and pickups were parked around the barn. Must be 4-H day. He peeked in the doorway of the barn where he saw a half-dozen kids working lambs in the coral. A girl with long braids had her arms around a ewe's neck guiding it towards Olivia, who had her arms crossed, leaning against the fence, eyes focused. The ewe baaed, not sure she liked being led around.

"That's good, Charlotte. Now bring her close to me and set her feet. Make sure you get them straight. And the back legs need to show off the rump."

Charlotte confidently did as she was told. Peter wasn't sure this was the best time to present the pup to Olivia. Better not interrupt their learning. He could only imagine the disruption a puppy would cause. He turned and took the pup into the house.

Evelyn was placing lunch fixings on the table—deli meats, cheeses, condiments, and chips.

"Hey Mom!" He struggled out of his backpack, carefully placing it on a chair. The pup whimpered, her sad eyes seeking comfort.

"Peter—what have you got here?"

"Just got back from a fire call. Found this little gal stuck under a beam."

Evelyn gently lifted her out from the backpack.

"Oh my gosh—her paw. Is she gonna be okay?"

Evelyn cradled her in her arms and took her to the laundry room where she placed her in the large sink and let the warm water run over her. She soaped up her hands and gently scrubbed the soot and grime from her fur.

"It's okay, sweetheart. I'm going to wash you up and we'll see if we can get that leg fixed up."

Peter watched a tear roll down Evelyn's cheek.

"You okay?"

"Yeah."

She swiped the tear with the back of her hand. "It just makes me remember the first time I saw Olivia. She was so tiny because she was premature. And when I saw she didn't have a hand—"

"That must have been shocking."

Peter couldn't imagine seeing Olivia when she was born. He was sure he would have focused on her beautiful round eyes and long lashes. Since he had always known her without a hand, this thought had never entered his head.

"It was. And I didn't want to say anything, you know, take the chance on making Nicole feel bad."

She rinsed the puppy off, being careful of her damaged paw and Peter handed her a towel.

It wasn't bad, though, having only one hand, was it? She could do so many things. Most things, really. He was sure that was because of Brad and Nicole's upbringing. Always encouraging her. Pushing her to do her best. To overcome.

THE RAUCOUS LAUGHTER of middle school voices came from outside.

Olivia opened the door and kids barged in. They headed for the food table, chattering about the upcoming county fair. Olivia made eye contact with Peter, and he nodded his head towards the hall. She raised her eyebrows and followed him to the laundry room.

"Awww."

Olivia picked up the injured pup and stroked her clean blonde head. "What happened?"

"I found her after the house fire. Her front paw was stuck under a beam. Vinny Carloni and I wrapped it. If you help me, we might be able to save it."

He slowly unwrapped the paw.

"Oh. This is really bad. Do you think we should try and stitch it?"

"Daniel and I stitched a man's thumb back together." He shrugged. "I'm hoping that will work."

A deep voice growled. "You gonna leave a bunch of wild kids unsupervised in the kitchen? What are you thinking?"

Ross stepped into the laundry room. He paused.

Evelyn turned. "Sorry, we have kind of a situation here."

"Dad—I'm so glad you're here. Don't you have some Telazol or some type of sedative we could use? We want to try and stitch the paw and I'm pretty sure she's not gonna sit still for that."

Ross placed his hand on his chin.

"I'm sure I have something. I'll go look."

Evelyn ran to her sewing room and returned with a curved needle and strong thread.

"Will this do?"

She set them and a shaver on the drier lid.

"I'll go help with the kids."

Olivia cradled the pup in her arms.

"Thanks Mom. I'll be there in a sec."

"Hold her paw and I'll carefully shave it. We don't want it to completely fall off."

Peter picked up the shaver and switched it on. The pup glanced at it and started to shiver. Olivia stroked her head as bits of fur fell to the ground. Peter looked up from threading the needle as Ross walked in and handed him a filled syringe. Peter parted the hair and quickly administered the sedative. It didn't take long for the little girl to fall asleep.

"Olivia, hold the paw and leg together while I stitch it up."

She watched him gently begin to stitch the broken paw. This felt so natural to her. Now this is what she was intended to do—not accounting. She needed to use her gifts. Compassion. Caring. Sensitivity. Quite the opposite qualities of an accountant.

Peter drew the needle through and pulled the string taught.

"Okay, I think this is it. Let's cover it with betadine, and rewrap it. She'll need to rest."

He snipped the string and let his eyes fall of Olivia.

"You are a natural."

He smiled and touched his shoulder to hers.

WHEN THE DROWSINESS WORE OFF, Olivia gently picked the little gal up and snuggled her head into the soft golden fur. The pup turned her head and licked her chin. She giggled.

"Did you name her?"

"No. I was hoping you'd like to have her."

"Oh, Peter. Yes, of course. You know I would."

She gazed into the pup's eyes and stroked her head.

"How about we name you Hop-a-long," Peter said, scratching her ear.

Olivia shook her head.

"No."

She stroked his soft fur.

"You need a name that doesn't define your limb difference. I think I'll call you Bella. It means beautiful."

Bella licked Olivia's chin, instantly accepting the name.

WILLOWBROOK COUNTY FAIR WAS BUSTLING. The lower fields had been mowed to create a parking lot. Guides riding horses led eager participants to empty slots, where parents followed their boisterous kids onto the tractor drawn ride to the entrance.

Peter walked past the ferris wheel and bumper cars to the front gate. Excited expectation surged through his body. He hadn't been to this fair since he was in high school, but the sounds and sights were as comfortable and familiar as his worn-in muck boots. It felt like home. He knew the sounds of carnival music coming from cheap speakers, carnival barkers calling for participants for the ring toss or ball throw. He knew the smells of sweet-smelling fried bread and cotton candy as his feet shuffled down the dirt paths to the animal pens.

He spotted Olivia, eight 4-Hers surrounding her, soaking in her wisdom. She was pretty darn cute in overalls, a ball cap covering her French braided pigtails. She glanced up at him as he leaned against the fence and crossed his arms.

"Make sure your sheep are completely clean. Not even a speck of mud or hay left anywhere. Peter's here—he'll help you fine finish shearing their coats. The judge will be looking for beautiful animals."

She looked from face to face searching for questions.

"Okay, you've got two hours."

Peter clasped his hands. "Alrighty troops, pair up and get your lambs ready to wash. This will go quicker if you help each other.

When you're done, bring them over to this stand and I'll close shear them."

He remembered his dad giving the same advice to him and Olivia as kids. Funny how things came around.

"Olivia, think we have time for a lunch break? I can smell those barbecued hamburgers in the Chicken Coop. Makin' my mouth water."

"Yeah. I could use one of their milkshakes, for sure. We can sit outside in view of the wash area."

They carried their orders to a picnic table, a slight breeze making the rising temperature comfortable, fluffing the tendrils of Olivia's hair. Moms and dads meandered down the aisles, pushing strollers and holding hands with their mesmerized children.

"When was the first time you came to fair, Ollie?"

"Hmm, must have been when I was around fourth grade. You had probably been coming long before then since your dad was leading 4-H."

Peter hadn't needed to ask. He remembered the first time he saw her. Almost the same look—pink jean overalls and pigtails with bows. But at that age, she had a nose full of freckles. And her confident ability to do whatever anyone else did—well, right then and there he was pretty sure she was the girl he wanted to marry. Peter looked away and swallowed.

Peter was halfway through his ketchup-and-relish-covered hamburger when Jake appeared, his ball cap covering all but a few curls over his ears. He carried a plate of curly fries and sat down beside Olivia. She frowned and scooted away. What was that about? Had something happened between them?

"Hey, how's it going? You got your kids organized?"

"Yep. They're doing great. I'm proud of them. Peter's going to shear their lambs in a bit."

"Oh. Well of course. That would be pretty hard for you to do."

He dipped a long fry in ketchup, stuffed it into his mouth and bit a chunk off.

Peter frowned. "Olivia could manage fine on her own."

He gave a slight shake of his head.

They looked up as three of Jake's friends bounded up to their table. Bill reached for a fry and Jake slid his plate closer to them. Gus stared at Olivia's arm.

"Hey nubs, if you don't mind me asking, were you born like that?"

Olivia double blinked.

"Yes. Yes, I was."

Her eyes bore a hole into Gus's. She picked up a fry and bit into it, yanking away what remained like an exclamation point.

"Wow. That must be hard. What do you do with your extra glove?" Hunter said. He ribbed Gus with his elbow and smirked.

"She probably finds someone with only a left hand!" Gus said.

Jake laughed.

"But really, why don't you just wear a fake hand? Like, how would it attach to you?"

"Wait, are you right or left-handed? Cuz that's gonna be a problem Jake, if you don't have nowhere to put a ring on her left finger." Gus glanced at her hand.

"Yeah, you'll save a butt load of money if you don't have to buy a ring." Hunter laughed so hard he rolled over at the waist.

"Besides, you'd have to be worried about your kids having only one hand." Gus slapped Jakes's back.

Peter felt like he'd been kicked in the gut. What was wrong with these guys?

Olivia stood.

"That's not going to be a problem, Jake, because there won't be a need for a ring. You and your friends are fixated on my limb difference, but I'm more focused on what's in my heart and mind —something you clearly lack."

Jake held his hands out, palms up. "What did I do? They were just fooling around. It's just what guys do. Geesh! It's not that big of a deal."

The look on Olivia's face could strike lightning. She straightened her posture, turned, and walked off.

Chapter Eight

Olivia had just finished uploading video clips of her fair day to YouTube. She had caught a particularly endearing photo of Peter shearing sheep. He could be so serious sometimes. A contrast to his usual funny self. But she supposed that's what made him likable. She had to admit she enjoyed having him back home.

She switched to her phone and brought up Instagram.

"What? Really? That scum ball!"

She tightened her hand into a fist.

Someone had videoed the encounter with Jake's friends and had edited snippets so that there were dozens of individual slams. They had gone viral in a matter of hours. And tons of comments with more *clever* jabs. She pushed share to Peter. Woof.

She threw her phone onto the bed like a hot potato. Why did people have to be so cruel? She had spent years working on comebacks to rude comments. The constant reminder that she was less than. As much as her parents had tried to normalize her life, there were always the nagging questions. How had she been born without a hand? Was it a DNA failure? And bigger than that, what had God been thinking? Why her?

When she was thirteen, she had prayed that God would do a miracle—restore her hand. It would be an opportunity for Him to show His miraculous works. Think of the impact that would have on others, bringing them to Him.

That never happened. Her dad had sat her down on the couch, wrapped his arm around her. Helped her see that her greatest disability wasn't physical. It was her mindset. She needed to see what God's plan was for her, what His purpose was. And to always remember that He loved her above all else. Just. As. She. Is.

Still, there was always someone glancing at her. Or whispering. Or, more often than not, saying something dumb just because they were trying to wrap their mind around her lack.

Oh my gosh, are you that surfer who was bit by a shark?

My uncle is missing his hand—his name is Joe Clark. Do you happen to know him?

How do you even tie your shoes? Or cut your steak?

Olivia, you're such an inspiration to me!

Can you swim? Or do you just go in circles?

Maybe this is why her bio mom chose adoption. She didn't want to live with the stigma of a kid with only one hand. Made her thankful for Nicole. Olivia knew *she* loved her.

But would she still love her when she told her she was giving up on accounting? The idea had been ruminating in her mind, causing her to feel both free and anxious. But Peter was right.

That's not even you. What had he seen in her? What *was* even her?

One thing she knew for sure. She was through with Jake. He couldn't even have stood up for her? Nope. There was no place in her life for a relationship where she didn't feel valued. If that meant she was going to remain single, so be it. If she was ever to fall in love again, it would be with a man who loved her completely—limb difference and all. Not someone who just waves it off and pretends it doesn't matter but recognizes that what she doesn't have is just as much a valuable part of her as what she does have.

A cool but clammy breeze swirled through the huckleberry bushes, the sound of rustling through the pines restoring a calm to Nicole. She followed Bree up the trail to where they would put the finishing touches on a small bridge over the stream.

"Olivia has changed her mind about her career choice. Again."

"Really? What was she pursuing?"

"Accounting."

Olivia had timidly approached her with the news. Had she been worried about her reaction? Nicole had to admit she was disappointed.

"I'm not sure why she was taking those classes anyway. Numbers are not really her thing."

"You didn't tell her that to begin with?"

"No. Sometimes it's better for her to figure that out on her own. She is an adult, after all."

Bree picked up a branch and set it off the trail. "That's something I should get better at with my kids. Maybe once they become adults, they'll have it figured out."

"Possibly. At least you have more than one kid. The first one is for practice, so you know what to do with the second, right?"

"I suppose. I actually should have had three."

Bree pulled the pruners from her hip pocket and snipped off a branch working its way across the trail.

"Did you miscarry? I had several miscarriages before we adopted Olivia."

"No. I had an abortion."

Nicole double blinked. An abortion? How could she say that so casually? Nicole couldn't even fathom that. She'd have given anything to have a baby.

"Oh. Well, I suppose you had your reasons."

Where did that comment come from? It was not at all what was really on her mind.

"No worries. It's all good. I made the best decision I needed to at the time."

They reached the stream crossing, the water bubbling over mossy rocks. A butterfly flitting from tiny white shamrock blossoms. Sights and sounds that soothed a mom's soul.

The area had already been cleared of the rotting pilings and two by sixes, making ready for the new. Battery operated drills, radial saws and other tools sat in a wheelbarrow, waiting for creation to happen.

"It's just the two of us?"

Nicole sat on a stump and stretched, entwining her fingers, and reaching her hands over her head.

"Yep. That's all we need. It'll take a couple of hours and we'll walk away with the joy of finishing a project. That's what I love about this job. Working in nature, breathing in the fresh fragrances, and creating a place for others to enjoy and make memories."

Nicole looked up the path, wondering what types of conversations the old growth cedars held in their rings. Would they remember her conversations with Brad while hiking this very trail? Their angst at not being able to get pregnant and keep a baby? Their desperation to have a child? Or the trust it took to raise someone else's daughter? Nicole would have been ecstatic to raise Bree's baby had she had the chance.

Bree slogged on some boots and took one end of the piling while Nicole grabbed the other end. The stream was low and gentle as Bree made her way across.

Suddenly, she slipped on a mossy rock, causing her to lose her footing. The end of the piling slid to into the water and Bree curled her body over it to avoid falling.

Hysterical laughter rang out causing Nicole to let her end of the log fall as she unsuccessfully held in a giggle.

"You okay?" Nicole asked.

"Yeah." Bree took a breath between giggles.

Nicole allowed the humor to override her angst from their former conversation.

Chapter Nine

"Hey Mom, I picked up your new prescription."
Peter pulled out the bottle from the white bag, took a moment to read the information and went for a glass of water.

"This should make a difference in your energy and some of the nerve pain."

"Thanks, Peter. I'll try it. I don't know. I've tried so many things and nothing seems to work."

"Well, let's give it a whirl. Are you coming to the fair with us today? We'll be showing sheep. It would be good for you to get out and do something other than farm work. See some friends. Check which ribbons you received on your flowers."

Peter would give anything to see her feel better, to have pain free days. To be the mom he had grown up with. It was hard seeing her suffer. But somewhere amid it all, she was always cheerful. Joyful even. He needed to learn that. But the mistake he had made, not telling his dad about the frayed wires. How could he be joyful when his guilt was always there nagging at him. Pulling him under.

Peter glanced out of the window when he heard the rumble of

the pickup. The back was packed with hay, tubs of grain, a cooler inevitably filled with drinks and sandwich fixings.

Olivia jumped out, her blonde pony sticking through a red ball cap. She started towards the front door. Her sculpted shoulders showed through a sleeveless plaid shirt. Admiration swelled clear through him. This girl was so much more than what others saw in her. So capable. He couldn't accomplish half of what she did with both his hands.

"Hey—just let me grab my sweatshirt and I'll be right there."

Peter kicked up dry dirt as he walked to the truck. They needed rain. Not only for the crops, but right now the fire danger was high. He grimaced and moved some folders and a coffee can full of feed from the seat before jumping into the passenger side. Bits of straw and gravel littered the floor, the nature of a true farm truck.

"I told Mom I was quitting accounting." Olivia side-eyed Peter.

"Really? How'd she take it?"

"I thought she'd freak out. But she didn't. She just gave me the look—the one that said she was disappointed in me. It's like there's always this underlying, unspoken thing that we never talk about. I know she loves me. She's always tried to make me see that I can achieve anything. But—"

"And you have. You've been at the top of your game in everything you've touched."

"I know. But it's like I'm always supposed to prove something. Sometimes I just want to be able to pick something *I* really like instead of her suggesting what my path should be." Olivia looked out the window.

"But you seemed to like swim team. And soccer. And everyone loved having you on their team."

"I did. But I don't know. I just don't feel like I've found my place, you know? I mean really, me and accounting?"

Peter's laugh bubbled over the sound of the engine.

"Yeah, that's not really you. Maybe something with animals,

though. Look at you. It's like you're a different person when you're around them. You have everything here—you are so talented with them. You have the setting and all the space to meet their needs. You're right about defaulting to what your mom wants you to do. What she wants you to be. You need to choose a career that you look forward to each day. Something that fills your mind and stretches you. Something that makes your heart sing."

Olivia sucked on her bottom lip.

"Just think about what you really enjoy. And, um, I'm thinking maybe Jake isn't on that list?"

"Way to turn the subject!"

Olivia's mouth turned in a wry grin.

"No, he's definitely not on the list. What a jerk!"

"My thoughts exactly. I mean, what did you even like about him?"

Olivia leaned against the truck door and crossed her arms.

"You can't deny that he's gorgeous. Strong arms. Nice smile."

"Looks aren't everything, you know."

"Obviously. I'd seen signs of him being controlling but just passed them off. Until the other night when he came over and I was studying for my exam. He was ruthless."

"And when he didn't stand up for you with his imbecile friends, I about decked him."

Olivia smirked. "Almost?" She giggled. "He's twice your size. Good choice to walk away."

THEY PULLED into the fair entrance and stopped near the pens to unload. The barn was filled with the raucous sounds of a couple of preteens chasing a wayward ewe.

"Olivia, get on that side and try to keep her from getting out of the barn."

Olivia ran to one side and held her arms out to try to keep her in place.

"Oh noooo—she got away!"

Olivia and Peter ran towards the ewe slowing to a walk as they got closer. Sheep are not always the smartest animals on the planet. And without Zip to help round up the runaway, this was going to be a chore.

"You guys spread out—one on each side of the aisle. Extend your arms. Olivia and I will try to urge her back towards the pen."

They took slow steps toward the ewe, who let out a baa and ran back towards the kids and stopped. Her eyes flitted, trying to decide her next move. The kids flapped their arms trying to shoo her in the direction of her pen. She bolted through them and out the other end of the barn.

"Dang!" Peter took off his hat and slapped it on his leg.

"Just gotta be patient."

"But now she's not contained. She'll be running all over the place."

They hustled outside to where she grazed on a small patch of grass, acting as if she'd found a little piece of heaven. Olivia and Peter simultaneously jumped on the ewe, pinning her down, Olivia's arms wrapped around her neck.

The rich smell of lanolin filled his senses. But the citrusy scent of shampoo of the girl under Peter did him in. He could stay like this forever. Possibly would have, had she not burst into laughter.

Peter pulled a piece of Olivia's hair out of his mouth before he rolled off her.

"Eww—you didn't get enough to eat for breakfast?"

"Just thought I'd try something new. Hair's not bad. You should try it sometime." He grinned.

"Well, I guess we caught her."

Olivia got to her knees. The lamb baaed and tried to jerk away but Olivia held tight to her. Olivia led her back to the empty pen where she immediately went to the grain bucket.

"That was some show." Evelyn leaned over the fence.

"You two are something." She laughed. "You were right Peter. I haven't had this much fun in eons."

Peter brushed the hay from his jeans.

"Did you have a chance to look at the flower exhibits? How did your entries do?"

"Not yet. Do you have time to wander over there with me?"

"You two ago ahead. I've got to get the kiddos rounded up for showmanship." Olivia nodded at them.

They stopped by the Chicken Coop, and each got ice cream cones, Peter's, strawberry cheesecake, Evelyn's, vanilla bean, before they wandered over to the exhibits.

"It looked like you were enjoying yourself with that catch."

Peter's chest warmed when he saw the grin on his mom's face. The one that said there was more to that statement.

"With the ewe. And possibly with that neighbor of ours." She licked her cone.

Peter's felt his ears burn. Was it that obvious? He'd never had a serious girlfriend. Tina had been on his mind at Mercy. But God had other plans for her. Olivia? Now that he was back, he saw a whole new meaning to possibilities.

Evelyn stopped by each colorful quilt admiring the fine stitching and designs. The photos and art displays showed hours of talent and creativity. Peter smiled watching his mom's enjoyment. It was good to see her energized. Hopefully the new meds would kick in. If not, he'd check in with Daniel and see if he could recommend something else for her.

"Peter, thank you for coming home. I know that was a sacrifice for you. Leaving your job and I'm sure it was hard to leave your friends."

Peter nodded.

"You didn't have to. But I want you to know I appreciate it. I haven't been able to keep up all the time. It's been incredibly frustrating. I just don't want to be a burden."

Leaving the Invincibles, yes. Leaving his job? That was another story. The fast pace, the entitled patients, his constantly questioning his ability to make accurate decisions? Not so much.

"I'm happy to be here for you Mom. I should have been here for you more before now. You've got a lot on your plate—keeping up your flowers and pumpkin patch. Not to mention keeping up with all Dad has to do."

Maybe his dad was right. He did belong on the farm.

"Look, here are your flowers, Mom. Grand champion ribbon on your gladiolas. And blues on your dahlias and flower arrangement."

Yep, he'd missed out on the little things. Like the glow of pride on Evelyn's face.

Peter's phone buzzed.

"Son, I need you to come home. I've got a calf tangled up in some barbed wire. She's not going to make it without you."

Chapter Ten

P eter turned as Olivia grabbed his arm.

"I'm going with you! I want to help."

In the field, their boots crunched the dry grass, Peter's long legs moving him towards the fence. The calf letting out a mournful moo.

"Aww, he's so small. Poor little thing." Olivia ran to him and squatted down.

Large dark clouds were forming, threatening rain. The sky brightened as a flash of lightning struck. Rain would be a blessing for the parched earth and crops, and better yet, would prevent wildfires. There was no doubt that had plagued Peter's mind. But releasing a calf in a downpour would make things that much more difficult.

"Here are some gloves, son. Grab the clippers while I try to calm her down."

Large brown eyes pled with Peter—her long lashes blinked. Olivia placed her arms around her neck and spoke softly to her.

"The barbed wire between those old, weathered poles was loose so she managed to get her legs twisted between the strands. We'll have to make fixing that fence a priority."

Ross shoved his cap down further as the rain slid down the brim to the front of his Carhartt jacket.

Thunder boomed and the calf struggled to free herself, but the barbs stuck her, and each struggle brought the strands tighter.

Peter opened the long handles of the snips and with a crunch, released the wire. The calf jolted and Olivia held her tighter. Big drops fell from the sky bringing the scent of petrichor to the earth.

"You're okay. Let Peter get the wire untangled from your legs."

Olivia stroked her head. Peter was glad for the gloves as he gingerly unwrapped the strands, jumping back as she kicked to try and free herself. A quick glance caught Ross' eyes giving Peter affirmation this was where he belonged.

"You're fine. We'll get you fixed up here."

Peter unwrapped the wire several times to free her.

"She's got quite a gash there. Do you think you can get her to the barn so I can treat her? She'll need stitches."

"I can help." Olivia stood. "We already had practice on Bella."

"Yeah, I guess so."

Ross removed his hat and ran his hand through his damp hair.

"You think you could manage that? It would sure save a bundle on a vet bill."

Maybe his dad would appreciate the skills he had learned while he'd been away.

The calf bellowed, scrambled to her feet, and ran towards her mother. The rain kicked in, large drops pouring down, soaking them. Ross looked up at the sky and let the refreshing water stream down his face. He lifted his hands.

"Thank you, Lord."

SUN SHONE through the thinning clouds, creating a double rainbow that reached from one end of the horizon landing in the pumpkin patch where bright yellow flowers bloomed, promising a full crop of happiness for kids in the fall. Olivia had missed the wet, loamy smell of soil. Drops of water fell from the eaves splashing into a rain barrel. Olivia breathed in the freshness of the moist earth and smiled. God was so good, the rainbow reminding her of promises and new possibilities. He had been there for her before. He would be again. She felt a peace come over her. He would direct her path. And it would be good.

She filled a bucket of grain for the heifer and stopped beside the calf pen. She set the bucket down, slid the gate open, and held her hand out, letting the calf come to her. She stroked her soft head and ran her hand down her back. Peter had been so adept at treating the gash and stitching her up. It had been fascinating to watch. He was such a natural.

"Hey little babe, are you feeling better?"

She poured the grain into the trough for the mama while her thoughts flitted to Peter—landing on top of her and the ewe. She shivered, the feeling zinging through her chest and into her stomach.

She shouldn't have enjoyed it as much as she had. Longing sprung up, surprising her by its suddenness. It was unsettling. And then who should come walking up behind her. Blood rushed to her cheeks. She forced herself to look down and set the bucket on the dirt floor.

"That little gal looks like she's doing okay."

Peter leaned his arms over the fence.

Olivia found it difficult to picture the teenager he had once been—gangly limbs and cocky swagger. He had the same brown hair. Same hazel eyes. But now, she couldn't miss his broad shoulders, the line of his jaw, his muscular forearms, his denim sleeves rolled up to his elbows.

"Yes." She cleared her throat. "She seems like she doesn't even notice it."

"I'm glad you were there helping, Ollie. She really calmed

down with you. I had the chance to watch dozens of surgeries. Seeing the experts stitch up the patients came in handy."

"For sure."

The heifer nuzzled her calf.

"They're so cute together." Olivia said.

Made her wonder about her bio mom. That was always a longing in her heart that had never been met. She paused and looked at Peter.

"I wonder if I could ever find my bio mom. Tell her thank you for choosing adoption. I landed in the best spot with Dad and Mom."

"I'm sure it would be possible. Would you want me to help you?"

Olivia turned to him. "You would do that?"

"Yes, of course. Ollie, I've known you since forever. Why wouldn't I help a good friend?"

A good friend? Well, he said good, not just a friend. Wait, what am I thinking? He is just a friend. That's all. Okay, stop. Don't muddle things up.

"How do you think I could go about it? Look up ancestors online? There must be a record somewhere."

"Don't you want to ask your parents? They probably know who to contact. It might be easy."

"Do you think they'd get mad? I don't want them to think I don't love them."

"Just tell them that. I'm sure they'd be okay."

Olivia bit her lip. "What if I find her and she doesn't want to talk to me?"

"Yeah. That might hurt. It's a risk you have to take if you want to find out."

Memory lane flooded her with painful thoughts of how, in the early years of school, her classmates had hurled questions at her about being adopted. Questions she hadn't known how to answer. And truth be known, that aching uncertainly lingered and left an occasional yearning. Who were her people? Why didn't her mom choose to raise her? Did she look like her?

Olivia nodded slowly, then looked up, determination in her eyes.

"I do. I want to find out."

Chapter Eleven

Olivia hiked the wooded North Peaks Parks trail, sandwiched between her mom and dad.

"There's something I want to ask you."

Nicole had wanted to show them how she had restored the bridge. Olivia breathed in the fragrance of the pines. The wind made a soft rustling through the trees causing needles to fall at their feet.

"What is it, honey?" Her dad turned—his eyebrow cocked.

"First of all, I love you both so much. And I know that you love me."

"Good to know. Sometimes I've wondered about that," Brad winked.

"What's on your mind, sweetheart?" Nicole turned.

"I was watching the calf with her mama the other day. It was so sweet—she licked her face and nuzzled her. And it made me want to know if I could find my bio mom."

"Let's sit down on this log. I need a rest anyway."

Brad put his hand on her shoulder and guided her.

"We were wondering when this conversation would take place."

Nicole brushed a leaf from her sweatshirt. Olivia let out the breath she had been holding.

"We can tell you what we know," Brad started.

"Which isn't much," Nicole clasped her hands over her head and stretched.

"Where was I born? And do you know anything about her? Why she chose adoption?"

And why she didn't want me? Olivia swallowed. Talking about this was harder than she thought.

"You were born at Mercy Hospital, in Portland," her dad began.

"Brad and I had tried so hard to have a baby. Each month when my period came, I would cry. And when I finally got pregnant, I miscarried at six weeks. And several times later. I was miserable. It just seemed like—like life had no meaning."

Brad put his arm around Nicole's shoulders. "So, then we decided to pursue the path of adoption. And it wasn't long before we got the call."

Olivia nodded. "Was my bio mom there when you showed up? I mean, sometimes the bio mom wants to see who will raise her baby."

"No, we never met her. And to tell the truth, we weren't sure if we wanted to or not," Brad said.

Olivia wrinkled her forehead. "But why?"

"I had mixed emotions. I was over the moon that she had chosen adoption. She was the reason my dream was coming true. But then, I was afraid that we would lock eyes and she'd change her mind. Realize that giving you to another parent wasn't really what she wanted to do."

Olivia rubbed her hand over her face. This was a lot to take in. She watched a swallowtail butterfly land on a skunk cabbage, the yellows blending in with the blossom.

"What did you think when you saw I didn't have a hand?"

She held her arm out and rubbed it. "Did you want to change your mind? I mean, really, you can tell me."

"Can't deny we were a little shocked. It would have seemed that the nurse or someone would have prepared us for that. You were a premie and only weight five and a half pounds. Your little arms were tucked inside the receiving blanket, and you had a tiny pink knit hat on. And your face was beautiful. Rosy cheeks, bright alert eyes."

"I swear I saw you smile when you looked at me. And it wasn't until we changed your diaper for the first time that we saw it. Your stump was bandaged." Nicole locked eyes with Brad.

"Wait, I wasn't born without my hand? What happened to me?"

Moisture formed in Olivia's eyes. She could picture her as a tiny baby and the shock on her parents' faces.

"No one would tell us. It seemed like kind of a big deal that they should have shared."

Brad put his arm around Nicole's shoulders where Olivia leaned into her.

"But Mom—Dad—you kept me anyway. You didn't have to."

Olivia's lips trembled and tears slid down her cheeks and she choked out a sob.

PETER KNELT on the other side of the row from his mom. Her gloved hands deftly pulled the weeds surrounding the pumpkin plants, the long tendrils beginning to reach out to grab the plant beside it. The sun-kissed yellow flowers starting to bud, some already opening, waiting for the baby pumpkin to form inside. The soil was warm underneath Peter's fingers and soft under his knees.

"I'm glad you're back home, Peter. I really appreciate the help. Not that Olivia hasn't been a godsend."

"Yes, I feel peaceful here, like this is where I'm supposed to be.

At least for now. I can't tell you how crazy our hospital floor was—heck, who knew there was such a thing as IV drug users?"

He shook his head and yanked up a handful of weeds.

"Anyway, you seem to be feeling better. Looks like those new drugs are kicking in."

"I am. I have a lot more energy. It's nice to have my own nurse."

She grinned and adjusted her sun hat.

"It's not like your dad doesn't care about me. He does. He's the best man in the world. But he's anything but medical."

That was true. He could do anything around the farm. Well, maybe not everything. He wasn't the one who stitched up the calf.

"I can't wait till the pumpkins are ripe. They're always so cheery. And I'm sure Ollie helps decorate the patch for the kids and their families."

"Mmhmm. She's got a gift, that girl."

"October was always so much fun growing up. You guys made it the real deal. Hayrides, corn maze, all kinds of pumpkins and gourds. Great memories. Say, would it be okay if I invited my nurse friends for a barn party in the fall? They would love it here."

"Yes, of course. I can't believe you feel like you have to ask. Of course, I'd love to meet them."

"So, a little segue here. I'm glad Jake's out of the picture. He seemed okay at first, but there was just something about him."

"Yeah, I know what you mean. I didn't much care for him either. He was a hard worker, but I don't know, sometimes he would say things to her that were insensitive. Made me uncomfortable."

They moved down the row, parting the vines to pull more weeds.

"Did you know Nicole and Brad when they adopted Ollie?"

"Sure. In fact, they moved next door about four years before that."

"What was the story?"

"Well, let's see. Seemed like they had tried for a year or two to get pregnant. I'm pretty sure she miscarried once. Maybe twice. It was a long time ago, so I'm not sure. We used to pray for them every week at our Bible study."

"And then they decided to adopt?"

"Not right away. They went to a fertility specialist. But in the end, it was just too expensive. So, it was after that they filed for adoption."

"Hmmm. I bet they were happy when they got Olivia."

"I can't even tell you! They were beside themselves. We had a big baby shower and—" Evelyn looked out over the field.

"And what?"

"Well, I was just remembering how afraid they were to let anyone know about her hand. I guess they weren't sure if everyone would accept her."

"But she had to have been beautiful. I mean, look at her! That long blond hair, gorgeous brown eyes." With golden specks. And long eyelashes.

Evelyn put down her handful of weeds and looked at Peter. A hint of a smile played on her lips.

"What made you ask about this?"

"Last night, we were in the barn—I was checking on the calf that I stitched up. She couldn't take her eyes off the mom and babe. And then she said she wanted to find her bio mom. She wanted to tell her thank you for choosing life."

"Well, that's normal. I suppose that was bound to happen sometime. Seems like most adoptees want to know about their biological parents, who they are, what they look like, if they have any siblings."

"I told her she should talk to her parents first. They could show her birth certificate to her and tell her anything they know."

"Wise counsel, son. It wouldn't do for her to start looking and then have them find out."

"Yeah, I didn't think so. She has a good relationship with them. She loves them both so much and the last thing she wants to do is to hurt them."

"They'll be fine." She looked at Peter and smiled. "I think I'm not the only one who's glad you're back."

Chapter Twelve

Bella limped to Olivia. Olivia stroked Bella's soft golden fur, her warm head resting on her knee. The irony. She stroked her head. Her paw hadn't healed as they had hoped. It had been too late for the stitches to take. Still, Bella hadn't seemed to mind. She just went on with life like running three legs was how she was supposed to be. It was so sweet that they had something like that in common.

Only Peter would think to bring her an animal that she could instantly bond with. One like her. Warmth traveled to her heart. He always knew the way to her heart. She turned the video on, the red record button blinked.

"Hey guys, I wanted to update you on a new thing. Most of you know I'm adopted. And I absolutely love my parents. But we don't look anything alike. I want to know where I came from. So, I've decided to search for my bio mom. I'm a little nervous. I know this could take a long time. And I know nothing about how to search. So, if any of you have gone through this and have

suggestions, I'm open. Hope y'all have a great day! Oh, and look at my adorable puppy! Her name is Bella. Isn't she the cutest thing ever? Okay, really, I'll see you next time!"

She clicked stop, watched it, and posted to her YouTube channel. She sat back in her chair, hopefulness tingling in her soul. Bella licked her arm.

"My bio parents are out there, Bella. The people I'm a physical part of."

She ran her hands over her soft ears.

"I just want to know who they are."

Bella turned her eyes towards a tap on the door.

"Hey Olivia. Thought I'd stop by and see if you wanted to start your search."

Peter's t-shirt stretched across his chest and fit comfortably over his faded jeans. Olivia's eyes jumped back to his face and coughed.

"You startled me!"

"Sorry. I thought you heard me come in."

A cool breeze swirled through the window and over her desk. It flipped the open pages of her journal. She nonchalantly closed it and swiveled her chair to meet him.

"Uh, yeah. I just posted a video on my channel saying I was gonna do it. It's starting to feel real."

And not just the search. Her cheeks grew red. Peter was a friend. She shouldn't be looking at him as anything else. She didn't want to ruin a good thing.

Peter pulled up a chair next to hers.

"Where should we start?"

"At the beginning."

He laughed. She joined in and together they said, "And go on till you come to the end. Then stop."

"I can't believe you remember that." She laughed.

"Of course—how many thousands of times did Mr. Graham say that phrase from Alice in Wonderland to us? Fourth grade, right?"

Yes, she remembered. Each time he had come to that part she and Peter would lock eyes and hold in a giggle.

"Okay, I guess the beginning is searching how to find my birth parents.'"

Olivia held in a deep breath, sat up straight and whooshed it out. Peter swiveled his chair, put his hands on her neck and rubbed, then slid his hands to her shoulders—the same move he had done through high school when she was anxious.

"My friend Kaitlyn, when she got nervous, would stand tall, spit over her right shoulder and ptooey. You should try it."

"Was she one of the Invincibles?"

"Yeah. You'd like her. Tina too. You'll get to meet them next month when they come to the Pumpkin Patch. But anyway, type it in, will you? We don't have all day!"

Their knees touched, his right to her left, like when they had been in grade school, paired up as reading buddies. Olivia had to admit she liked the feeling. It was comfortable and ordinary. In contrast to the door she was about to enter through.

Olivia clenched her teeth and began typing. Dozens of links showed. Search Birth Records for Free. US Birth Record Search. Biological Parents Records—Just Enter a Name Now. Sign up! Your birth parents may have already registered if they're searching for you, too.

Was that even a possibility? She was afraid to hope.

"Holy moly! So much information," Olivia turned to Peter.

"Okay, give me your notebook. I'll start a list."

He reached for her journal. She grabbed it back and put it in a drawer.

"Uh—use this."

Olivia felt the blood rise to her cheeks. That seemed to be happening a lot lately.

Peter double raised his eyebrows and grinned.

"What, you don't want me to see what you wrote about me?"

Olivia frowned and looked away. Letting Peter see her last few months entries? Never gonna happen.

He wrote a list of steps as they perused the web. Birth certificate. Pre-adopted birth certificate. DNA test. He stretched. Not much of a list, but so much wrapped into each item. Olivia rolled her shoulders. It was easy to go from site to site with just another click. She knew this would take time, but maybe this was going to be a bigger challenge than she thought.

"Maybe you should go ahead and order the DNA test. That's the easiest thing to do first."

Peter tapped a few keys. "Here you go."

Olivia inhaled, held it, gave an affirmative nod and let it out.

Bella rested her head on Olivia's lap, her squeaky ball in her mouth. Olivia stroked her soft fur. She couldn't stop the chuckle as she looked into those loving brown eyes. This little girl was just what she needed.

They looked up as Nicole tapped on the door frame.

"Hey, I found your pre-adoption birth certificate."

Olivia's heart's thumping accelerated. Did she really want to see it? She took it from her mom's outstretched hand and opened it slowly, as if an ogre would jump out at her.

She focused on each line, taking in the scrawl of the signature, wanting to memorize each curve.

Birthdate: March 1, 1993. Mother's name: Bridgett Madeline Thompson. Father's Name: Unknown. Place of Birth: Mercy Hospital, Portland, Oregon. Sex: Female

Olivia let out a slow breath and lifted her eyes to her mom's.

"Well, I guess I know her name. That's a start. I already knew the rest."

Nicole rested her hand on her shoulder.

"I wish I could tell you more. Are you okay?"

Olivia nodded. "Yes. Thanks Mom. You'll always be my favorite mom." She leaned her head into her mom and smiled up at her.

"Whew! I'm glad to hear that." She grinned. "I knew this day would come. Let me know how I can help."

She started for the door.

"Oh, and could you guys pick a bucket of blackberries for me? I want to make a pie."

"My mouth's watering already!" Peter stood.

"Yeah, okay. I've got to go walk this puppy anyway. She hasn't been out yet today."

Bella tapped her tail and smiled up at her.

"We got a good start though."

Peter reached his hand in the air and high-fived her. Then reached in for a hug.

SOMETHING HAD SHIFTED. It was just a quick hug. He could smell the scent of her shampoo lingering, light and citrusy. The same shampoo she wore in high school. But why did that hug feel like so much more? Maybe that moment when her eyes met his? Was she feeling it too? And did he even need to shy away from the feeling?

Bella ran ahead of them, stopping now and then to sniff and piddle. She had quickly learned how to get around despite her foot not lining up properly. An orthopedic surgeon he wasn't. But he had done his best at the time. And she didn't seem worse for wear. Peter picked up a stick and threw it ahead of her. She raced after it and returned it.

"Good puppy! Here you go." Olivia tossed it again. "Let's head down by the creek. The blackberries are biggest there. Plus, this day is like an oven, and it will be cooler there."

"I had no idea there was so much online about finding bio moms." Peter glanced at her.

"I know, right? But I'm glad to have my pre-birth certificate and know my mom's name." She whistled for Bella who turned and ran to her. "I feel funny calling someone else *my mom*."

"For sure. That would be kinda weird. Maybe you can refer to her as Mama Bridgett."

Olivia nodded. "Do you think maybe she registered to try and find me?"

Peter watched Olivia's shoulders tense.

"I guess you'll be able to find out the next time you're on the site."

"Yeah."

She looked down at her sandled feet as she walked.

They reached the blackberry patch, nestled in the shade of a massive oak tree. The sound of the creek burbled in contrast to the stillness of the air. A bee buzzed and landed on some wild sweet peas.

"This shouldn't take long. The berries are big, and the bushes are loaded."

The sound of the berries pinged in the metal bowl.

"Only one more day of fair. Just the market animal auction."

"I always felt kind of sad when that day came. One, because of selling my animal that I worked so hard to raise. And to think it was going to be slaughtered. My little 4-H'ers might have some tears."

"Remember Ollie, when you sold your chicken? That was the first year you had a market animal."

"Yeah. I'll never forget that. I had babied that thing and carried it around since it was just a little fuzzy chick. I could call it and it would come."

Olivia's face had been a blubbery mess when she had to hand it over to the buyer.

"You handed me a wad of paper towels and put your arm around my shoulder. It was so sweet." Olivia looked up at Peter.

That penetrating look—it was more than a moment in time. It was wrapped up in a lifetime of memories. He couldn't keep his eyes from tracing the softness of her jaw, moving to her lips, and bouncing back to the depth of her eyes. He caught himself, inhaled and reached for another handful of berries which he placed into the nearly full bowl.

Then Peter picked one and lobbed it into the bowl like a basketball. He repeated with several more and then tossed one at Olivia where it hit her arm. She looked up, alarmed, and set the bowl down.

"Why you—"

One look at his smirk and she tossed one at Peter which hit him on the cheek. He pulled off his shirt. Before long, a full-on blackberry fight ensued, squeals and laughter filling the air.

Olivia backed Peter to the creek where he lost his balance and fell in. He righted himself, ran his hands over his wet face and caught her arm. She wriggled out of her sandals.

"In you go, missy. You're not going to get away with that move."

She squealed, wriggled out of his grip, and ran down the bank where she threw herself in and swam to the deep pool where the creek curved and eddied.

She dunked her head under and let the water refresh and cleanse, her hair billowed out resting on the top of the water.

He joined her and stretched his arms out behind him where he supported himself on a rock.

"I guess we needed to get cleaned up before we went back home."

"Yeah, thanks to you."

He loved that scowl, the one that played between anger and love.

Peter moved his hands to her shoulders where they locked eyes. He glanced at her open lips and moved closer. Bella jumped into the creek and dog paddled up to them. Olivia pulled away, crimson rising to her face.

"Bella! Come on girl, time to get these berries home."

Chapter Thirteen

Peter had almost kissed her. And she had come close to letting him. And if Bella hadn't interrupted, she would have absolutely let him. What in the world was she thinking? Peter was her best friend. She couldn't let this turn into something more. Something like a relationship, as in, cute guy falls for cute gal. Or vice versa. It would ruin everything. Still—

Bella watched Olivia pull her green 4-H leader sweatshirt over her tank top. Better to be prepared if the temperature dropped tonight, what with fall setting in.

"Come on, girl. We've got to get ready for the auction."

Bella stood and wagged her tail.

Nicole held a plastic tub.

"Are you going to take these cookies? I made several batches for your kids."

"They'll love those. Thanks Mom." Olivia gave her a peck on the cheek. "You didn't have to do that, you know."

"I know. It's just my way of being a part and supporting you."

"And even if you didn't do those special things, you'll still always be my favorite mom." She smiled.

It was a tricky spot, searching for Bridgett. What would it be like if she didn't have the support of her parents? Would she have to hide every move, worrying about them finding out. Worrying about hurting them? She hoped they were telling the truth when they gave her their blessing to continue.

She had made the next move. The DNA package should come in the mail any day now. Anxiety traveled from her chest to the pit of her stomach. *Lord, am I doing the right thing?*

OLIVIA PULLED INTO THE FAIRGROUNDS, going up and down the rows trying to find a parking spot. So many people here on the last day. She waved at a group of her kids headed to the ferris wheel, tapping her watch, reminding them what time they needed to show up to get their animals ready.

She went from pen to pen checking each animal. Were they clean? Trimmed? Did they each have food and water? The judges would be making the rounds, and she wanted her club to be top notch. It wouldn't do for them to receive white ribbons.

She checked the sheep's teeth and feet, making sure they were in good form. She stood back, taking them in. Everything looked okay. More than okay. She had done a good job of training up this lot and if felt good.

Maybe something with animals. It's like you're a different person when you're around them. You are so talented with them.

Peter was right. She realized then and there that she wanted nothing more than to become a veterinarian. She could do it. She knew she could. Tomorrow she would take steps to develop a plan.

PETER HAD ALMOST SLIPPED UP. He had let thoughts of Olivia consume him, so much so that it seemed natural to want to kiss her. To almost kiss her. The sun shining diamonds on the ripples in the creek, her wet hair matting on her face, purple berry staining that spot next to her lips, almost begging him to lick it off.

The thing of it was, it seemed like she would have let him if Bella had not interrupted them.

Man, he had it bad.

Peter threw his jacket into his backpack and jumped on his motorcycle, letting the wind breeze past him. When he arrived at the animal barn, they were just announcing the Mutton Bustin' contest. Brought back memories of when he was a little kid. Olivia had beat him by a few points and got to do the happy dance holding up her prize belt buckle. One that was almost as big as she was.

"Here they are, the kids coming into the gate. Cowboy number one is seven-year-old Travis Murphy from Brownsmead. Where is Brownsmead, anyway? Anybody know?"

Peter watched the helmeted boy with his cowboy boots and safety vest lifted onto the back of a ewe. He grabbed onto the thick wool with both hands.

"Hold on Travis. You can do it."

The ewe raced around the pen until Travis slid off her back and rolled onto the soft dirt. His dad picked him up and Travis waved at the crowd and ran back to the bleachers.

"Good job Travis. He's got eighty-eight points everybody! Next, we have Rosalia Gonzales from Madras."

She was lifted onto the back of the ewe who took off running. It was only a matter of seconds before she slid off. She waved at the crowd, dusted herself off and ran to her mom, pigtails flying.

"Eighty-nine points. She just took first place. Look at the smile on her mom's face. Okay everybody. Next up is five-year-old George Baldwin from right here in Willowbrook. Oooohhh! Hop back up, kiddo. He'll do better next year, I'm sure. Sixty-eight points."

The volunteers rounded up all the kids and put them in a line, their vests emblazoned with large numbers and faces full of hope. Their smiles reached their ears when they each received trophies.

"Let's give these brave kids a hand. It takes a lot of guts to do what they did."

Peter turned to leave and bumped into Olivia.

"Oh! Sorry. I didn't see you there."

"I didn't know you were going to turn around just then." She laughed. "Do you want to go with me to get the final night barbecue ribs?"

They made their way through the crowds—kids tugging on their parent's arms to go somewhere more interesting than where they were at present, a teen pushing his grandmother in a wheelchair showing her the displays, music from the country band on the grandstand coming over the loudspeakers. Peter had missed this the last few years when he'd been cleaning up puke and changing IV's. Kaitlyn's daughter Claire would love this. He'd make sure they came next year.

They waited through the long line and carried their ribs, Cole slaw, berry pie and lemonade to a grassy area near the music.

"You helped me make a decision today." Olivia took a bite of her roll.

"Yeah, what's that?" He wondered if the decision had to do with his almost kiss.

"You helped me realize how much I love being around animals, and that I could pursue a career as a vet."

Olivia put her hand on Peter's arm.

"And do you know that when I said it out loud, my lips turned up. I felt confident it was the right choice."

Peter grinned. "That is great. Have you thought about where you want to study?"

"I think I can start at the community college. I'll check and if so I'm going to register tomorrow."

Peter was drawn to the sparkle in her eyes, the animation of her hands. He took her hand and planted a kiss on it.

"I'm proud of you, Ollie. You're gonna be the best vet in the county. And you know, I'm here for you when it comes to medical terms."

The look in her eyes seemed to say so much more. She didn't come right out and say it, but he got the sense that things were already changing between them. It excited him—maybe a little too much.

Olivia looked at her hand and slowly pulled it away. In just that moment, it seemed something had passed between them.

THE BOOMING VOICE of the auctioneer echoed over the speaker, rising above the cacophony of voices, baaing of sheep on halters, grunting of pigs and squeals of those escaping their pens as the participants tried to head them to the show arena.

Peter crossed his arms and smiled as he remembered those high school days. He took in Olivia. She was in her element. Surrounded by animals. Loving the smells—the lanolin mixed with manure and hay. Smells only farmers and 4-Hers would appreciate.

"Okay folks, we've got a real fine ewe here. This young lady has obviously fed and worked her well."

Charlotte braced her thigh into the lamb's shoulder and set her rear feet straight.

"Let's start the bid at three dollars. Three dollars a pound, folks."

The cadence of the fast-talking auctioneer was like a song. A call here, a response from the crowd. Another call with a higher bid, a laugh and response from the crowd.

Peter moved his arm around Olivia's shoulder. She slid a glance to him.

"Marry me." She double blinked. He'd caught her off guard.

"You want me to marry you?"

"I want you to marry me."

"Hmm."

Her head turned to the auctioneer as she heard him call her name.

"Hold that thought..."

Chapter Fourteen

Olivia walked to the auctioneer. She glanced back once—her brow wrinkled, and one eyebrow cocked. Was there the hint of a smile?

The auctioneer spoke to her. She pointed to Charlotte and beckoned her over. Charlotte was a mixture of joy and grief. She had gotten way more money than expected for her lamb. But tears slid down her eyes as she watched them take her pride and joy away. Olivia gave her a hug and stroked her French braids. She pulled back and handed her a hankie.

Olivia made her way back to Peter.

"Let's go for a walk."

As they strolled out of the barn, Peter reached for her hand. There was a niggling telling her not to fall for his charm. Risking their friendship was something she wanted to avoid.

"Can we just talk about what I thought I heard you say?"

"I'll repeat what I said. Marry me!"

She pulled her hand away.

"Peter. We can't."

"Why not?"

"We just can't."

She turned and looked at him, her arms accentuating her words.

"It won't work."

"But what if it *does* work?" Peter wrapped his hands gently around her wrists, gazing into her eyes.

"What if it doesn't? We'll never be the same. We've had this amazing friendship all these years. I don't want to risk that."

"But it could work. We could make it work. And still be friends."

"I'm scared."

Olivia took a few steps. Then turned.

"Peter, you need to find a real girlfriend. I don't know, someone who is whole. It can't be me."

PETER'S HEARTBEAT thundered in his chest. Impulsive. That's what he was. Once again, he acted before thinking things through. And what the heck—*find someone who's whole?* She is whole. Peter didn't even see her without a hand, he'd known her for so long. But it obviously bothered her. For being best friends, she should know that wasn't an issue. Would never be an issue.

So now, what was this supposed to look like? Was he supposed to avoid her? Or was it okay to pull back and pretend this never happened. Reverse the scene. At least for a while. Because he knew that he knew he would marry her someday. And he would wait as long as he had to.

Besides, he wanted to still be with her every step of the way in her journey to find her bio parents. And help with her vet studies. No. She wasn't going to be able to just walk away from him. He wouldn't let her.

OLIVIA LOGGED into her YouTube channel and clicked on the record button.

"Hi guys. Fair is over. It's always a sad-glad day. Sad to not have the daily contact with the kids and both the hustle and down times at the fair. Glad that I can get back to my life and move forward because guess what? I've decided to become a vet. Yeah. I'm so excited. And that's what tells me this is the right move. I'm filling out my college application today.

And — I got my DNA kit in the mail today! I'm a little nervous about doing it. Cuz it's going to open doors I'm not sure I'm ready for. It's a weird place to be— wanting something so badly, then taking the step, and then being worried about the outcome. I have to believe that God will be with me along the way, good or bad.

See you next time!

SHE UPLOADED her video to her channel and sat back in her padded office chair. The sky out her window had a few lazy clouds slowly drifting along. A humongous flock of swallows flew in, swirling and diving, like a ballet. That's what she wanted her life to be like—a dance. Perfectly choreographed. She hoped these journeys she was embarking on would flow like that.

And now, what was she going to do about Peter? What was he thinking? That she would say yes right there in the barn in the middle of the auction surrounded by a bunch of people?

It wasn't like she hadn't begun to think about him as more than a friend. She had. Just the thought tied her in knots. He was truly the only person who knew her inside and out. But what if they got married and it didn't work out? She would lose him. She would lose her best friend.

And maybe, with her walking away, she was going to lose him

now. Unbid moisture beckoned to roll down her cheek. Her phone buzzed. Peter.

I'm sorry

Olivia wiped the tear from her cheek.

Yeah. Me too

I'm afraid I ruined everything. I don't want this, us, to be awkward.

Me neither

Can I come over?

Olivia stared out of the window. How should she answer.

Yes. I got the DNA test in the mail. You can watch me do it

Be right there

Olivia took the DNA kit to the kitchen. She made a cup of orange pekoe tea and swirled some honey in it. Peter knocked on the door with two raps, and came in. He stood with his hands jammed in his pockets before he stepped any closer.

Olivia looked at him, a small smile on her lips.

"It's okay. Come on in. I'm not mad."

Peter's shoulders relaxed and he removed his hands and let them rest by his sides. He sat on the swivel stool at the counter and rocked it back and forth.

"That smells good. Can I have a taste?" Olivia handed her cup to him, a move she would only make with a good friend. He took a sip and then went to the cupboard and took out a cup.

"The tea kettle is still hot."

Peter took a tea bag out of the box and poured the steaming water over it.

"Okay, you ready?"

Olivia slid the directions out of the DNA kit.

"Do not have anything to eat or drink within 30 minutes of administering the test. Well, good thing I didn't drink it yet."

She pulled the small vial out of the envelope and gathered a glob of spit. She glanced at Peter with her mouth full.

"Ewww. Careful now."

Olivia held the vial to her lips and let the saliva slide into it.

"Step one is successful."

She took out the other capsule that had liquid in it and combined it with the other. Peter set the timer on his phone for thirty seconds. She shook until it beeped, then placed it into the provided box and sealed it.

"How are you feeling right now?"

Olivia hugged herself. "Okay. I think. Well, maybe a little nervous."

"I can only imagine how I'd feel."

Peter started to reach his hand to touch her shoulder and pulled back. He cleared his throat.

"I'll walk beside you as much as you want. Or not." He raised his eyebrows.

Olivia nodded. "Thank you, Peter. Really."

He was doing it again. Being a safe fence around her tossed-about heart.

Chapter Fifteen

Olivia swiped the sweat off her brow with the hanky in her pocket. She rolled it up and tied it into a headband, then pulled it over her forehead. September wasn't supposed to be this hot, but it seemed the weather was changing into a new normal. She filled Bella's bowl with water, and she lapped it up like there was no tomorrow.

"I know. It's so hot. But I've got to get the fall décor up."

Olivia stroked her soft head and marveled at how much she had grown. She was getting around just fine on her three good legs. She smiled, remembering Peter's surprise gift to her. She did love him. But it was the love of a best friend, right? Nothing more. Of course not.

Evelyn rounded the corner pushing a wheelbarrow.

"Come help me fill this with pumpkins."

"Of course. How are you holding up? You look like you're feeling well today."

"Pretty good. Peter's got me on some new meds and my energy level is way up. I feel a little guilty, but I'm so glad he's home to help me. He told me you're looking for your birth mom?"

She stopped and put her hand over her mouth.

"Oh, I hope that was okay to bring up."

Olivia smiled. "Of course. Mom and Dad know. They're okay with it."

She took some clippers and started cutting the pumpkin vines.

"So, you'll need to do a little detective work, then."

"Yeah. I can't believe the rabbit hole of the internet. One thing leads to another and the next thing you know, you've been at the computer for several hours."

"I'm sure you've thought about what happens if you find her and she doesn't want to see you."

Evelyn followed behind her, setting pumpkins into the wheelbarrow.

"Yeah, I know. I just want to tell her thank you for giving birth to me. I mean, she didn't have to."

"I'm sure you've thought about what happens if you find her and she doesn't want to see you." She just had to be ready for all possibilities. She checked her phone. No messages from Ancestry.

"No, I suppose not. Well, I wish you the best. I'll keep you in my prayers for a good outcome."

"Thanks. And, Evelyn, I need to tell you that after the Pumpkin Patch is over, I need to buckle down and study. I've been admitted to the college to begin veterinary studies."

"Olivia! That is perfect for you. You love animals—everyone can see it. You'll be a natural."

The rumble of the tractor had them turning their heads to see Ross with several bales of hay stacked on the forks.

"Where do you want these?"

Olivia pointed to an open area beside the barn.

"We'll need about two dozen, if that's okay."

"For you? Of course!"

He tipped his ball cap. Olivia laughed. What wasn't to like about working here, being around ordinary folks who knew how to make a girl feel comfortable. Validated. Loved. Never once did she feel like they looked at her differently. Or coddled her. They just treated her like—like a regular girl. She grabbed the bale with a hooked pole and slid it in place.

Peter hopped off his motorcycle and removed his helmet. He took long strides toward them.

"Say, do you need a hand with that?"

He gave an exaggerated wink.

"You might say I always need a hand." Olivia returned the wink. Peter grinned.

As Peter stacked the bales, Evelyn and Olivia arranged pumpkins and gourds of all sizes decoratively around them. Olivia had painted an arched welcome sign that visitors could enter through. She brought out a large black tub full of clothes for the scarecrow.

Peter looked at his phone. "The Invincibles are coming for an overnight next weekend. They just sent a group text. I know how much Kaitlyn likes holidays. I'm sure she's going to want to have a good family photo shoot."

"I can't wait to meet them. Tell me about them."

She stuffed a plaid shirt with patches on the sleeves.

"Kaitlyn, Luke, and little Claire. They've been married a couple of years. Tina and Nate got married last summer, and there's Daniel."

"Daniel doesn't have a girlfriend?"

"He did, but Miya ended up moving to Florida. You're gonna love these guys. They're a lot of fun." Peter stared at the open field.

"You miss them, don't you."

"I do. But I don't miss working at that crazy hospital." He shook his head.

Hey friends. . . Well, I did it... sent off the DNA test. I must admit it's a little scary. I know I've got a mom out there. At least I hope I do. I suppose it's

possible something could have happened to her. Anyway,
I'm just sitting back and waiting for the mailman to
bring me results.

Fall is here! It's a little crisp in the mornings and
I'm getting the Pumpkin Patch ready for you all to come
visit. Here's the photo spot. Even have this cute scare-
crow cutouts for you to put your happy little faces in. All
kinds of fun for you and yours.

Evelyn's grown those cute baby pumpkins for your
table and quirky gourds. We'll be having a pumpkin
carving contest coming up. More on that later.

"Beep beep, beep beep, beep beep beep." Olivia looked up from her computer. Peter's friends must be here. She shut down her computer and went outside into the glorious sunshine where she hopped on her 4-wheeler and made her way to Peter's. An SUV pulled up next to the barn and six bodies piled out. Peter was grinning ear to ear, slapping the guys on the back and side hugging the gals. A toddler ran to his knees and held her hands up.

"Claire! You remember your uncle Peter?" He lifted her up where she grabbed his ball cap and put it on her curly head, then squiggled down. But not before Kaitlyn snapped a photo. She picked Claire up and placed her on top of her bulging belly. Peter looked down and then up.

"Yeah, Claire's gonna have a little brother soon."

"Congratulations!"

Olivia joined them.

"Hey guys, this is Olivia. She's—" he paused, "my neighbor."

That wasn't at all awkward. "Hey. Peter's been counting the days till you got here. So glad to finally meet you."

"Hi, I'm Tina and this is my husband Nate."

"I'm Luke, dad to this little rascal and husband to Kaitlyn." He held Claire's feet in place on his shoulders.

"And I'm Daniel. Pleased to meet you."

Olivia looked from one to the other, memorizing their names and features. Nate, tall and scruff on his face, Tina's red hair. Luke's gentle smile and Kaitlyn's curly brown hair—Claire must have inherited the same. And Daniel with his blue plaid flannel shirt.

Peter pointed to a spot in the field where they could set up their tents.

"Olivia, Mom's in the kitchen making dinner. Would you mind helping her?"

OLIVIA FOUND Evelyn peeling potatoes for potato salad, a cool breeze drifting in through the open window.

"Hey Evelyn. Could you use some help?"

"Boy could I. Could you cut the rest of these potatoes? I've got burger in the fridge to make into patties and we need celery and carrots cut for the salad."

Olivia picked up the knife.

"Peter's pretty pumped about his friends being here."

"That's true. I'm sure he misses the camaraderie at his job. It will be fun to have them here for the weekend. I love having you young kids around. You bring a nice energy."

"Speaking of energy—how's yours been? We've gotten through the flower festival and the fair, but we still have the pumpkin patch and that's going to have crowds of people for the month of October."

"Yeah. I've got my ups and downs. Yesterday I crashed but I'm pretty good today."

"Glad I can be here. I'm sure we can get Peter's friends to help get the rest of the Pumpkin Patch ready. Families will start coming next week, right?"

Olivia pulled out the bowl of burger and added onions, seasoning and a little barbecue sauce. She smooshed her hand through it and mixed it up, then formed patties. She turned as Peter entered.

"Want me to start the barbecue?"

Chapter Sixteen

Olivia handed a plate of burgers to Peter. Their fingers grazed as he took it. Peter quickly pulled the plate away. Was this how it was going to be? Always questioning what to do with the sensations of being around her? Maybe it wasn't such a good thing to be back home where he couldn't avoid her. Watch her confidence. See her cute smile. Want to touch her. To breathe in the citrus fragrance of her hair.

He pulled out the lighter and started the grill. The happy sounds of his friends drifted his way. Laughter. Jostling. Antics. All the things he missed about being a part of them on a regular basis. Well, he'd take what he had here and enjoy every minute of it.

"We've got the tents set up."

Nate shoved his hands in his pockets. Tina sidled up and wrapped her arm around his waist. He turned and kissed the top of her head.

"Are you thinking what I'm thinking?" Tina lifted her eyes to his.

Nate's grin reached his ears. "Our first kiss?"

"Yep—maybe we should repeat that—Tina planted her lips on his.

"PETER, what do you need help with?" Nate asked.

"I'm gonna have you check with Olivia. She's in the kitchen. And could you bring out the rest of the food?"

"Hey, what's that great smell?"

Kaitlyn hopped behind Peter and tackled him, as much as she could over her round belly.

Peter laughed. "Now that's one of the things I forgot about you—"

"What?"

"How exuberant you are."

"You love me. I'm not even sure you know how to live without me."

She gave her head a shake causing her curls to bounce.

Luke laughed. "Woah, wait a minute there. You're *my* wife. I'm not sure I want to share you with this guy."

Kaitlyn went to her husband and wrapped her arms around his large frame.

"I know. I'm just giving him a hard time."

They loaded their plates with potato salad, chips, corn on the cob and burgers, and saved room for Evelyn's famous berry cobbler.

"Did anyone tell Peter about the guy we just did surgery on?" Daniel spread butter on his corn.

"You mean Randall? Peter remembers Randall. You know, the guy that got hit by a bus?" Tina said.

"The one with dreads? That broke most of the bones in his body?"

Peter swigged his bottle of pop.

"Yep, that's the one. Remember how he cussed us all out?" Kaitlyn cut up Claire's burger into small pieces.

They laughed. "Well, he was back. This time with a broken hand. I guess he tried to punch someone. The bones were poking through his skin, and we had to put all the pieces back together."

"Figures. I'm not so sure I miss all that."

"Gotta say though," Daniel said, "It's not the same without you."

Olivia stood. "Who wants ice cream on their cobbler?"

That girl knew how to break in at the right time. Peter did miss them. But he knew in his heart that being here was where he belonged for now. And not just for his mom.

THE NIGHT STARS shone bright against the inky sky, a sliver of moon shining. Everyone sat in camp chairs, circled around a fire pit. Peter had made sure there was a screen over it. He wasn't taking any chances on embers lighting the dry grasses. Nate was strumming his guitar, singing a lullaby to Claire who was wrapped in her daddy's arms, snuggled under his bearded chin. Kaitlyn had wrapped a quilt over them.

Olivia turned to Tina. "He's got a nice voice."

"Yeah, that was one of the things that won me over."

Tina's red hair had tendrils flowing under her stocking cap.

"We were at a fundraising event in the park, and he walked onstage and sang the most tender song. It just melted me. What about you, do you have a man?"

Olivia looked at the flames licking the log, and her eyes were drawn to Peter. He sat on the camp chair, relaxed with legs extended and crossed in front of him. What was the right way to answer. The answer was yes if she wanted one.

"Naw." She held up her arm. "This pretty much scares guys away."

"Losers!" Tina scrinkled up her nose. "Are you serious?"

"Yeah. You wouldn't believe some of the things people say."

"I can't even imagine. If you could, would you choose to have your other hand?"

"Good question. I'd say no. I've lived this way my whole life. And I'd say it's helped me become who I am. It's helped me have a deeper walk with God. He knows who I am, and He knows the reason. I think my limb difference can be an inspiration because it hasn't stopped me from being successful in what I've been able to do."

Tina nodded. "Tell me more about you."

Olivia zipped up her hoodie.

"I'm adopted. I have truly great parents. But I was watching Peter stitch up a calf and then the mom snuggling it afterwards. It made me want to find my bio mom. I just want to tell her thanks for giving me life."

"So have you started your search?"

"Yeah, Peter's been helping figure out how to do that. I sent in my DNA a few weeks ago."

"What about you? I know you're a nurse and you obviously have a great group of friends."

Tina took a sip of her cocoa.

"Yeah. It hasn't been the same without Peter. But I understand his wanting to return home. Me? My brother died when he was a kid from Batten disease and my mom died from cancer when I was a teen. But ya know, God works good things despite the bad. He helped me create a new relationship with my dad and I got the bonus of marrying Nate. I can't complain." She smiled. "I guess I was able to truly find *my* Dad through all that."

Nate had quit playing his guitar and walked to Tina, putting his hands on her shoulders.

"You girls solving the problems of the world?"

"Yeah, I think we've got things pretty much covered." Tina placed her hand on his.

"Peter said to ask you what needed to be done tomorrow."

"Oh, um, maybe you and Tina could work on the corn maze. And we need to set up the pumpkin slingshot," Olivia said.

Tina started to giggle. "Remember when we came here, and you tried the slingshot?" She grinned up at Nate. "It was quite hilarious."

"Uh, yeah. Maybe to you."

He squeezed her shoulder.

"That was you? Slipping in the mud? I videoed that and put it on my YouTube. It got a bunch of likes and shares." Olivia laughed.

"Great! Thanks so much. Glad I found some fame." His wry grin was cute. "Tina, ready to turn in?"

The moon had sunk to the horizon turning the sky even darker. The stars twinkled and winked over their conversations and bonding. Tomorrow would be a good day.

Chapter Seventeen

P eter handed Daniel a warm blueberry muffin. "Let's get to work on the corn maze."

They rode four-wheelers to the entrance, kicking up dust as they went.

"So, today we need to do the final clearing of the paths. People will start coming next week and we need to make sure there's nothing to trip anyone up. And make it accessible for those in wheelchairs."

The corn was at least seven feet high, blocking the morning sun. They left their vehicles and Peter pointed out the task.

"We'll take the riding mower with the drag harrow and make sure the paths are clear."

"How in the world did you even make this? That has to be a lot of work."

Peter handed him a map of the maze.

"First Evelyn and Olivia design it based on a theme. This year was the universe, so it has stars and planets and such. Then we have a GPS on our tractor that we can program the design into."

"Wow, that's slick. How long does it take to put the whole

thing together? This is several acres, right?" Daniel took a bite of his muffin.

"Ten acres. Yeah, it takes about a week. A lot of work, but people love it and come from all over. And we make quite a bit of income from it. That and the pumpkin patch and activities. Brings a lot of smiles."

Peter replaced the maze map into the stand. He watched Olivia and Tina laughing from the display area as they arranged gourds and pumpkins on the hay bales. He was glad Olivia had hit it off with Tina. They were well matched.

"Tell me about Olivia. Is she on your radar?"

Peter placed his hand on the back of his neck.

"I've been friends with Olivia since we were in grade school. Well, more than friends."

"With benefits?" Daniel smirked.

"No, we've just been really close."

Peter glanced at her again. Her jeans fit her just right and her tank top accentuated just the right places.

"The way I see you looking at her makes me think there's more there."

Peter faced Daniel and locked eyes.

"I asked her to marry me."

Daniel slapped him on the back.

"Dude! You did? And you didn't say anything?"

"She said no." Peter dipped his head.

"Wait? Why?"

"First of all, it was impulsive. I can't stop thinking about her as more than a friend and I caught her off guard. She thinks it would ruin our friendship if things didn't work out. And she's scared to take a chance."

"Want me to talk to her? Tell her you're the best thing since since sliced cheese?"

Peter huffed out a breath. He wished.

"Dude, no. I'm just gonna give her some time. Keep showing

up for her. She's got a lot going on. She's trying to find her bio mom and starting vet school."

"That's a lot. But I guess you can take as much time as you need though."

"Yeah. And what happened with you and Miya? I thought you guys had a good thing going."

Daniel sat down on the mower.

"We did. But then she got this job offer she couldn't resist in a hospital across the country. We just didn't think long distance was gonna work. And I didn't want to move. Someone else will come along. I'm not worried."

AFTER A LUNCH OF A TACO BAR, fresh apple cider and great conversation, Ross commanded their attention. He clasped his hands together.

"Okay, you city kids need one more great experience. I need help worming the sheep and giving them shots. I'm pretty sure that's something you nurses should be capable of." He grinned.

Peter looked at him and palmed his forehead.

"I'm in!" Kaitlyn raised her hand.

"Me too." Tina high-fived Kaitlyn.

Nate looked at Tina and shrugged.

"Totally out of my comfort zone, but I'll give it a whirl."

It didn't take long for Zip to expertly round up the sheep and pen them. The racket of baaing shook the corrugated tin roof. Luke stood right behind Claire with his body holding her onto the fence she had climbed. Ross brought out several containers of wormer attached to tubes and syringes. Olivia stepped beside him.

"May I?"

Ross nodded. Now was a good time to show what Olivia had learned so far in her vet studies.

"We need you to pair up into three groups. Two people will grab the ewe and administer ten mils of wormer, then shove them into the next pen where two of you can give tetanus shots. After that, someone will chalk their backs to show they've been done. Ross and I will demonstrate."

Ross filled the syringe with wormer while Olivia manipulated the ewe onto her back and held her against her stomach so that Ross squirted the wormer into her mouth.

"This isn't hard. Just place the wormer in the back corner of her mouth. Push it in slowly so she doesn't get it in her lungs and aspirate."

The ewe licked her lips.

"Now while you've got her there, check her eyelids for anemia. The more pink, the more anemic. Check her gums to see if they're swollen, which is another sign of parasites."

Ross held a plastic bottle and inserted a syringe to fill it, then shot it into the ewe's chest floor. He let her go and Olivia chalked her back.

"I think we can do this," Daniel said. "It actually might be easier than dealing with patients." He laughed.

Olivia and Peter paired up. They made it look like a carefully choreographed ballet.

"Dude, you and Olivia should form a business together. It's like you were made to work together," Daniel said.

Olivia ducked her head and hid a smile. He *was* easy to work with. To be around. She didn't want anything to interfere with their friendship.

Chapter Eighteen

Olivia sat on the couch with her back against the pillows on the arm rest, her legs in front of her and her computer on her lap. The page was open to the eye structures of dogs. A third eyelid? Bella had her head resting on her legs.

"Bella, let me see your eyes." She pulled her eyelid up. "Will wonders never cease. I guess you do have a third eyelid."

There was going to be a lot to learn if she wanted to become a vet. But really, it was probably a lot of the same things Peter had learned in nursing school. Maybe not about eyelids, but still—

Olivia looked up as the door opened and Nicole sat down beside her with a stack of mail.

A tingle of nervous energy zinged through her. Did she have what she thought she might?

Nicole thumbed through the mail and gave her a brown envelope with Ancestry for the return address. Olivia's hands shook as she slid the envelope open. She stopped and closed her eyes as she slowly pulled the letter out. Olivia felt the warmth of her mom's hand on her shoulder. She looked up at her, where their eyes met. Olivia moved her feet to the floor and patted the cushion next to her. Nicole sat down and put her arm around her.

The page contained a match. Olivia inhaled a deep breath.

"A first cousin on my paternal side?"

"That's what it looks like. Does it tell you anything else?"

Olivia held the page between them.

"It's a female. I don't see anything else. That must mean that my cousin must have had a DNA test as well. And I guess my mom didn't."

She felt a thud in her gut. What would it take to find her mom?

"Well, that's some progress. Especially since your dad was not listed on the birth certificate."

Nicole stood. "Okay, well, I've got to run. I need to be at the park by noon today."

She took Olivia's face in her hands and gave her a kiss on her forehead.

"I love you, sweetheart."

"Thanks Mom, I love you too."

It wasn't long after Olivia texted that Peter showed up.

"You got your results?"

"Yes! And it shows my cousin. Come, sit down here on the couch."

She patted the spot beside her and slid her computer towards Peter to show the Ancestry site.

"Look here—there's a match to my cousin. I don't see a name."

"Try clicking on the dot."

A name came up. Maria Murphy.

Olivia opened Facebook and searched the name. Six options popped up. She eliminated several who appeared too old. Peter moved closer to her.

"Click on this one."

A girl playing with a golden doodle puppy in a huge yard

where long strands of moss hung from a bald cypress. She scrolled through more photos. The girl with multiple selfies, playing a guitar, another at the beach.

"What do you think, Peter?"

"I don't know. There aren't any of her with family. And I think you want to find a picture of her dad."

"Yeah, you're right. Because her dad would have to be my uncle, right?" Peter nodded.

She clicked on the next one. There were only two left. She raised her arms over her head and stretched. Peter went to the fridge and pulled out some soft drinks. He popped the lids and set them on the coffee table.

"Thanks—how'd you know I needed that?"

Peter raised his eyebrow. Olivia shoved her shoulder into his.

"I'll try this next one."

She clicked and Maria Murphy, who appeared to be in her twenties showed up. There were some selfies of her and a boyfriend kissing. Some with a group of silly girls with goofy expressions. And then one with her and a family sitting on a picnic table. Olivia enlarged the photo to the whole screen.

Peter pointed. "Look at this guy. He must be her dad because he looks just like her. Same brown hair. Same eyes."

"Yeah, he does."

Olivia read through the comment.

"His name is Kurt Murphy." Shivers ran through her arms to her fingers. She typed in his name in the search and his page popped up.

She took a sip of her drink and handed her computer to Peter.

"I'm too nervous."

Peter looked at the bio. Kurt Murphy. Works as a truck driver. Lives in Colorado Springs, Colorado. Went to Harrison High School. Peter clicked on family members. It listed Maria—daughter, Ezra—son, Sandra—wife, Jack—only sibling.

"Only one sibling. A brother." Peter looked at her. "He lives in Colorado, too."

"That's not enough information. How do I narrow down that he might be the one?"

Peter clicked on photos and scrolled. Halfway down, he found a photo of Kurt and Jack standing on a dock, grinning ear to ear, holding fresh caught trout. Peter enlarged the photo. He looked at Jack. Then looked at Olivia. Then back at Jack whose vivid blue eyes the color of bachelor buttons were unmistakably Olivia's.

"I think we found him." Olivia grabbed Peter's hand and squeezed, her heart kicking into high gear.

PETER'S MOTORCYCLE roared as he sped down the road towards town. What if they could find Olivia's father? That would be one piece of the puzzle. He could picture Olivia meeting him—nervous, excited, relieved. Or, what if she contacted him and it wasn't really him? She'd be deflated. This search had to be nerve wracking. And yet, she seemed upbeat at every turn. Nervous, yes, but excited about the possibilities. He was glad she was letting him be a part of her search. Part of her finding out more of who she is.

He pulled into the drive-thru at Cool Beans. Phoebe stuck her head out.

"You here for your usual double latte with almond?" Peter nodded. Maybe he'd been coming here too often if she knew his regular. Phoebe gave his order to a curly headed teen next to her. She crossed her arms on the ledge and leaned towards Peter.

"Hey, how are things with you and Olivia?"

Did he want to say? They were good. Good enough for now. He shrugged.

"Okay. Why?"

"Well," she drew the word out like taffy. "I'm going to a wedding and need a plus one."

She waited a beat.

"Could I convince you to go with me?"

Her green eyes shone, and her glossed lips curled into a hopeful smile.

He shouldn't. But what would be the harm? Olivia made it clear she didn't want to have *that* kind of relationship. Hadn't she told him to pursue someone else?

"I suppose I could do that."

Phoebe jumped up and down and clapped her hands.

"Thank you, Peter. You're a lifesaver. I'll text you the deets."

She handed him his latte. He nodded and sped off.

Chapter Nineteen

Phoebe, looking absolutely gorgeous, opened the door. Peter's eyes slid from her smile to her bare shoulders and followed the lacy blue bodice and full skirt that stopped below her knees.

"Wow! You look nice."

Peter had had to search through his closet to find anything appropriate for wedding attire. He had plenty of working-the-farm clothes, scrubs, and t-shirts, none of which would work. His dad had loaned him a pair of dark slacks, a white button down and some dress shoes. The shoes fit but the shirt was a size too large. Well, he'd have to make do. No sense in spending money on a shirt he wouldn't need again.

Peter thought that it was amazing his dad even owned those. He was sure he rarely dressed up. In fact, he couldn't remember him ever dressing up.

"You're not so bad yourself."

Phoebe smiled, a dimple indenting her cheek.

Peter put his hand on the small of her back and guided her to his dad's car—his motorcycle wasn't exactly an option. He held the door for her, and she slid in.

"Tell me about the couple getting married."

He figured he should know something about them before he got there to prevent some awkward conversation.

"It's actually my ex-boyfriend, Ben. He's marrying Cora, the girl he left me for."

Peter cocked his head. She didn't sound resentful. He was sure *he* would have felt that way.

"And why, exactly, are you attending his wedding?"

"He sent me an invitation. And I still think of him as a friend. Cora is really a better match for him than I was."

Phoebe adjusted the pearled barrette in her hair.

"So, that's why you wanted a plus one. So he'd see you with someone?"

Peter wasn't sure what he had gotten himself into. Was he just a pawn?

"I guess this looks bad."

She looked out the side window, then turned.

"But Peter, we could still have fun, couldn't we? I mean, I don't have feelings for him anymore. Maybe this was just an excuse to dress up and party." She side eyed him. "And be with you."

Peter frowned, puzzled. He wished Daniel or Tina were here to give him perspective. He wasn't always the best at navigating relationships. Well, he'd just make the most of it and see where things went.

They sat outdoors on white folding chairs facing a trellised arch where the couple and pastor stood, flanked by three matching bridesmaids and grooms. Peter studied Ben's grey tux and Cora's cream wedding gown with the long—what did you call all that fabric at the hem of the dress? This was not the type of wedding he wanted to have. Too fancy. He pictured getting married on the farm when his mom's flowers were in bloom, tables set outside with barbecued ribs and plenty of room in the barn for dancing.

Olivia had said no to marriage. But did that mean she didn't love him? He knew he loved her. Not thoughts he should be having while sitting next to a date at a wedding. He sighed. Why was life so hard?

They sat down to a full dinner of salmon and roasted potatoes, asparagus spears and arugula salad. Peter picked up a spear and took a bite.

A girl wearing a slinky satin dress stopped at their table.

"Phoebe, I'm so glad you could come."

"Oh, hi. Peter, this is Bethany, an old friend."

Peter nodded at her his mouth full of salmon.

"I wasn't sure you'd," Bethany paused, "you know, want to be here." She cocked her head towards Ben.

"No, it's fine. I'm over him. We're friends now."

Bethany glanced at Peter.

"Bethany, this is Peter. We've known each other since high school. He just moved back from Portland."

Peter held his hand out.

"Nice to meet you."

Bethany smiled and took his.

"Well, looks like you've found yourself someone better, anyway."

Rose crept up Phoebe's cheeks as she slid Peter a glance. Music began playing.

"Come on, let's dance."

Phoebe grabbed Peter's hand and pulled him to the floor. He followed her lead, self-conscious of his moves. The next song was slow, and Phoebe put her hand on his shoulder. He pulled her into his arms, and she rested her head on Peter's chest. The beat of his heart matched the rhythm of the song. With one hand on her waist, he wrapped hers close to his chest. He thought of Olivia. He would love this to be her. But she was the one who told him to find someone else. Time would tell. Meanwhile, he should just enjoy the moment.

PETER'S FINGERS tapped a rhythm on the steering wheel, the amber of the streetlights lining Central Avenue passing over his face one by one. His lips curled up and he glanced at the passenger seat where Phoebe had sat just moments ago. He had enjoyed the feel of her lips on his more than he had anticipated. Soft, warm, inviting. Then his brows turned to a frown. It was enough to flummox him. The light scent of her Jasmin perfume hadn't hindered him from wanting more. But was this the more he wanted?

He slowed as a deer crossed the road in front of him. The young buck stopped and stared at his headlights, then meandered on. He certainly hadn't spent a lot of time thinking about what he wanted, other than to spend time with Olivia. But she had made herself clear that she didn't want to ruin their friendship by going deeper into a relationship. So, that left him with the bird in the bush, or the bird in the hand. And the bird in the hand was starting look pretty good.

As he rounded the corner to his driveway, his heart raced as he saw red and amber lights whirling. What was this about? Medics were wheeling a gurney to the open back doors of an ambulance. Who were they here for?

He slid the car to a stop and jumped out. His dad stood beside the gurney, holding someone's hand.

"Dad?" Ross looked up.

"Your mom. She wasn't feeling well."

Peter looked at her pale face, her skin pasty—a shade off the color of the white sheet draped over her. Her languid eyes searched his. His jaw tightened.

"What were her symptoms?" Peter's nursing skills kicked in.

"She was complaining of blurred vision, dizziness, and headaches. She took some aspirin, but it didn't help."

This wasn't good. It could be a stroke. Low blood sugar? Maybe a brain injury?

"Did she fall? Hit her head? What preceded the symptoms?"

"You need to step back so we can load her up." The medic shooed them away with his hand.

"Ross, you can ride up front with me. Don't worry, we'll get her taken care of."

Peter sent a quick prayer and a text to Olivia, then stood back and watched them leave, the siren blaring. He jumped back into the car and followed them.

Chapter Twenty

"How do you think Evelyn will look?"

Olivia slid one leg under her other and watched the orchards whir past—fat with apples, the ground clean of weeds and grass.

Nicole's hands were placed at two and six on the steering wheel.

"Not sure. She was weak when they took her away. At least that's what Peter told me."

"I know Portland is kind of far, but I'm glad we're going to see her. She's kinda like a second mom." Olivia chuckled. "Maybe a third mom."

Nicole put her hand on Olivia's and smiled.

"Have you found out anything else?"

"Not really."

She pulled out her phone and scrolled through.

"Peter and I looked through Facebook and found who I'm pretty sure is my cousin Maria. And there was a photo with her mom Sandra, and uncle Kurt—my cousin looked just like him. And then we found one with Kurt and his brother Jack holding some trout."

"I'd say that's progress. I want to see!"

Nicole checked her mirror and passed a semi, the wind jiggling their SUV.

"I'm not showing you while you're driving." Olivia laughed.

Olivia searched Jack Murphy on Instagram. Nothing popped up. She tried Kurt. Still nothing. She shared a play-by-play as she searched.

"Try Sandra. If she's on, she'll surely have photos of her and Kurt."

"True. But I would have to assume that was him. They look a lot alike."

She searched Sandra Murphy.

"Four choices. This shouldn't be hard since I've already seen her."

She clicked on one. Photos of flowers, reels of a cocker spaniel, more reels of her canning jelly. She went to her profile and scrolled through photos there. Her throat constricted.

SHE RELEASED A SLOW BREATH. A closeup of Jack. That had to be her dad. When she looked in his eyes, she was sure of it. She felt an instant connection.

"I think I found him. My dad. What should I do, Mom? Pull over at the next rest stop. You have to look at this."

Olivia sent a text to Peter with a screen shot.

> What should I do?

> Contact Sandra. See if she would call you

Her heart hammered.

"Peter thinks I should contact Sandra and see if she'd call me."

Nicole turned on her blinker and pulled off at the rest stop. She shut off the engine and held her hand out for the phone. Her eyes locked on the man who could possibly be her daughter's father.

"Are you going to contact Sandra?"

"I'm thinking about it. But what if she thinks I'm crazy?"

"She might. But if God wants you to find your parents, he'll make a way."

"My bio parents." Olivia corrected. "You guys are my parents." She whooshed out a breath and sent a message.

> Sandra, my name is Olivia. I'm thirty and was adopted as a baby. I've been searching for my bio mom and took a DNA test. The results showed a cousin, your daughter Maria. I think that your brother Jack is my dad. Would you mind calling me?

Olivia released a slow breath and showed it to her mom.

"Looks good, honey. Go ahead and push send."

She reached over and wrapped her in a hug.

WHEN THEY FOUND Evelyn's room, she was sitting up in the hospital bed, an IV in her arm, slow blips on a monitor. Olivia set a vase of flowers she had picked on the table next to her.

"Hey Evelyn, how are you feeling?"

Phoebe stood beside Peter with her arm around his waist. Olivia's heart skipped a beat. Sure, she had told him to find a girlfriend, but she didn't think it would have been this soon.

"Better."

"Her doctors still haven't figured out what's wrong. They're running more tests. They've ruled out a stroke."

Peter slanted her a crooked glance.

"Phoebe, you remember Olivia."

"Of course, we went to high school together." She smiled.

"Weren't we on swim team together?"

Olivia was sure she had been the one who had encouraged Phoebe.

"We were. I was always amazed at how fast you were. All those trophies. You were kinda my hero."

Phoebe shrugged her shoulders.

"She's pretty amazing, for sure." Peter slid a glance to Olivia.

Olivia cleared her throat.

"So, Evelyn do you feel up to planning the details of the Pumpkin Patch? I'm not trying to take over, but until you're back on your feet, well—"

"Evelyn sat up straighter. Olivia, I am so glad to have a right-hand gal. I think Peter's nurse friends got a lot done. Peter? What else do we need?"

"Don't ask him. Remember, he hasn't been here for a few years."

"True."

Olivia pulled out her phone and started taking notes while Evelyn ticked things off.

"Corn maze, maps, trivia questions?"

"Yep."

"Stems cut off the pumpkins? Price signs? Photo booth? Scarecrow? Sling shot?"

"Still need the price signs. And cash box. Better outline the parking places too. Do you think it would be too much to add a petting zoo? Just a small one—a few miniature pigs, a lamb, and the kittens are the right size. I'd be happy to man it, or shall I say, woman that." Olivia smiled.

"I suppose so, if you think you can handle that."

"I'd be happy to help too," Phoebe said. "Just tell me what to do."

Her nurse entered pushing a cart.

"Tina? You're her nurse?" Peter's mouth dropped.

"I wanted to make sure I was assigned to her floor. Can't have just anyone giving her care. Daniel's on night shift so we've got her covered!"

NICOLE SLID into a parking spot in front of Rose City Bistro.

"Let's sit outside. The weather is perfect."

Olivia nodded and pulled out a metal chair, curlicues and flowers embedded in the seat back.

The server handed them menus and told the specials after pouring water in their glasses.

"Okay," Nicole set her menu down. "What's the deal with Peter?"

Olivia looked away and sucked in her lower lip.

"And Phoebe?"

"Uh, yeah."

This conversation was not going to be easy.

"Isn't he allowed to have a girlfriend?" Olivia crossed her arms.

"I suppose. But somehow, I'm thinking there's more to this story. I've seen the way he looks at you."

The way he looked at her. As in, past tense.

"Did you say something to him? Tell me what happened. Because something had to have happened." Nicole took a sip of water.

"Okay, well," Olivia hesitated. "When we were at the auction, he asked me to marry him."

Nicole choked and spat some of her water.

"Mom!"

Olivia handed her a cloth napkin.

The server returned. "Have you made up your minds?"

"I'll take the garden salad, minestrone and strawberry lemonade, please." Olivia handed him her menu.

"Same please."

Nicole placed both hands flat on the table in front of her.

"Talk."

Olivia locked eyes with her mom.

"I don't know what got into him. It was right in the middle of the auction, and as soon as he said it, the auctioneer called me to the front. I didn't even have a chance to take it in."

"You had to have talked to him later, though."

"Yeah. I did."

Olivia looked away, then back.

"I told him no."

"Why did you do that? You know you two were meant for each other. Are you the only one that doesn't see that?"

"I, I started seeing him as this man, you know, instead of just the kid next door. I didn't want to screw up our friendship."

The server brought their food, carefully balancing a tray on his arm.

Nicole dipped her fork into the minestrone and blew on it.

"I screwed up. I was afraid that if we became a couple, it would ruin the friendship we have. I told him to get a real girlfriend."

"Okay, so how are you feeling about that now?"

Olivia worked her way around her salad, sticking her fork into a cheese square, a beet, a cucumber. What exactly was she feeling? Was she missing out on something more? She had to admit she was a little jealous. Peter had to go for someone she knew? Someone cute, gregarious personality, full-bodied?

"I don't know Mom. I'm fine. We'll still be friends. He's been helping me with my bio mom search."

Nicole stirred her lemonade, the ice cubes clinking against the side.

"I hope you've prayed about it." Nicole's right eyebrow raised.

Had she? Once again, she should listen to her mom's advice. But praying about it was a scary thought. What if God said she should pursue Peter? Take that road? Did she trust God enough to follow his answer either way?

"Hey, what's going on?"

Olivia stood and looked down the street where a crowd of

people marched towards them. Cars had slowed, heads were hanging out of the windows.

Women chanted and waved signs.

Keep abortion safe and legal!

Abortion is healthcare!

End the war on women's rights!

You are not pro-life; you are pro-control!

"Abortion is worth fighting for! Abortion is worth fighting for!"

"Not your uterus, not your choice."

Olivia's face darkened. Her stomach clenched. What was wrong with them? She couldn't wrap her mind around why killing a baby was ever okay.

"Mom," Olivia nodded her head toward the line. "Isn't that your friend? The one you volunteer with?"

Nicole searched the marchers, a sharp intake of breath and then put her hand over her mouth.

"Bree? Oh my gosh." She locked eyes with Olivia. "She told me she had had an abortion when we were talking about kids. I never imagined she was part of this, this—"

"Planned Parenthood? Well, it looks like she's a big part."

Chapter Twenty-One

P eter was up before the sun peeked over the horizon, the lone orb blinking in the morning sky. He pulled his jean overalls over an orange plaid shirt, his usual fare for helping with the pumpkin patch. It had been a few years since he'd helped, but clicking the straps brought a smile to his face. This was his favorite time of year—he air crisp, a few soft clouds dotting the sky and the special smell that fall brought—apples? Corn stalks? He loved it all.

There were days it was difficult to remember why he had given up his job at Mercy surrounded by his closest friends and using his hard-won nursing degree to return to this Podunk town. But not today.

The green John Deere hummed when he turned the key. He had checked the hitch making sure it was safely secured with the trailer, and he drove to the parking area where it would be ready to carry excited kids and families to the entrance of the patch. He and his dad had mowed an area of the field, knowing there would soon be dozens of cars.

Ross took the straightforward job of guiding rigs to keep the space efficient. He didn't want people parking in random angles or leaving just enough gap that no one else could park beside them.

Golden rays of sunlight peeked over the hill, causing the corn stalks to shine, their opaque golden leaves curling, shadows beginning to form on the dry earth. A perfect day for fun and shenanigans.

It wasn't going to be the same, not having his mom here. He couldn't understand why the doctors hadn't been able to pinpoint what was wrong with her by now. At least she was in expert hands at Mercy Hospital. Tina and Daniel sent text updates regularly, for which he was grateful.

But he'd almost lost her. His mom. Peter had to become more intentional about noticing things about her—how the skin on her hands was beginning to thin and wrinkle, the smile lines around her eyes, her wonder at the beauty that surrounded them. He had been more cognizant of being there for her, being more attentive to her needs.

OLIVIA PARKED her four-wheeler and jumped off. She carried two travel mugs and handed one to Peter.

"Thanks. Just what I needed. Of course, you knew that." He slid a grin.

"A spot of vanilla creamer." She looked over the grounds. "Can you give me a hand," she gave an exaggerated wink, "with the table?"

Peter grabbed one end and they carried it to the entrance.

"I'm glad I got to see your mom. She seemed better, but still not herself."

"Yeah, I wish they'd figure out what the deal is and get her started with a treatment regimen."

"This is hard on you."

Olivia set the legs and placed a chair by the table.

"Yep. But I bet you and your mom had a great day."

"We did. It was good until—Olivia opened the lid on a cardboard box and began to unload jams and jellies.

Peter situated them on the table.

"Until what?"

Olivia looked up and put her hand on her hip.

"There was a Planned Parenthood rally that marched by where we were having lunch outside."

"Ugh."

"Right? But then, I saw Mom's friend, Bree waving a sign and chanting in the march."

Peter's hand rested on a jar.

"What did your mom think?"

"She was a little shocked. But then she remembered Bree saying she had had an abortion. When we talked about it in the car, she felt like she should continue to be friends with her, because who knew if that's where God had placed her."

Olivia shoved another box to the table and took out drinking cups and napkins.

"I'm going to the house to get the lemonade."

Bella's gait matched Olivia's as she returned, her arms around a large beverage dispenser. Peter jogged and took the container from her. Bella jumped up on him, knocking him into Olivia as he dropped the plastic dispenser. Lemonade splashed all over Peter. Bella started barking and then began licking Peter, enjoying the treat. Olivia broke out laughing hysterically.

"Hi, uh, do you guys need help or anything?" Phoebe stood over them.

Peter choked out another laugh and held his hand up.

"You might not want to touch me. I'm very sticky."

Phoebe's forehead formed a vee.

"I'm just going to go get the cookies from the car. You need to take a shower." She smiled and shook her head.

Olivia locked eyes with Peter and they both snorted a laugh.

CARS LINED the field and excited voices melded together as one as the hayride brought them to the entrance. Olivia had changed and settled herself on a camp chair in the petting zoo, where a Nubian goat nibbled on her shoelace. Nicole and Phoebe manned the entrance, collecting fees and selling homemade goodies and merch. If Evelyn had been here, she would have made dozens of her famous pies. Peter had volunteered to man the slingshot and Brad, Olivia's dad, worked the corn maze.

Olivia loved everything about this. Being with the animals, the smell of the hay, the feel of the crisp fall air, surrounded by happiness. She motioned to a small girl.

"Come on in. You can sit on this stool. Let the animals come to you. Then you can pet them, or just watch."

A bunny hopped to the young girl.

"Do you want to hold it?"

"Could I?"

Olivia carefully placed the mini lop into her lap, where she gently stroked his soft brown fur. The chime of Olivia's phone alerted her. She checked the screen. Sandra? Her heart hammered. She looked at the girl's mother.

"I've got to take this. Do you mind staying with her while I get my mom to take over?"

She nodded, and Olivia stepped outside, carefully latching the gate.

"Hello? This is Olivia."

"Hi Olivia. It's Sandra. I saw your message."

Olivia allowed a tiny intake of breath.

"Can you give me a minute?"

"I can call back later if this isn't a good time."

Olivia didn't want to take a chance at losing this opportunity. She glanced around for Nicole.

"No, it's fine, I just need to ask my mom to take over for me. I'm manning a petting zoo. It'll be just a second."

"Mom," she whispered. "It's Sandra—you know, my 'aunt'?"

Nicole's eyebrows raised.

"Can you take over in the petting zoo?"

"Of course!"

"Sorry, I live on a farm, and we've got the pumpkin patch open today."

"That sounds like fun. So, tell me more about your DNA search."

Olivia walked to a hay bale and sat down.

"Well, I'm adopted. I love my parents, but I've always felt like there was so much more of me I didn't know about. What's my medical history? Do I have natural siblings? Anyway, I talked to my parents, and they were okay with me searching for my mom. And then when my DNA came back, and it gave a match to your daughter, well, I have to admit I did some Facebook stalking."

"And that's how you found my name."

"Yeah. I hope you're not mad."

"Oh honey, no, of course not. We had no idea Jack might have had a kid. I'm not sure he even knows he had one, if this is really true."

Olivia drew in a breath. He didn't know about her?

"Sandra, how are you feeling about the possibility?"

There was a moment of silence.

"Well, you sound sincere. And I suppose if the DNA test is true, then you're probably my niece. I only have my older brothers —Kurt and Jack. So, I don't have any connection with whoever gave birth to you. But I'd love to meet you. Would you mind sending me your photo?"

"Yes, of course."

Olivia quickly scrolled through a few photos, and not finding one that was acceptable, snapped one of herself.

"Okay, I just sent one."

"Got it."

The seconds ticked by.

"Olivia? Your eyes are just like Jack's! Wow. I can't believe this. So, how do you want me to proceed?"

Olivia's voice grew quiet.

"Do you think you could ask Jack to contact me?"

"Yes, of course. I can imagine how nervous you must be. Honey, he's not scary. I'm not sure what he'll say, but I'll show him your photo and we'll go from there."

"I'm on all the socials. You can look at my posts."

"Okay, I'll do that. You probably need to get back to what you were doing. I'll get back to you as soon as I can."

"Thank you, Sandra. You don't know what this means to me."

"Yes, of course. Take care."

Olivia could feel the smile in her voice. She held her phone to her chest and closed her eyes. She turned in a circle and sighed. Each step brought her closer to the possibility of finding her dad. Not the result she had initially hoped for. But a parent, anyway. And if Jack was her father, it would most definitely lead to her mother.

She was sure God knew where they were. She raised her eyes to heaven. Thank you, Jesus. Then texted Peter.

Chapter Twenty-Two

"Give me your arm."

Evelyn had returned home, and Peter was back in his stride.

Evelyn pulled up her sleeve for Peter. He noticed the waning strength of her upper muscles and glanced at her scar. He frowned. He couldn't bear to see her deteriorate. What else could he do to help her? To fix her?

"I'm pretty good at giving shots–I've had a lot of practice. Especially after that epidemic. You won't even know I inserted the needle."

Evelyn rolled her eyes and Peter, true to his word, had the needle in and out before she knew it.

"See? Piece of cake."

Peter rubbed the spot with alcohol and placed a bandage on it.

"Thanks. I guess I'll keep you around." She grinned. "So, tell me about Phoebe."

"Well, I was her plus one at the wedding and we hit it off. She was a great help with opening day of the pumpkin patch, by the way."

"She's a cute girl. Be sure to take your time. Relationships can be tricky."

"Agreed."

Especially when your heart was still holding out for another girl.

"What does Olivia think of her?"

Peter didn't exactly know. He couldn't read her emotions when Phoebe was around—something that had never been a problem before. He pretty much always knew what she was thinking.

"Olivia told me to find a girlfriend."

Evelyn's eyebrows raised.

"There's more to that story, I'm sure."

Peter sat down on the plaid wing-tipped chair and crossed his arms.

"Yeah, well—at the fair, I impulsively asked Olivia to marry me."

"Ohhhh?" Her mouth dropped open.

"Mmhmm. And she said she was scared to take us to that level, that it would ruin our friendship and she didn't want to compromise that. I don't agree. But anyway, she said I should find a *real* girlfriend and then Phoebe asked if I would go to a wedding with her."

Now that the story was out, Peter whooshed out a sigh.

"Well son, I guess we'll see where things go. I know where your heart is. Be careful not to hurt Phoebe."

Yeah. That was something he hadn't considered. He'd take things slow and see where they went.

"Let's get some breakfast—I made waffles and bacon and the coffee's hot. Then you need to get out there to man the entrance. I'll help with the slingshot but just give me a holler if you need help with anything."

OLIVIA BROUGHT UP YOUTUBE. Excitement bubbled over and her hands shook as she began to type.

> Hey friends, I just wanted to tell you I'm so close to finding my bio dad! Can you believe it? My DNA showed a cousin and I traced that to her mom. I talked to her on the phone the other day. She's so nice! She's going to talk to her brother-in-law and ask him to take a DNA test. I'm not gonna lie, it's got my stomach doing calisthenics!
>
> Here's what I'm worried about—maybe he'll deny that I exist. Rather, deny that he could be my dad. He might remember and not want to see me. I might meet him and then wish I never had. I mean, what if he's an ax murderer?
>
> Well, anyway, God knows, and we'll see where things go from here.

OLIVIA CLOSED her YouTube channel and searched for family reunion success stories.

> "I couldn't believe that my mom had been searching for me for years. All this time, I thought she was embarrassed to have me, or never wanted me. I just could not believe that I had been wanted. She was forced to give me up for adoption. She never wanted to do that."

OLIVIA REACHED for a tissue as tears streamed down her cheeks. She shouldn't be so moved. Olivia had mom and dad that truly loved her. But seeing the connection of that mom and daughter? She couldn't help but rejoice with them. Had someone forced her mom to give her up too?

PETER LISTENED INTENTLY as Mac described their fire drill— one that was going to train them to be that team member who could pull everyone through the challenge. Together, each training through adversity would toughen them to be there for each other.

Mac continued. "A four percent increase in a degree of diffi- culty is all it takes to top your ceiling—where you max out. And this is what happens, people, when you hit that level. Your sympa- thetic nervous system kicks in and anxiety starts and before you know it, your cognitive ability is toast, and you can't troubleshoot. We can't have you in that situation. You become a danger not only to yourself, but to your teammates and to any victims."

Peter crossed his arms, leaned back in his chair, and crossed his legs in front of him. Somehow, it made the tough floor he had worked on at Mercy seem like a cakewalk. Mac went on to explain that tough training through this series develops dopamine—the feel-good hormone, oxytocin—the bonding hormone, serotonin that keeps you calm in tight spaces, and endorphins that give you a second wind so you're there for your mates.

Mac led them to another room where an obstacle course, constructed from two by fours and plywood sat. It had a small entrance which led to a hole in the roof, on to a tunnel and through various levels of spaces and sizes. Peter didn't think it would be that difficult.

Until Mac held up the blinding mask, they had to wear to get through it, fully clothed and outfitted with their gear.

Vinny Carloni ribbed Peter.

"You think you can do that in less than ten minutes? Mac'll have us doin' it again until we get it right."

"I hope so. I'm not too good in tight spaces. Guess I'll have to take some deep breaths."

He watched Jordan don the mask and make his way into the structure.

"Say, did I tell you I found my mom?"

Vinny put his hand on Peter's shoulder.

"Your mom?"

"Yeah, I'm adopted. And I've been wondering about her all my life. So, I started searching. And last night I got a call. I'm going to meet her tomorrow."

"Really? That's amazing. How did you find her?"

"There was this person called a search angel. She did the investigating. I'm all butterflies to finally meet her."

A search angel. Olivia may not want him as more than a friend, but sharing about a search angel was a friend thing to do, right? He could take this on. See what he could find out. Maybe a search angel could find her mom and she'd have some closure.

Chapter Twenty-Three

Orange Maple leaves twirled down around Peter as he sat on the park bench scrolling through his phone. He was so engrossed he didn't hear Phoebe sit down beside him. She bumped shoulders with him.

"Hey."

"Oh, sorry. Hi."

"What's got you so intrigued? It doesn't look like a game."

"No, Vinny Carloni from the fire department, told me he had a search angel to find his mom. I was looking that up."

"For Olivia?"

"Yeah."

Peter glanced at her long enough to catch the eagerness in her eyes.

"I'd like to help. I can't imagine wondering about who my birth parents were. There's so much you'd want to know. A lot of unanswered questions."

Phoebe took out her phone and brought up YouTube.

They locked elbows and sat in silence as they searched different sites.

"This looks like it may be a possibility."

Phoebe showed it to Peter.

"You could at least fill out an application."

OLIVIA ZIPPED her hoodie before she slid the barn door open. The air was crisp and invigorating. She still hadn't mustered the courage to call Sandra back to find out if Jack had taken the DNA test. Each hour turned into impossibly long days, the waiting constantly swirling from her mind to her stomach.

Maybe he wouldn't want to know. Or maybe it was a one-night stand, and he doesn't even remember it. Or vanish the thought, what if he was married and had an affair when she was conceived? Olivia ran her hand through her hair and clutched her pony.

Well, the best thing she could do was focus on her vet studies and attempt to get her mind off the waiting and wondering. Things would happen in God's time. Not hers.

ROSS WANTED Olivia to check the ewes. They were bred in June and were ready to lamb any day now. Olivia was excited about this part. What was more fun than newborn lambs? Newborn anything, really.

"Ready to roll?"

Ross had gathered the ewes into the barn where he poured grain into a long wood feeding trough. The sound of their munching created a rhythm, and their wooly sides rubbed each other, their rears visible.

"First, we look to see if their girl parts are swollen. This is why we dock their tails when they're born. It makes birthing way easier, and keeps them cleaner, especially when they're lambs."

Ross spread some of the wool aside with his hands.

"See how she's getting pinker and beginning to swell? I'd give her another week. Now, reach down and feel her bag. It should be getting firm, and her teats should be pointing down."

Olivia felt the bag. If what she was feeling was any indication, she was sure Ross was right. It would be soon.

"When they go into labor, you'll see some of the water bag show. If you watch her stomach, you'll see the contractions. She may move around a bit to try and find a comfortable spot. But, if possible, I'll call you in when the first lambs come. I'd like you to learn how to deliver them on your own if they need help."

What was labor like for Olivia's mom. She hoped it had been easy. Or maybe it was rough and gave her another reason to give her away. She shrank into herself.

Ross turned to leave.

"Oh, and Olivia," he turned his head towards her, "I'm praying for the outcome of your search for your birth mom."

JACK OFFERED Sandra a glass of iced tea and pointed to the couch. She looked nervous—a shifting of her eyes, leaning her head as if to stretch out a kink. Nothing like what his baby sister was usually like.

When she had been born, it was all he could do to protect her from his brother, Kurt. Jack and his brother who was barely a year younger than him had been in the limelight for four years and it seemed his baby bro wasn't too keen on stepping out of it. When Sandra was a baby, Jack had caught him throwing a blanket over her face, pushing her swing too hard, even trying to feed her worms.

Over the years, Jack had maintained his protective stance, to the point where he kept an eye on who she dated and had to approve of who she eventually married. Turned out to be a great catch and her teens were well rounded and successful.

"What's going on? You look like the time you told me Kurt got in an accident while drunk."

"It's not that bad."

She took a swallow and set the can on the wood coaster. She inched to the edge of the cushion.

"So, I got a message from a girl I didn't know. I called her back, and we had a long talk."

"And? I guess somehow this has to do with me."

Sandra nodded and tented her fingers.

"She's been searching for her biological parents, and she thinks you're her dad."

Jack double blinked. That couldn't be possible. Could it?

"I'll just give you a moment."

Jack stood and walked to the picture window. He pulled the curtains aside and watched the neighbor boy wheel his bike down the sidewalk. The cat crouched and then sprang toward an unsuspecting robin.

A video of his life rewound through his mind as scraps of memories he hadn't sifted through in years dropped, stopping at his senior year in high school. His brother and friends had all given in to hormonal lust, but he had kept solid boundaries. That is, until he was in college.

Jack turned. "Why does she think I could possibly be her father?"

Sandra shrugged her shoulders.

"She started searching for her biological mom. She's been adopted since she was a baby and loves her adopted parents. But she wanted to find out some medical history and wanted to tell her bio mom thanks for giving her life."

Jack couldn't take his eyes off his sister. His forehead wrinkled.

"So, she did a DNA test. The results showed a cousin on the paternal side. She said she searched Facebook and narrowed down to our family photos. When she saw you, she was sure you had to be her dad. Your eyes are identical to hers."

"How did she know it wasn't Kurt that was her dad? That would be significantly more likely."

"Her eyes are blue. Kurt's are green. Here's a photo of her."

Jack couldn't believe what he was seeing. It was like his daughter Ondrea was looking right at him. They weren't exactly the same, but still—

"That still doesn't mean anything."

Jack's adrenaline was racing, shooting blood through his veins. This couldn't be true. Could it? What would he tell Lisa? Or his kids? He shook his head and raked his fingers through his hair.

"Well, I'm here to tell you, there's a really easy way to find out."

Sandra pulled the DNA test out of her bag and handed it to him. He held it in his hands, staring like she had handed him a bomb.

"I'll leave you her contact. Her name is Olivia. In case you think you want to talk to her."

She picked up her bag and stood.

"This isn't necessarily the worst thing that could happen to you. It might be an adventure. New opportunities."

She smirked and punched him in the shoulder.

Chapter Twenty-Four

"This is so exciting. It's like being a detective or something." Phoebe pulled her scarf tighter around her neck and leaned into Peter as he clicked on the questionnaire for the search angel registry. He paused.

"Should I use my email? Or Olivia's?"

"Use hers. No, use yours. If you use hers, she'll wonder how her information got in there."

Peter scrolled through the questions, answering each.

Who are you trying to find? Peter's fingers flew as he typed birth parents.

Which best describes you? I am the adopted person.

Indicate your gender. Female.

Indicate your birth year. 1993

Indicate your birth month. March

Indicate the day of your birth. 1

In which country did the adoption take place. USA

In which state did the adoption take place. Oregon

When did the adoption take place? Within a year of birth

TEN MINUTES later he pushed submit. Peter looked at Phoebe and tensed his shoulders. He pulled his knit beanie tighter over his ears.

"Olivia is going to be glad you did this for her."

Phoebe's smile held his gaze. She kissed him.

Would Olivia be glad? Or was Peter pushing the boundaries?

OLIVIA SHOVED the vacuum over her bedroom carpet. Her room wasn't that dirty. Stacks of books on the floor. A dirty sock or two. A box of stuff that needed to be put away. How long had that been there? Her room hadn't had a deep clean in way too long. So much had been going on, and, well, to be honest, sometimes cleaning was on the bottom of the list. She glanced out at the grey sky. Bits of light snowflakes fell. It put a smile on her face. Perfect for December.

It seemed she was at a standstill as far as finding her bio mom went. Maybe she should just accept that it wasn't going to happen. She didn't need to pursue it. It had been a whim, anyway. She had a perfectly wonderful family. Why should she be searching for something more? She was fine. She didn't really need to know the rest.

At least, that's what she told herself.

She shoved the vacuum under the bed where it knocked into a box. She got on her knees and pulled it out. She'd forgotten about this box of photos. Shutting the vacuum off, she rested her back against the dresser, crossed her legs, and set the box on her lap. She wiped dust off the lid with the back of her sleeve and pulled it off.

Bella padded in and looked into Olivia's eyes. She sat, her tail wagging.

"You are so adorable. Wondering what I'm doing? Sit down here."

She tapped the floor beside her.

"You can look through these photos with me."

The box was a mishmash of photos. Now was as good a time as any to organize them. She pulled out a handful and turned them right side up. A photo of her in a walker by a Christmas tree, her two blond ponies sticking out of her head wrapped with red bows. She reached for an ornament. On closer inspection, it was a bear on a bulb with Baby's First Christmas painted on it.

Olivia started a stack to organize them into a time frame.

Next, she was dressed in a scarecrow costume sitting on a large pumpkin. Must have been around four at Peter's farm. A photo of her racing to the finish line in a high school swimming event. Man, these were really out of order. This one, she remembered—the adrenaline push to the finish line, taking first place. A proud moment. She should create a pile of proud moments. There had been a few over the years. There must be photos of track and soccer too.

Now here was a cute one in black and white. She and Peter from the back, holding hands, each dressed in coveralls and walking towards the barn. What were they? Six years old? Five? It would make a cute Insta post.

Oh, here's what Mom must have been talking about. Dad with Mom holding her in the crook of her arm as a newborn. A little pink knit hat on her head, wrapped in a receiving blanket, her bandaged arm visible. What had happened to her? And why didn't the hospital or adoption agency tell her parents the cause? It was so strange.

Her phone buzzed. Not a number she recognized.

"Hello, this is Olivia."

"Uh, hi. My name is Jack Murphy. Do you have a minute to talk?" A deep voice.

Olivia's heart raced, and her fingers tingled. Jack? Her dad?

"Yeah. Sure."

Could he hear the shake in her voice? She cleared her throat.

"My sister, Sandra gave me some interesting news last week."

It was his turn to clear his throat.

"She says you think I might be your bio dad."

"Mhmm. I took a DNA test, and the results came back as being related to a paternal cousin. So, I started searching socials. Which led me to a photo of you and, possibly, your brother? Would you like me to text you the photo?"

"Uh, yeah. I'd like to see it."

Olivia heard his phone ping. Then silence.

"This is us alright. Sandra, me and my brother Kurt." There was a pause.

"When were you born?"

"March 1, 1993. In Portland, Oregon."

"That would have put your mom as being pregnant in July, 1992. Let me think on that."

"Take your time."

Olivia stilled her breath. She was talking with her dad! *Her dad!* This had to be shocking news for him. Or maybe not. She let out a slow, silent breath.

"I hate to say this, but I don't know how that would be possible. I've never been to Oregon. And I have no recollection of being with anyone at that time. I'm sorry to disappoint you, but I think you have the wrong guy."

"Oh, okay."

She took a moment to take this in.

"But would you mind taking the DNA test anyway? I know you don't know me and have no reason to do something like this for a stranger, but I would be so grateful if you would at least erase the possibility of doubt."

NICOLE TOOK her poles from Brad after she had stepped into her cross-country skis. The deep, pristine snow on Mt. Hood was picture perfect. She tucked her scarf into her down jacket and pulled her ski cap tighter on her head. They had invited Bree and her husband Phil for a weekend at a cabin. Brad had wanted to get away and it was good to see what Nicole's friend was like.

The snow was dry and powdery. Made Nicole remember the time they had come here when Olivia was in fifth grade. She and her friend Phoebe were disappointed that it wasn't good for packing, putting snowball fights and snowmen on hold. Come to think of it, this was the same Phoebe that Peter was dating. Interesting.

She glided ahead on the silky snow and caught up with Bree.

Bree glanced at Nicole. "It's so quiet out here."

"Lovely, isn't it? It's nice to get away and see different scenery."

"We've really got the best of all worlds—working in the woods, you living in the country, me living in town."

"What are you doing for Christmas?"

Nicole shoved her poles into the snow, enjoying the smooth glide.

"We'll put up our fake tree next week. It's easy peazy, and already has lights on it. I don't really go all in for decorating. You?"

"I guess we fall into the opposite category. Brad and Olivia put the lights on the house right after Thanksgiving. He's got them rigged up in the trees, down the driveway, all over the bushes. And puts out deer and tree décor as well. I like it. Winter is so dark, it's nice to have the lights."

They rounded a bend where deer's antlers peeked out from the leafless branches.

"What are you getting your kids for Christmas? I imagine it's easy to think of things for teens."

"Both of them are easy. Maddie and Matt are both in basketball. New team shoes, iPods, laptops. The ushz."

"Maddie and Matt—are they twins?"

"Nope. We named them after Phil's and my middle names. It had a ring to it." Bree smiled.

"What does Olivia want for Christmas?"

"That's a good question. I found a cute sweatshirt that says It's a Good Day to Save Animals. And she'll need a nice stethoscope."

"So, she's enjoying her new vocation venture?"

"She is. And truth be told, she's really a natural at it. Our neighbor Peter rescued a pup from a fire several months ago who lost one paw. He gave it to Olivia, and she is so smitten with it. It follows her everywhere like they were made for each other."

A snow rabbit hopped across the trail in front of them, stopping at the side to watch them pass.

"I'm sure you noticed at her birthday party that she only has one hand."

Nicole glanced at Bree.

"I did. What caused that?"

"I have no idea. The hospital only warned us that she only had one hand. They never said why."

"Odd. But she seems to get along fine without it, right?"

"That she does."

Brad and Phil slid up behind them.

"You guys ready to go back? I could use a hot cup of cocoa and some popcorn."

"And a warm fire," Phil said.

THEY WERE on their third round of Farkle, where Phil had been trailing behind by several thousand points. He cupped the six dice, shook them vigorously, looked around at each of them and spread a cheesy grin before he blew on the dice. They rattled as he rolled, and wouldn't you know it, he got three pairs. He fist pumped, rolled again, and got a straight. Rolling once more he landed five aces and stopped there. Brad patted him on the back.

"Way to come up from behind. We should have played teams."

Nicole went to the kitchen and set out bowls for the steaming chili in the instant pot.

Bree set out some grated cheddar and corn bread.

"That smells heavenly. You gals are the best."

Phil wrapped an arm around each of their shoulders.

They sat at the table where Brad had cleared the game and returned it to the shelf. Snow fell in light flakes. Flames licked the logs, shedding the warmth needed on a winter day.

"Say, I wonder if you two would be interested in joining us at the Planned Parenthood convention."

Phil loaded cheese and olives, onto his chili.

Nicole pointed a look at Brad, who took the cue.

"That's not really our thing. But thanks for thinking of us."

"Really? You're not for women's rights?"

Nicole looked at Brad who seemed to be sucker punched.

"Uh, yeah. But we're also for baby girls' rights."

"You mean, as in, unborn girls?"

Brad nodded. Nicole felt her insides implode. Could she really be friends with someone whose opinions she was diametrically opposed to?

"They aren't really even people yet. Not until they're born, anyway. Why should it matter?"

Nicole wanted to jump up and scream. Doesn't matter? They obviously didn't know the science of the unborn. She was thankful for a husband that could and would stand up for right.

"I would encourage you to research prenatal life from a science perspective. You might be surprised. Three weeks after conception, organs are developing."

Nicole was surprised at how even his voice was.

Bree set her cornbread down.

"That may be so, but women have the right to their own bodies. No one should be telling them what they can and cannot do with them."

Phil reached his hand towards Bree's.

"I guess everyone has a right to their own opinions. We just happen to be on opposite ends of the spectrum. Let's not let this ruin our weekend. Nicole, you made brownies for dessert, right?"

Chapter Twenty-Five

D*ear D—*
No, she couldn't write dad.
Dear Jack,
That didn't feel right either.
Hi,
Olivia straightened her shoulders and ptooeyed over her left shoulder. If it worked for Kaitlyn, she could certainly give it a try.

I wanted to thank you for taking the time to talk to me. I can't imagine what a shock it was for Sandra to suggest that you had a child you didn't know about. And I hope you'll consider taking the DNA test. Because if it's not you, it will be good for each of us to know. And (I pray I'm right) if it is you, I can't wait to meet you.

I want you to know that I was adopted as an

infant by a very loving couple — Nicole and Brad. They had tried repeatedly to get pregnant and after many failed attempts, decided to adopt. I'm an only child — I guess it was a lot to go through and they didn't want to undergo the process again. Anyway, they raised me in the country and have given me every experience and opportunity I could possibly want. I played soccer, won awards in track and swimming. I was valedictorian of my class of four hundred and have pursued several vocational directions. (I hope this doesn't sound like I'm bragging.) But, well, I guess I am a little.

I settled on vet studies. I've been working at the neighbor's flower and pumpkin farm. They also raise chickens sheep, pigs, and beef cattle. I love being around animals and think this is the best fit for me. It puts me in my happy place and makes my heart sing.

I want you to know that IF I am your daughter, it would be an honor to meet you. I don't want to disrupt your life but would like to know possible medical background and traits we may have inherently the same.

And well, if I'm not, it was nice to meet you and I thank you again for taking time to talk to me.

LOVE,

Nope.
Your daughter,
Ugh.
Your friend,
No.
Sincerely,
Olivia

She added her phone number and email, folded it, held it in the air and asked God's blessing.

PHOEBE JUMPED out of Peter's truck and shoved the door shut.

"I am so excited about being a volunteer firefighter. Fire girl. Fire gal."

She bubbled a laugh and hooked her elbow through Peter's.

The door slid open, and Peter introduced her to Mac. He held out a large hand and shook hers.

"Glad to have you here. We could use another team member."

He looked over her slight build.

"You sure you're up to the physical portion?"

Peter slid her a glance, the corner of his mouth curving up. He couldn't wait to show them what she could do. She had talked him into joining her at the gym twice a week. It had taken awhile for him to catch up to her strength, but she inspired him. Let's just say he didn't mind sweeping his eyes over her abs when her belly was bare during a workout. He silently thanked Olivia for refusing him. This was working out A-okay.

She filled out the required fire service paperwork, and then spent the next twenty minutes going through the obstacle course. First, her cohorts ran up and down a flight of eighty stairs. Then rolled under a log set a foot above the ground and jumped over another set two feet up. Phoebe ran ahead to a structure that had her crawling, then propelling herself by her forearms through a claustrophobic tunnel. Peter led, swinging arm to arm across a horizontal ladder, jumped off and picked up a fifty-pound bag of sand, hoisted it to his shoulders and ran a hundred yards. He wiped sweat off his brow with his sleeve. Phoebe jumped onto his back, where he carried her to the finish line and fell laughing.

Peter handed Phoebe a Gatorade.

She took a swig and said, "That was fun. We should do that every day."

"Maybe you could, but I'm fine for once a week."

Peter took a chug on his drink. They sat down to watch a training video showing different techniques on hose management.

"Don't get too comfortable. We're going to model what is taught, step by step."

Mac motioned for everyone to circle up.

The video showed the handling of the hip grip—they should start with their left leg bent with their bottom resting on the heel of their right foot. There was one practice hose for each two volunteers.

Phoebe squatted and got into position. Peter followed suit. He handed the hose to Phoebe, who placed it in her left hand, which rested on her left knee and her right hand gripping the hose near her waist, pushing the hose into her right hip. Peter watched her as she followed the video and grabbed the bale to open the nozzle. He blurted a snort as the force of the water knocked Phoebe back. She glared at him as he grabbed the hose, allowing her to right herself.

"Sorry, I just didn't expect the power of the water."

Mist from the hose rested on her false eyelashes. Peter wanted to brush his fingertips across them, but instead shut off the water and handed the hose back.

"I did the same thing the first time I tried it. No worries."

Next the video showed the clamp position where he placed the hose under his right ankle to hold it in place. Phoebe got into position, lifted the hose, and glanced over her shoulder at Peter. He smiled reassuringly, and she placed her hands into position to turn on the hose.

Yes. He was going to enjoy having her on his team.

EVELYN HOISTED the five-gallon bucket of grain and poured it into the calf trough, then set it down beside her with a thunk. She leaned her forearms over the fence and huffed a few breaths. It seemed she couldn't pull her weight since that stint in the hospital. Things like this had been so easy in the past, but lately everything had her out of breath. She hoped Ross hadn't noticed. She really hoped Peter hadn't. He was hovering like a hummingbird over her all the time as it was. Evelyn couldn't quite put her finger on why he did that. She knew he blamed himself for not being there for here with the fire. But that shouldn't be his burden. Lord, give me understanding. Raising kids, even grown kids, is not always that easy.

"You're growing up, Daisy. You'll soon need to go to pasture and give up this soft life."

She hoped this wasn't an allegory of her life. No, it was just a bump in the road. Things were easier during winter when she didn't have as much gardening to do. The Pumpkin Patch was over. Throngs of people came now to cut Christmas trees. But Ross and Peter managed that most of the time. She sighed and relaxed her shoulders. Healing takes time, girl. Give yourself some grace.

Chapter Twenty-Six

Olivia reached for the blueberry syrup and poured a generous amount on her French toast, letting it swirl and mix with the glob of butter melting in the middle.

"How was your weekend with Bree and Phil?"

Nicole took the syrup from Olivia.

"It was great. The snow was oh so beautiful and getting out there on the skis was refreshing. I enjoy that crisp air." Nicole held her coffee mug in both hands, her eyes focused on the memory.

"I'm glad you had a good time, Mom." Olivia swirled a bit of toast through the syrup and slid it into her mouth.

"Did Dad hit it off with Phil?"

"He did. Until Phil asked if we wanted to join them at a Planned Parenthood convention."

"What? How did he react? What did Dad say?"

"He handled it way better than I would have. He just calmly said that we were on the opposite side of the equation." Nicole took a sip and set her cup down.

"Yeah, I could see him saying that."

Olivia rested her hand on Nicole's shoulder. She knew that abortion stole lives, and there was no doubt that wasn't God's plan. But it seemed like talking about it hit her mom hard. Why was that, anyway?

"I need to get out and check on the ewes. They should lamb over the next few weeks."

"I know. I can't wait. They're so cute. I'll get these dishes washed up and then I've got to get groceries. There's a Christmas party for the park volunteers and I stepped up to organize it."

OLIVIA SCOOPED grain into several buckets and shlepped them onto the back of her four-wheeler. She slid her leg over and started the engine. A family of four followed Ross to the Christmas trees —a pruning saw in the man's hand. It reminded Olivia that she should ask her dad today if they could pick one out. December was ticking away, and it wasn't really Christmas without a live tree.

Olivia scanned the field. The grass had taken a toll when freezing weather set in the previous week and the frozen blades lay on their sides.

She held a feed bucket up, shook it and hollered, "Hey lambies! Come and get it."

A field of raised heads and a chorus of baas sprung up and she hoisted a bucket and poured the grain into the trough. Ewes came running, some followed by their offspring. She made a visual check of those who were still pregnant, calculating the closeness of their birthing time.

A new set of triplets hung out in the field with a string of gooey afterbirth trailing from the mama's rear. Olivia set the bucket down, climbed over the fence and walked towards them, her boots making a sucking sound in the fresh mud. The mama had done a good job of licking the yellow goo off the triplets. One ran to his mom, butted his head into her bag and started nursing. Another followed. Olivia squatted by the third lamb. It was a runt —its wobbly spindly legs shorter than her siblings'. She made no effort to join them.

"What's going on there, sweetie? Let me take you to your mama."

She gently lifted her and set her beside the others. The lamb just stood looking at her brothers.

"I might need to take you in and bottle feed you. It's not looking like you're gonna have a chance next to these alpha males."

Olivia slid a bander from her back pocket and took hold of the first ram lamb. She held him with his back to her stomach, placed a band on the tool and slipped it over its testicles. It protested with a baa. She took the bottle of worm wound spray from under her arm and squirted some onto the area. It baaed again.

"No worries, little guy. You'll be fine in a few days."

Easy for me to say. She laughed.

Taking the ewe lamb under her arm, she set it on her lap after she mounted the four-wheeler.

"We'll get some formula into you, and you'll soon catch up to your bros."

JACK STOOD IN THE KITCHEN, sifting through the mail. He slid an opener through the top of an envelope. His heart sped to the rhythm of the pendulum wall clock. He shouldn't be nervous. It was just a letter from that girl he had talked to the other day. What was her name? Olivia? It was a nice name. And she had a pleasant voice. He moved to the living room, where he sat on the couch. Would this letter represent a fork in his road? One he would take?

Or not.

He slowly slid his finger under the flap and pulled out a piece from a writing tablet.

Hi, I wanted to thank you—

He finished reading the letter and set it on his lap. His eyes traveled to the window, where the sun peeked through the clouds.

Streams of light sifted through the tall cedars and into his front yard. Maybe this was a sign.

None of it really made sense, though. He didn't remember a relationship with anyone at that time. His previous fling, Lindsey, had broken it off with him. Had he had a rebound? *Lord, I need some discernment here. Bring this incident to my memory—if it's even true.*

But it couldn't be true. July 2019. Where was he? Preparing to start his senior year at Colorado State. He lived in an apartment a few blocks from campus. His engineering classes kept him busy, and he rarely ate out or went anywhere. He wanted to keep his head in his studies. Kurt had been the party animal and barely graduated. But Jack was focused, like his dad.

"Hey babe, what are you up to?"

Lisa, Jack's wife, sat beside him.

Jack shook out of his revery.

"I told you about the girl who called me the other day—take a look at this."

He handed the letter to her and felt the comforting warmth of her shoulder on his, soaking up her trust in him.

Lisa looked up. "What do you think?"

"I don't know. I'm racking my brain through my past, trying to think of an incident that matches. I'm not coming up with anything."

"You know, if you *are* her biological father, I wouldn't hold that against you. God only knows the things I did in college that I wish I hadn't."

Lisa reached for his hand.

"I think you should do the DNA test. What's to lose? If you find out you're not a match? You go on with your life. If you find out that you are? Then maybe God's opening a door for a new relationship."

Jack nodded. "And this," he rubbed noses with her, "Is why I love you."

Chapter Twenty-Seven

S now had drifted softly through the night, creating a white wonderland. Olivia had gotten up in the middle of the night to go to the bathroom and soaked in the beauty of the full moon which cast shadows on the fluffy, magical field. It was a reverent moment—the purity, the perfectness of it all. The stillness.

Nothing marred the untouched landscape. Is this what heaven would be like? She had always envisioned walking by streams or down pathways with tall cedars. Or wide-open meadows with sunflowers and lupines. But this had a beauty all its own. Like it eliminated every care in the world.

She rubbed some sleep from her eyes and crawled back into her bed, and snugged under the flannel quilt her grandma had made for her.

PETER HOISTED the pitchfork and scooped cow puckies from the stall, tossing them into the wheelbarrow. Daisy watched him, her long eyelashes crowning her large brown eyes. Made him think of Phoebe with her fake lashes. Why she thought she needed to improve on what God gave her was beyond him.

She was a good fit as a fire volunteer. So in shape. He almost couldn't keep up. There was more than one volunteer that couldn't keep his eyes off her. Peter was one lucky guy.

Peter had heard nothing from Search Angel. He thought he would have by now. It had been several weeks since he and Phoebe had initiated contact. And, truth be told, he had spent little time with Olivia lately. Where was she with contacting her dad? He felt a ping of loss. Was he drifting away from his best friend? And should he even have taken the lead to contact Search Angel without consulting with her?

He checked the time. He needed to get back and give Evelyn her shot.

Peter removed his Carhartt jacket and hung it on the hook by the front door. He kept his beanie on, still enjoying the warmth.

"Hey Mom, time for your meds."

Peter walked to the kitchen where her Betty Crocker cookbook lay on the counter open to sugar cookie recipes.

"Okay, just let me clean the flour off my hands."

She ran the warm water.

"How's Daisy this morning? The cold didn't bother her?"

"It didn't appear to. But you know cows have thick skin. They're used to any type of weather. She is awfully cute."

Peter took the syringe from a box in the cupboard and tapped the side.

Evelyn pulled up her sleeve and looked away.

"I'm not sure this stuff is helping. I don't notice any difference."

"Remember the doc said it might take some time to kick in?"

"Yeah, that was three weeks ago. How much time should it take? I feel like that sharp point is vindictive, just waiting to make me miserable."

Evelyn stuck out a pouty lower lip.

Peter pulled out the needle and tossed it into the sharps container. He put his arm around her and gave her a kiss on her cheek. Sometimes, that was the most he could muster. He hated watching her go through this—whatever name they wanted to pin on her. The doctors just didn't seem to pinpoint what was going on. It had to be frustrating for her, but she rarely showed it. Just trooped on. He mustered a wan smile.

"How about helping me with these cookies? Nothing like a snowy day to bring on the cookie spirit."

"I'd love to."

Lately, he felt as if he needed to spend as much time with her as he could. There were days when she seemed so frail. Then others where she would rouse, and no one would have guessed there was an issue.

Peter handed the carton of eggs to Evelyn, who cracked several into the Kitchen Aid mixer where the blades swirled the butter and sugar into the sweet-smelling mixture.

"How are things with Phoebe?"

"Good. Great. She joined the Fire Department. She is really a trooper. There's nothing physical that phases her."

"That sounds like fun. How did the guys take her being on? Are there other gals in there too?"

"She's the only one. At first, they thought she wouldn't be able to do anything cuz she's so slight. But they soon changed their minds when she went through the obstacle course." Peter laughed.

"Nicole said Olivia contacted the man she thinks might be her dad. Of course, you probably already know that."

Peter washed his hands and sifted flour onto the counter. He *should* know that. But he didn't.

"I bet she's excited. Probably nervous."

What was keeping him from talking to her?

Evelyn scooped out some dough and plopped it onto the marble slab. Peter handed her the rolling pin.

"Phoebe and I went online and found a site for Search Angels. They help connect those searching for their birth families."

"Really? That sounds good."

"Yeah, I think it is. But," he looked in the drawer for the cookie cutters. "I'm not so sure I should have done it. I didn't check with Olivia first to even see if she wanted me to."

"Why wouldn't you have done that first son?"

"I don't know. I guess I wanted to help her out, but it just seems," he looked out the window, "a little awkward. You know, me and Phoebe and all."

Evelyn rolled the dough to the edges.

"Check your heart. Spend some time with your Papa. He will show you what he wants from you."

OLIVIA'S BOOTS crunched on the snow as she and her dad made tracks towards the Christmas trees. Bella romped through the snow, ignoring the frigid temperature—not a care in the world.

Olivia glanced at Peter's kitchen window as she passed. Had she done the right thing? Telling him to find a *real* girlfriend? He had certainly done that. She had hoped they could have kept their same friendship. It seemed possible at the time. But now? Well, he spent all his free time with Phoebe. Regret settled at the tip of her heart.

Her dad stepped up beside her.

"What are you so deep in thought about? You're so quiet."

"Nothing much. I'm a little anxious about hearing from Jack."

"About the DNA test? Did he do it?"

"That's just it. I don't know. And I feel a little nervous about even searching for him."

She stopped and slid her arm through her dad's, her puffy coat bunching up at the elbow.

"You're thinking if he is he might not want to know you?"

"That, but I'm also wondering if me pursuing this is hurting you."

They walked through the rows of trees.

Brad turned to her. "Baby, you're my daughter. You always have been. It doesn't take me physically being related to you to love you to pieces. I don't feel threatened in the least. In fact, maybe, if he truly is your bio dad, he'll want to meet me." He grinned.

Tears found their way to the corners of her eyes. Bella nuzzled her snout in Olivia's hand.

"How about this tree?"

Olivia scrutinized the Nordmann Fir, her favorite. The branches were symmetrical and gave enough space for the ornaments to be seen. She pulled off a glove and ran her fingers over the soft needles.

"This will be just perfect."

Chapter Twenty-Eight

Christmas songs were cued on the music app. Ondrea and her boyfriend, Hunter, held wooden spoons like microphones and belted out *All I want for Christmas, is youu-uuuuu—*. He took her hand and twirled her around, the full skirt of her dress standing out like she was on Dancing with Stars.

They burst out laughing. Owen rolled his eyes as any junior high boy would do, grabbed a decorated sugar cookie from the plate and headed to the living room, where he plopped down beside his older brother Otis who was watching Elf.

Jack grinned and wrapped his arm around Lisa's shoulder.

"We've done all right, haven't we?"

"That we have."

Lisa turned and kissed him.

"Help me get the dishes cleaned up so we can open gifts."

They had decided years ago their Christmas tradition would be a dinner of homemade pizza, then go to church and finish the night with gifts that Santa snuck under the tree while they were away. That way, they could all sleep in, open stockings—filled by Santa, of course, eat Lisa's homemade cinnamon rolls slathered with cream cheese icing, and binge watch Christmas movies.

Otis switched off the TV and pulled out his guitar. He strummed, his long fingers moving expertly over the frets. His hair, parted on the side had longer back strands which hung down to his denim collar.

The music was magical, and he was so immersed in it he didn't look up until voices joined in with Go Tell it on the Mountain. Hunter sat on the floor, his legs creating a space for Ondrea, who rested her back on his chest. Owen positioned the djembe drum between his knees and beat out the rhythm. Jack sang the verses and the rest joined in on the chorus.

The ten-foot Grand Fir nearly reached the vaulted ceiling, the white lights reflecting in the floor-to-ceiling windows. Lisa had decorated it with soft full ribbons between the collection of ornaments, each with a story behind it. Piles of presents sat balanced on the tree skirt, inviting curious fingers and sneaky package shaking.

Otis segued to Silent Night, and Lisa harmonized with Jack. What could be more perfect?

"Hey, before we open gifts, I thought it would be fun to look at some old photos. Reminisce a little."

Jack brought out several boxes and set them on the teak coffee table. He took off the lids and handed one to each, where photos were lined up evenly, separated by dates. Otis and Owen shared one box, pulling out photos one by one. They laughed at seeing them together in the bathtub, Otis pulling Owen in a wagon attached to his skateboard, all three of them in their swimsuits, covered head to toe with goopy mud.

Ondrea held a photo showing her at a middle school dance dressed in a long satin dress with a slit up the leg. Two girls stood with her on one side, and a boy with a goofy grin had his arm around her shoulder.

"Wow, what happened to him?"

"We split ways when we entered high school."

Ondrea looked up at Hunter. "And I'm glad I did, or I wouldn't have you, now, would I?"

Jack held up a photo of all three kids sitting on St. Nick's lap. Ondrea with her blond hair in two high pony tails with red and green bows. Owen pushed out his bottom lip while the others smiled. Otis had probably teased him about what he wanted for Christmas.

The next photo was one of all three dressed in nativity costumes—they must have been in grade school. Otis as a Wiseman, Owen a sheep and Ondrea played the part of Mary.

"They were so cute. I miss those days." Lisa took a sip of her cider.

"They were. But so busy! I kind of prefer the age they are now. Just as fun. But maybe even cuter now." Jack smiled.

"We should start in on the gifts. It's eleven already!"

"Who wants popcorn? I'll go make some before we open presents." Ondrea looked from face to face. Three hands raised.

"Make sure to put on lots of butter."

"And bring napkins." Jack's eyebrows raised.

Lisa gathered the loose photos and replaced them in the box. She picked up the lid and turned it over.

"What's this?" She glanced at Jack.

A folded sheet of paper slid inside a baggie, taped to the underside of the lid.

"Not sure—pull it out. Let's see."

Lisa slid her red polished fingernail to separate the zip lock and took out the yellow sheet. She unfolded the lined page and held it between them.

To my unborn child:

In a mere four words, the memory came crashing back, obscuring everything in the room. Jack's pulse quickened, and he sucked in a breath.

There may never be a chance for you to see this, but I feel I need to explain.

Jack continued to read to the end, the memory taking over, filling him with remorse.

Lisa set the letter down and turned to Jack.

"Are you okay?"

He slowly locked eyes with her.

"It's her, isn't it—the girl that called? She's alive. I don't even need to take the DNA test. I know."

Lisa nodded slowly, recognition in her hazel eyes.

"Isn't God good? His timing is always perfect. What a precious Christmas gift!"

He nodded. "I guess I just repressed the memory. Too painful to hold on to."

"I think you should take the test. You both need the confirmation. But I have one question. Did you ever see Bridgett again?"

Jack shook his head.

"No. I asked around and one of her friends said she had moved to Oregon."

Ondrea had returned with a large popcorn bowl and red silo cups.

"Dad, when can we open our presents? Don't you think we've waited long enough?"

Waited long enough? Yes. He had waited long enough. Long enough to connect with his daughter. To meet her. To see her and get to know her.

"Presents! Presents! Presents!" A chorus of excited little kids in enormous bodies.

Chapter Twenty-Nine

Olivia slid an ornament off the tree branch and carefully laid it in the plastic tote, sectioned off to protect each precious item. Christmas had been a mixed bag. Her family had spent it with Peter's family like hundreds of other times. Only this time, Peter had Phoebe. Olivia reminded herself that he had Phoebe because *she* had told him to find someone else. Still, she couldn't shake the feeling that she had made a mistake. A huge mistake.

She removed an ornament of a girl in a swimsuit from the branch. Peter had given it to her when she had placed first in the final meet. She had perfected her one-armed stroke by keeping her body facing the left side of the pool, keeping her left arm limp, and kicking powerfully in time with the strong pull of her right hand.

Peter had been there for her, cheering her on every stroke of the way.

Like he had been for her track meets.

Like he was there for all her soccer matches.

Olivia hadn't minded Phoebe's being at the Gunderson's. Mostly. Olivia watched how she was at ease helping Evelyn with dinner. She had a fun sense of humor. She was cute. And whole. And just right for Peter. And Olivia was okay with it.

Until Phoebe opened her gift from him, a heart necklace, and she full on kissed him.

Olivia placed the last ornament in the box and snapped the plastic lid closed. *Buck it up, buttercup.*

The snow had melted and now the rains had come, grey clouds obscuring the sun. The east wind that had begun slowly, was now hollering and hurling raindrops against the windows, the sound like hundreds of tap dancers.

A horn sounded, and she glanced outside. Bella stood from her soft cushion on the floor and followed her to the door. The mailman parked in her driveway. She grabbed her raincoat and hustled out. He handed her a package and stack of mail, then Olivia scooted back to the house.

Olivia shook off the raindrops and hung her coat on the rack. She snagged a dishcloth from the kitchen and dried the package. Something for her dad. She set it on the counter and pawed through the letters, stopping on one from Jack Murphy. Her heart skipped a beat. She ran her finger over his handwriting. Held the letter up and inhaled the faint scent, then placed it against her thundering heart.

Bella nosed her hand, and she patted his head. She should call Peter and have him open it with her. No. It was too wet outside. And she didn't want to bother him.

She'd wait for her mom or dad to return. Read it together. Then if it was bad news, she'd have someone to commiserate with. Or, if it were good, they could rejoice together. She slid it into her back pocket.

Pulling out the vacuum, she stilled her shaking hand as she tried to plug it in. Needles scattered the hardwood floor. She shook the tree skirt and swiped at the stubborn few that remained. The vacuum whirred to life, and the needles pinged the sides of the hose as they made their way into the bag.

She jumped at the sound of her mom behind her and shut off the vacuum.

"Olivia? We're home. What a day! The wind is sure picking up."

Nicole hung her dripping raincoat by the wood stove, and unwrapped her scarf.

"You removed the ornaments."

Her mouth turned down, a little disappointed.

"I know. I hate Christmas to be over, but the needles were shedding. We don't want a fire hazard."

Olivia put her hand on her back pocket, feeling for the letter. Should she ask her to read it with her now? Or wait till tonight? No, she should wait. Her mom needed to get warm and dry.

"I know it's awful out there, but have you fed your bottle baby yet?"

Olivia shook her head. She should have done that earlier, before the storm set in. But she had been sidetracked by taking down the tree. And the letter. Well, she'd better go now. No doubt that cute little Rosie lamb was hungry.

OLIVIA MEASURED out dry formula into a bottle of warm water and shook it. Then fitted the rubber nipple securely over the top of the bottle. Pulling her orange coat and rain pants over her jeans, she stuck the bottle in her coat pocket and grabbed the keys. It was dark and the torrential rain pelted enormous drops. The wind knocked her sideways as she ran for her dad's pickup. This was the kind of night she would have preferred living closer to the barn, not having to go clear to Peter's. Her shoulders tightened. Water dripped from her hood down her nose. She swiped at it. Caring for animals seemed like the right choice. Just not right now. She yanked on the truck door and jumped inside. Not only was it wet, but it was also cold and her hand shivered as she tried to aim the key in the ignition.

"Come on!"

Was it the weather? Or the anxiety of the letter in her back pocket? Better that she wasn't home. She could hear her mom calling her Miss Grumpy Pants. *Just shake it off, girl.*

The light was on in the barn, shining through the wooden sliding doors. Maybe Ross had left it on for the animals. Whatever the reason, she was glad she wouldn't have to feel around for the light switch. At least that was one good thing. Olivia shut off the engine and ran to the doors. She grabbed the handle and heaved her right shoulder onto it to give an extra budge. The wheels squeaked and caught. It was time for Ross to grease the skids. This was not helping her mood.

Rosie bleated—her little voice small against the storm.

"I'm coming. Just give me a minute."

Her voice was harsher than she had intended. Olivia walked to the pen, her vinyl pants swishing as she went. She pulled out the bottle, showed it to Rosie, who kicked up her legs and bounced to it, grabbing onto the nipple with eager lips.

"I'm sorry it took so long. I just got wrapped up in some other projects. And guess what? I've got a letter from Jack. I can't wait to read it. I'm a little nervous too."

Rosie glugged the milk and tugged at the nipple. No! Too hard. The nipple pulled off, spilling some of the contents. Olivia grabbed the nipple from the hay below her.

"Seriously Rosie?"

She swiped pieces of hay from it and fit it back on the bottle. At least it hadn't spilled much milk.

The wind howled, and Olivia heard the crunch of a large branch breaking. The lights flickered. She glanced at the ceiling. She needed to finish up before the inevitable happened. Happy to have left her headlamp in her pocket, she pulled it out and fit it onto her forehead.

"Okay, girl. You're done. You're not going to get any more till morning."

She scanned the barn. A ewe bleated. Hmmm. Olivia hadn't put her in the barn. Maybe Ross saw she was getting close. She better check on her before she left. Olivia sighed. She just wanted to go home, cozy up to the fireplace, snuggle with a warm blanket —and read that letter.

She stomped past Daisy laying in her pen, unperturbed by the storm. Olivia reached the pen where the ewe lay on her side, her uterus pulsing. Great. She's in labor. Well then, she may as well get comfortable. This could take a while. She slid herself into the stall and leaned against the wooden fence. She reached into her pocket and pulled out her phone.

May as well make use of the situation. She videoed the ewe and told what was happening. Then uploaded it to Insta. She lost herself, scrolling through dozens of reels. Bleating brought her out of that space and back into the barn.

"Okay, mama, let's try standing you up and see if gravity will help you deliver. I'd just as soon get home. And I'm sure you'd just as soon get that lamb out of you."

Olivia tugged on her wool and slapped her back to urge the mama up. She wasn't gonna lie. This was one of those times when it would be nice to have two hands. She nudged her with her knee. The ewe just stared at her with glassy eyes. Olivia looked around and found a bucket, filled it with a little grain, and brought it to her. With great effort, the ewe shifted her weight and pushed herself up, the straw at her hooves pushed down into the dirt floor. She bleated and her muscles strained to support the bulk of her body and baby. She swayed slightly and shook her woolly coat.

Slimy goop was trailing from her rear. Olivia checked the time. She'd been in the barn for almost two hours.

"Okay, mama, you've got this. Let's get this show on the road."

Minutes later, a head peeked through between two small front legs, its eyes closed. It held there until the next contraction when the ewe lamb slid to the ground. The mama nosed it and started licking the yellow meconium covering the little one. She bleated again.

"Good job! Do you have another one in there?" It wasn't uncommon to have twins. Even occasional triplets. Olivia jumped as she heard another branch crash. The lights flickered. And went out.

Chapter Thirty

Great! What else can go wrong? Olivia clicked on her headlamp.

Come on God. I could use a little grace here.

Long minutes passed and still no baby. Olivia pulled out her phone and tapped on the camera. She may as well create a video for her next YouTube. As the lamb stood on wobbly legs and approached the mama's full udder, Olivia recorded the event. The lamb instinctively butted the udder, bringing colostrum down into her tiny pink mouth, the little tail wagging happily as she did.

Olivia's body relaxed as she watched. She felt her pocket for the letter. It was all she could do to not take it out right here. Right now. But no, she wanted to read it with her parents. It had to be good, this letter. She imagined telling Jack about tonight. Showing him the video. This might be new to him if he hadn't lived on or near a farm.

The wind continued to howl, hurling cracked branches across the property. Hopefully, no more would land on the roof.

The lamb lay down.

"Okay, mama don't be mad, but I'm gonna reach in and see what's going on. Is your baby stuck?"

Olivia removed her raincoat and threw it over the fence post. She knelt on her knees, shoved her sleeves up and slid her hand through to the uterus. It was wet and warm, and she felt a contraction constrict her arm. She was right. There was another lamb. This wasn't the head she was feeling. This was the tail and its bottom. She pulled her arm out and sat down.

"Okay, God, this is new to me. What am I supposed to do? If you and I don't get this baby out, the ewe might die and the baby with it. And if I can't do this, what kind of vet will I be? We've got to make this work."

Through the wooden boards, she saw a flash of light. Was that a sign from God? Stranger things had happened in the Bible. She nodded a thanks and returned to her knees. With her left shoulder leaning into the soft wool, she slid her right arm back inside. She closed her eyes, trying to visualize what she was feeling. Coming out backside would not work. Somehow, she had to get that little lamb turned around. Maybe if she could find the front legs, she could reposition them. She nudged the bottom, and it moved slightly to the right. That was good. Inch by inch, right? She could do this. She had to do this.

PETER PULLED up to Phoebe's duplex and sprinted through the rain to the passenger door. He held out his hand and they ran to the covered awning, where he pulled her to himself.

"Another great evening—great food, good company."

He cupped her face and planted a kiss on her lips. She responded in kind, running her hands through his coat and lacing her fingers behind his back, pulling him closer.

A lightning bolt lit the sky, shooting through the thick, dark clouds.

The radio at Peter's hip belted out "92376 Gunderson Rd. Structure fire." He backed up and his jaw dropped.

"That's my house. What? How? Not again."

He palmed his forehead.

"And my parents are out of town. How could this happen?"

They bolted to the pickup and headed for the station where the red and yellow engine lights were whirling, and doors open. After suiting up, they jumped into the truck.

He pulled out his phone and tapped on three, the speed dial for Olivia. She could go and check on things. His pulse raced as it rang—four... five... six, the sound muted by the siren. No answer. He left a frantic message.

We're on the way

Black smoke billowed, filling their noses with the acrid smell. An eerie glow contrasted against the dark, stormy night. Angry flames shot out the upper loft window of the barn. Panicked chickens squawked and scrambled frantically; their red feathers ruffled.

Peter jumped out of the truck.

"Why did the rain have to slow down now? We could have used its help."

A quick survey showed a large limb dangling on a power line.

"Somebody call the power company. Let's get that limb taken care of," Mac yelled.

Could they even do that? Sparks flickered and crackled, igniting the barn walls. It may be too dangerous.

Phoebe put her newfound training to use and pulled the hose to the barn while Peter sprinted to the open barn door. He was surrounded by the darkness, save for the flicker of flames now invading the entire roof. Startled by the crash of a fiery beam only yards in front of him, he jumped back.

Daisy and any other animals needed to be saved before they were engulfed. The smoke alone was damaging. He had to act fast.

Phoebe pulled the hose into the barn, kneeled, and pulled the bale to release the flow of water, aiming it towards the fallen timber. Peter gave her a thumbs up, flipped on his headlamp and scanned the room. Daisy's bellow called to him, and he grabbed the latch to release her. Her frightened eyes searched the room, and she kicked her hind legs, running frantically around the stall. She bolted, and he waved his hands to head her outside.

Through the flicker of flames, he noticed a small light. What could that be? His legs pumped as he bolted to the spot. Olivia— her head facing the wall, arm inside a ewe, a lamb lying beside her. No, no, no! No animal was worth risking her life for.

"Olivia!" The sound of his voice bounced back at him inside his helmet.

Anxiety rose through his chest, causing his shoulders to tense. Sweat trickled down under Peter's gear.

Olivia turned her head and coughed.

"You've got to get out of here. Now!"

"I can't. I've almost got it turned. Grab the lamb. Save it."

Peter pulled a hanky from his pocket, folded it in half and tied in around Olivia's nose and mouth to protect her from the smoke. It wasn't much, but it would help some.

There was no way she could move this ewe outside of the barn. He had to do what he could to protect the both of them. Olivia leaving the barn without saving the ewe and her lambs would never happen.

But it was all Peter could do to resist picking Olivia up and carrying her out. Bowing to her need for independence, he cradled the lamb and ran outside where he deposited it into the arms of an onlooker. He grabbed Vinny's sleeve and pulled him inside.

Peter took the hose from Phoebe and pulled it towards the pen. He sprayed water, circling the fences, the walls, completely drenching the area. He would do all he could to protect Olivia until the lamb was born.

"I've almost got it turned."

Olivia coughed and squinted through the smoke. She gave a yank on two front feet and the lamb slid to the ground.

"Quick, let's get you out of here."

She rose and handed a halter to Peter for the ewe and handed the newborn to Vinny. He set the lamb over his neck and grabbed the halter to lead the mama out. Peter put his arms under Olivia, picking her up where she wrapped her arms tightly around his neck as he ran out of the barn.

Chapter Thirty-One

Peter used his elbow to flip on the lights as he entered the house.

"I can walk. You don't need to carry me."

He liked the feel of Olivia's arms around his neck and wasn't anxious to put her down.

"Mmmhmm."

Peter went to his bedroom and laid her on his bed, glad he hadn't made his bed that morning. He pulled off her Romeos and set them on the floor. He wasn't sure if he should pull off her rain pants. But she was so exhausted. He tugged them at the hems and slid them off, grateful that she had jeans under them. Not the most comfortable to sleep in, but it would have to do. He pulled the covers over her and grabbed some sweats before he left the room.

He needed to call his folks and let them know. The clock on his nightstand blinked eleven-thirty. Too late for them. He'd let them be until morning. Why ruin their rare mini-vacay? Let them enjoy themselves. The embers had quieted and there was really nothing more they could do now. Thank goodness the storm had abated. He'd assess the damage in the morning.

The pounding in his chest and anxiety that had completely

overtaken his body had finally calmed as well. It was bad enough attending to someone else's burning house. But his own? He could only imagine how horrible it had to have been for his mom to be in the center of the last one. Looking at the house now, one would never suspect it had been an inferno. Except for that nasty scar on her arm, you'd never know Mom had endured that either.

Could Peter's rescuing Olivia be redemption for not being there for Mom? Could he trade one good deed for one bad one? But it was more than a good deed. Olivia could have died from smoke inhalation. That burning timber could have landed on her instead of the open area of the barn. Only by the grace of God.

He went to the garage and shrugged off his gear where the odor would remain outside the house. His phone rang. Phoebe.

He put the phone on speaker and slid his leg through his sweats.

"Did you get home safe?"

He tugged his sweats on the rest of the way.

"Yes. Are you okay? I was worried about you."

"Yeah. That was seriously intense."

"Peter, I didn't want to wait until morning to talk to you."

Peter frowned. What was so important?

"I saw how you carried Olivia out. How you rescued her." She paused. "She's your first love. And you need to go back to her."

Peter put his hand on the back of his neck. Did he?

"Olivia didn't want me."

"But she *does* want you. I saw how she looked at you."

"Phoebe, it's been a long, emotional night. Let's talk in the morning."

He hung up and tiptoed to his bedroom. He let his phone slip from his hand to his bed. Sleep. He just needed a good night's sleep.

WITHOUT OPENING HER EYES, Olivia turned and pulled the covers over her shoulder.

After that long night, it was too early to get up just yet. She wanted to go back to sleep, but thoughts of last night made their way in, a continuance of her wild and frightening dreams.

She had done it. Not only getting the lamb turned and saving it, and let's face it—it wasn't exactly the finest environment in which to accomplish that feat. There would be no stopping her now. The challenges of being a vet didn't look so overwhelming in the face of what she just gone through. This was where God evidently wanted her. He had been right beside her though the way had been horrendous. She might even have died in the fire along with the sheep. But she hadn't. God sent a rescuer.

Peter—frantic with concern. Despite that, allowing her to finish what she had begun. Knowing she *had* to save that lamb.

Picking her up and rescuing her. Making sure the ewe and lamb were safe. And seeing Phoebe's eyes follow them out. She let her lids slowly drift open.

Wait. Those weren't her curtains over her window. Or her desk next to the bed. And where was Bella who always slept at her feet? She sprang up, knocking a book off the end table, and threw off the comforter where she saw the t-shirt and jeans, she had worn under her rain clothes.

Why oh, why was she in Peter Gunderson's bedroom? In his bed? Her heart hammered and she could feel the blood rush to her cheeks. Mortified, she slowly slid a glance to see bare skin right next to her, rising and falling, in this bed that was not her own. There was no way she was going to wake Peter up. With any great luck, his folks were still gone.

She slid her legs out from under the covers, found her sweatshirt, and ran to the bathroom. She didn't know if she should flush — would it wake him? She swished water in her mouth, ran her fingers through her matted hair and opened the door.

Where Peter stood in his sweats, shirtless, his arm raised above his head and leaning on the doorframe.

"Well good morning, sunshine." He slid a wry grin.

"Peter! What is going on? Why am I here?"

She punched his arm.

"And you didn't have to startle me."

Her hand went to her hip.

His face grew serious.

"You don't remember what happened last night?"

Oh, she remembered all right.

"The lamb. The fire. The storm."

His brows formed a question mark.

Olivia put her fist to her chin.

"Okay. But why did I wake up here? In. Your. Bed?"

Peter's chest shook as he broke out in laughter.

"Peter!"

He took a breath.

"I think the emotions of the entire night got to you. You were exhausted. I could have taken you home, but you weren't fit for another moment. And this was more convenient."

"And if that's so, Mr. Conscientious, you could have slept on the couch."

"Yeah, I suppose I could have. But then again, I was exhausted beyond reason as well. And my bed was closer than the couch."

He took her shoulders in his gentle hands and paused. What was behind the depth of his eyes? And oh, the feel of his hands on her shoulders—how she had missed that.

"Look. Phoebe broke up with me."

Olivia double blinked.

"But why?" Her voice was barely above a whisper.

He shrugged.

"She says I'm in love with you. And you're in love with me."

Olivia objected, shaking her head. It wasn't so. Was it?

He put a finger to her lips and entwined his free fingers with hers.

And then, he kissed her. Softly. Then full on. She raised her arms and wrapped them around his neck, joining her lips to his with a passion she had only dreamt of.

BACK HOME, Olivia stood in the shower, letting the hot water soak her bones, cleanse the smoke and soot from her hair and every other particle of her body. She had concocted all sorts of excuses to tell her folks why she hadn't come home last night. None of them felt right. And in the end, lying wasn't something she made a habit of. So, she told them the truth. Peter had carried her out of the fire, and she slept at his house. Was it a sin of omission to leave out *in his bed*?

Or to say he kissed her? And she kissed him back? A tingle ran through her chest to her stomach. *But what if it did work?* She had hidden Peter's words deep inside, like a holding place within her soul, wanting to forget about that possibility. There had been all sorts of reasons why to reject that idea. But the bottom line was fear of losing what they had as friends. And why did she fear that? Couldn't she spend the rest of her life with her best friend? What could be better than that?

Olivia toweled off, dressed in clean jeans, and a sweatshirt, and picked up her clothes to deposit in the laundry, holding the smell and filth away from herself. She opened the lid to the washer and threw in her sweatshirt, top, and underwear. Holding her jeans over the tub, she suddenly remembered the letter.

The letter.

She gasped. What if she had washed it? After starting the cycle she searched for her mom.

"Mom—"

Olivia plopped on the couch beside her.

"Look what I got in the mail! I had planned to wait until after

I fed Rosie to read it. And then, well, when I saw the ewe in labor, I couldn't just leave her there."

Brad entered, a look of relief on his face.

"I, we, couldn't be prouder of you. You had to be scared out of your wits. From what we heard, there were flames all around and beams crashing."

"But you mustered on, despite it."

Nicole put her hand on Olivia's thigh. Moisture formed on her eyelids.

That her parents loved her was wonderful. That they showed her their affection. But did they realize how hard it was to live up to the standard of *mustering on?* It was good for her—she knew that. But was she only good enough if she mastered the challenge? What if she didn't? Would that make her any less able?

"Mom."

She hesitated and picked at her nail. This was going to take more courage than what had transpired last night.

"You always make me feel like I need to perform. Like, unless I don't, I'm never going to be good enough."

Like you'll love me less.

Nicole put her arm around her.

"Oh, Olivia."

Brad waved his hand motioning them to move over. He sat beside Olivia and looked at his hands lying in his lap.

"I guess I could see how you would think that."

He slid a glance at her.

"But honey, you have to know that has never been our intent. We just wanted you to be normal." Nicole caught herself. "I didn't mean that. I meant you were capable of doing whatever anyone else could."

Olivia took this in, and a tear slid down her cheek. She looked up, her voice above a whisper.

"But I feel like I have to hide not having a hand." Her voice rose.

"It's not always easy, but I feel like I have to make everything *seem* easy. To look like it's no problem. But it can be a problem. Like last night—I wasn't sure I could get the ewe to stand by myself so I could help her birth. And I didn't want to bother anyone for help."

Brad locked eyes with Nicole.

"It wouldn't have been a bother. We'd have been there in a flash. We're sorry, bug. We never intended to make you feel less-than."

Nicole ran her fingers through Olivia's hair.

"It was the opposite. Thank you for telling us this. We'll both work on changing. Your identity is *not* in what you can do. It's in who you are. Where your heart is."

"And you have the biggest loving heart ever."

Brad gave her a peck on the head.

Olivia wiped her eyes with the sleeve of her sweatshirt.

"Well, now that we've got that out of the way—"

She pulled the letter from her pocket and waved it in front of them.

"We have more important matters to attend to."

Chapter Thirty-Two

Olivia's fingers trembled. Was she certain she wanted to read the contents? She was, after all, the one who had opened the door to the unknown. He basically already said, *thank you very much, but you've got the wrong man. Please leave me alone.*

Or—she didn't want to believe an opposite scenario was even possible.

Nicole touched her shoulder.

"Honey, go ahead and open it. We're right here with you. Good or bad."

"Besides, bug, you have nothing to lose. If it's not the outcome you hoped for, you won't be any worse off."

Dad—always practical.

Bella stood from her bed under the living room window and bounded to Olivia. She must have felt the energy and knew her best friend needed her.

Olivia held the letter on her knee and slid her finger under the seal—the very place her father had licked. She pulled out the page which was folded in thirds. There were three pages—one, a photocopy and the other written on a piece of plain stationary.

She unfolded the first.

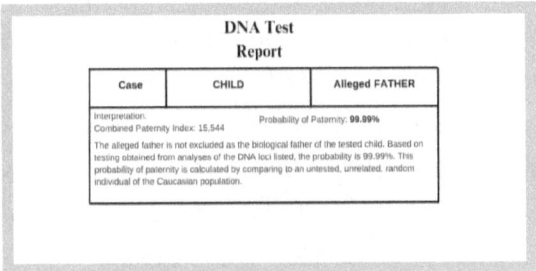

Olivia's eyes widened, and she reached for Nicole's hand. Ninety-nine percent match? She held the letter to her heart—the rate which had to have exceeded one hundred. Unbidden tears wet her lashes.

"He... is... my father."

Her words were slow and purposeful. She exhaled the breath she had held since the beginning of this journey. A smile spread, filling her lips to the sparkle in her eyes.

She turned to Brad, her eyes seeking his approval.

Brad smiled, his eyes reaching into her soul.

"I am so happy for you, sweetheart. This is exciting news."

The validation from Dad meant so much. She had always felt loved by him, known she was his little girl, but it seemed like the ultimate sacrifice for him to accept the man who had rejected her. Maybe that was too much. The truth was, if he didn't know the details, perhaps he hadn't rejected her.

"Open the other one. He obviously wanted you to see the good news first."

Brad wrapped his large fingers around her wrist.

She placed the first letter behind the others.

Dear Olivia,

How could I have ever known what a thrill it would be to follow through on a sample of a tiny glob of saliva. Before I even took the paternity test, I knew in my heart it would reveal that I was your dad. And I don't say dad lightly. I'm sure there's a man in your life who has filled the role I should have taken. And I hope one day to thank him—your real dad.

OLIVIA LEANED her shoulder into Brad's.

We spent Christmas eve in our usual way—playing games, eating good food, watching movies with our three teens (Owen, Otis, and Ondrea).

Nicole read over her shoulder.
"They named them all O names? That's kinda cute."
"Mom—It's more than cute. My name begins with an O!"
This was feeling so right. Like a little God wink.

But the divine interruption was when my wife, Lisa, brought out boxes of photos to reminisce with. We were ready to put them away when I found the following letter taped to the top of the box.

I can't tell you what a shock that was. I had totally wiped this from my mind. But after reading it, it was Lisa who urged me to pursue the DNA test. And the rest is history.

So, here I am hoping to connect with my firstborn.

The one I never knew existed. It could only be a God thing.

"Oh, my goodness. He's a believer too. And he wants to connect with me!"

Olivia set the letter down and stared out the front window, trying to take all this in, overwhelmed with finding a piece of her puzzle. A piece that seemed to fit exactly in place. Like it was made to happen.

As fathers, you're responsible for the life you created. When this is taken away from the start, we are blindfolded from that point on. We are left out of those months of feeling compassion and joy that we created something beautiful. I never had a choice about what was going to happen to you.

I would have chosen life. I want you to know that.

I live in Colorado. Could we meet through online video—get to know each other a bit? Then perhaps we could plan a person-to-person meeting. That is, if you want to. I'll leave that up to you.

Blessings daughter,

Jack

OLIVIA RAN her fingers over the writing, wanting to be as close to him as she could.

"One more page. Are you ready? Or do you want to take a break? This is a lot to take in!" Brad started to stand, and Olivia placed her arm on his.

"No, let's see the rest. I can't imagine what else he would have included. Pictures?"

She slid the last letter behind the others. This one was written on a page pulled from a spiral notebook. The ripped edges stuck out along the left edge. It had been folded in thirds and once again in half.

She held it a minute before unfolding the page. This would be good, right? The other two had been. She inhaled and let it out slowly.

January 1993

To my unborn child:

There may never be a chance for you to see this, but I feel I need to explain.

Your mom and I met in college. The term was just beginning, and she was sitting on the cement bench soaking up the sun and drinking a Kiwi Italian soda. I asked if I could join her. There were plenty of other places I could have sat, but there was just something about her. The sun illuminated strands of gold, teal, and blue woven through her dark hair.

I introduced myself and we hit it off right away, talking and walking through the afternoon and on into the evening. It wasn't long before we became intimate partners. I had assumed she was taking precautions. I was wrong. And admittedly, I should have taken precautions.

When Bridgett told me she was pregnant, she was

angry. She blamed me and didn't want to have anything to do with me. The last thing Bridgett told me was she was having an abortion.

You need to know that I begged her not to. I would have raised you by myself if I had to. She insisted it was her body and her life.

You would have been born in May 1993.

Words cannot adequately express how sorry I am. I pray that by some great miracle God will protect you.

Dad

OLIVIA WAS WEEPING by the time she finished the letter, the words blurring as she let the pages fall to her lap.

Chapter Thirty-Three

The engine rumbled to life as Peter started the tractor. He drove it into the barn—what was left of it. The back wall and part of the ceiling were toast, but it looked like most of the other three walls were going to be fine. He turned his cap backwards and adjusted it, then lowered the bucket to scrape the charred timbers into a pile. They splintered and fell, raising debris and the rank odor of smoke into the air. He coughed. These timbers that fell so near Olivia. His heartbeat rose as he remembered the horrendous night. Firefighting was one thing when it was at someone else's house. But when someone you love is in danger? A completely other matter.

That girl. What was wrong with her? She would put the care of animals over her own safety? Peter wasn't so sure he would have done that. Then again, he *had* done that for his patients during the pandemic. At any rate, he was glad that he was the one to find her. Anyone else would have forced her to leave. And they probably would have been right.

But they didn't know her like he did.

Peter scooped up a pile of burnt timbers and ash and drove them outside, where he deposited the debris in an open field.

Later, he and his dad could burn it down to ashes and use it for fertilizer.

A smile tweaked his lips, remembering Olivia's look when he stood at the bathroom door. Oh my, but she looked good for someone who had been through the wringer—her hair hanging with just enough mess to make it look like she had styled it that way. Fire in her brown eyes, little specks of green shifting in her gaze.

And he had to admit, if he hadn't been so utterly bone-tired, he'd have had a hard time staying on top of the covers rather than under them, where he would have wrapped his arm around her and tucked her head tightly snuggled under his chin.

He returned to the barn to scoop up the remaining charred wood. Olivia hadn't resisted his kiss, hadn't slapped him, or pushed him away. That was a good sign, wasn't it? Because when he'd proposed to her at the fair, which had definitely been too soon and impulsive, she had pulled away. Would she pull away now? He felt like he was on a tightrope, teetering above a canyon of uncertainty.

The bucket screeched along the dirt floor as he lifted the load. He backed it around and faced the doorway.

Evelyn waved. She looked dwarfed in her jeans and sweatshirt with the recent weight loss. Peter pulled the tractor to a stop and jumped down.

"Hey Mom, did you get some rest?"

He wrapped his arm around her.

"Yeah, a bit."

She spread her arm, gesturing towards the damage.

"This is a little Déja-vu. I'm actually kind of glad we were gone when it happened, so I didn't have to relive it."

Peter's Adam's apple lifted and fell. He cleared his throat.

"I called the insurance company. They'll send an appraiser out in a few days to look it over. Who knows, perhaps after we rebuild it, it will be better than it was before."

"True. The boards were weather worn."

"It might be best to replace them with corrugated siding. I can look into pricing materials for you. I know Dad has enough on his plate."

Preparing the fields for new crops. Tending to the calves and now, new lambs. Not to mention his silent holding in his worry about Mom.

"Peter, you've done so much. I've appreciated all the nursing help you've provided. Who knew I would be one to benefit from your education?"

Evelyn gave a crooked smile.

"Remember that time, you were about ten I think, when you ran the four-wheeler into the chicken coop and knocked it down? All the chickens were running around like crazy." She laughed.

Peter put his hand on his chin. His chest caught at the memory.

"I was so scared. I thought I had killed some of them."

"But you didn't. You must have felt horrendously guilty because you grounded yourself from riding the four-wheeler for several weeks. And then did what you could to repair the damage. You were out there with your hammer and nails, pounding nails in splintered wood and trying to reattach chicken wire to the boards. You did all kinds of extra chores without being asked."

Peter puffed out a breath.

"I *was* guilty."

"You were a little kid. You probably panicked and forgot how to slow down. It wasn't something to blame yourself for."

"You're right, I suppose."

Peter lifted his hat and ran his fingers through his hair before he replaced it as scraps of memories he hadn't sifted through in years dropped into his mind.

Evelyn put her hand on Peter's arm.

"I think you're doing the same thing here. You quit your job to help out. And I'm not saying your dad and I don't appreciate it.

You joined the fire department. Seems to me like you're trying to fix things."

"Mom, you don't understand. That fire started because of my negligence. There were frayed wires. I was going to tell Dad but then I forgot because I was in a hurry to get back. And then I wasn't there for you when the house burned. I was just thinking about myself."

Peter scuffed the toe of his shoe in the dirt.

"Well, that explains why you joined the fire department. Peter, you can't live with guilt. It's over. We got through it. Just like we'll get through my health issues. It seems to me that you've spent your life trying to be more than you are. Like you've been trying to prove something."

Peter felt his throat tighten.

"Look at me." Evelyn searched his face.

"Some things don't need to be fixed. I want you to listen to me because if I've ever said this before, you haven't heard me. It doesn't have to be you. You don't have to fix everything — try to make things right."

Peter's hands drew clammy.

"You don't have to be a hero. I'm just happy to have you as my son. And as a friend. I just want you to be yourself. You aren't responsible for everything—the farm, my safety, my health. You just don't have to feel the weight and responsibility of it all. I have a husband who's perfectly capable of filling that role."

TEARS THREATENED TO SPILL.

Evelyn linked her frail arm with his and walked outside.

"What I want—no, what I need is for you to be satisfied with who you are. Just be yourself, son. It's okay to be who you are. I am so very proud of you. You've accomplished a lot. But more than that, I love who you are—kind, caring, looking out for others, giving. I couldn't ask for a better child. Your dad and I love you, son. Don't you ever forget it."

Peter opened his mouth and let out the breath he'd been holding. The one that came from deep within and formed the moisture in his eyes. For the first time in as long as he could remember, Peter felt as if he there were light at the end of the tunnel.

"WHAT ARE YOU THINKING ABOUT? You're pretty quiet."

Olivia squeezed Peter's hand as they took a night walk. A half-moon shone through the clouds, casting shadows on the dirt path.

Peter shook his head.

"Mom had a come-to-Jesus moment with me." He glanced at her.

"What did she say?"

Peter took a few steps before he answered.

"I told her I had been responsible for the fire in her house."

"What? You? How could that be?"

Peter told her about the frayed wires.

"Does your dad know that?"

"I don't think so. At least, I never told him. And Mom didn't act like he knew."

Peter shook his head. "She said it didn't matter. They got through it and life goes on. But does it? Does it just go on like nothing ever happened?"

Olivia slid her hand around Peter's waist.

"It does go on, and there will always be scars. But scars are there because they've healed over the wound. Peter, you've been living with guilt and regret. And I get it. That's hard. Really hard. But God is the redeemer of those things. He doesn't stop loving you because you may have made a big mistake. He loves us despite it. Just like your mom loves you despite it. He's the healer. Not just of our bodies, but our souls. He's covered all our mistakes. Now it's up to you to forgive yourself."

They reached the truck, and he opened the door for her. He looked at her a moment and then kissed her.

"I love you, Olivia. Are you sure you want to spend the rest of your life with me? Cuz now's the time to run away if you don't."

"Isn't this what being in a relationship is all about? Working through the kinks? Being there for each other? Kinda like a best friend, wouldn't you say?"

Peter smiled. "You may be doing that a lot. I hope you're up to it."

"I'm sure it's gonna be a two-way street, babe."

Chapter Thirty-Four

O livia was sure she was only imagining things. Forty-seven more minutes and she would log into her computer for a FaceTime meeting with her dad. She drummed her fingers on the desk. How could she kill time to make it go faster? She logged into her YouTube channel.

"Hey friends, do I have exciting news to share! I received a letter from my bio dad! He sent the document that showed he was a 99% DNA match. Can you believe that?"

She fanned her face.

"We found each other! And he sent me a letter he wrote when my mom told him she was pregnant with me. It was a letter to his unborn child. Basically, it told how they met, and how my mom planned to abort me. He didn't want that to happen and prayed that it

wouldn't. So, I guess God does answer prayers, right? Cuz here I am!"

She checked the time. Twenty-three minutes.

"And guess what? We're going to FaceTime in just a few minutes, so I'll say goodbye for now and catch up with you later."

She ended the video, checked herself in the mirror. Loose strands of hair fell by her cheeks, so she redid her pony, decided her sweatshirt didn't look right, changed to a button-down red plaid flannel, plucked her eyebrows, and then brushed her teeth. Five more minutes. She logged into FaceTime, so she'd be ready. Her phone buzzed. Peter.

Thinking about you. Are you ready?

Thanks. I think so

Praying it goes well 🙏

It will. I just know it

She heard the FaceTime chimes, set her phone down and suddenly looked into the beautiful eyes of her father. Emotions welled up from her soul to her eyes, allowing tears to spill over.

"Olivia—I can't believe this is happening. I didn't think there was even an iota of a chance that you even existed."

He pinched the bridge of his nose.

"And yet, here I am!"

She shrugged, wearing a shy grin. There was so much she wanted to say, but she couldn't get her tongue to move.

"Tell me about yourself—I want to hear everything."

"Well," she paused. Where should she begin? "I need to start by saying thank you for taking the DNA test and for writing me. I can't begin to tell you how much that means to me."

"That makes two of us."

He leaned into the screen—his blue eyes sparkling.

"First, I need to let you know something."

She held up her arm.

His face went slack. Was he going to change his mind about wanting to know her?

"What happened?"

"We don't know. When my parents first saw me, I was wrapped in a blanket, like a sausage. It wasn't until they changed my diaper that they saw my stump wrapped in a bandage. No one would tell them what happened. Apparently, they rushed them to sign the paperwork and sent them home."

Jack shook his head.

"I'm not sure what to say. Tell me what that's been like for you."

"I've never known anything else. So, for me, it's normal. I'm not gonna lie. There were times growing up that people would tease me. But my parents have been great. They've always treated me like I was full-bodied, so I've learned to do everything anyone else can do."

"Now that's evidence that you have my genes. All the Murphys have a can-do attitude."

Olivia couldn't help but smile when she heard that. It was a connection she could grab onto.

"Anyway, I work at the neighbor's farm and am training to become a veterinarian. I just delivered my first lambs. Even had to reach in and turn a breach in the middle of a storm, with the barn burning down around me."

She laughed, covering the fear she felt that night.

Jack double blinked.

"And you lived to tell? Makes my life sound dull. But really, you weren't hurt?"

"A neighbor saved me."

Should she call Peter her boyfriend? Maybe it was too soon to say it out loud.

"Tell me about your family. Are you married? And you said you have kids?"

"I am married to Lisa, my wife of twenty-seven years. And I told you we have three teens, Owen's eleven, Otis is sixteen and Ondrea is seventeen."

"All O names. So, I could fit in, right?"

"Absolutely." Jack laughed. "In fact, they were really excited to hear about you. They are hoping you'll come to visit so they can meet you. Do you have siblings?"

"No. I guess my parents thought I would be enough of a handful."

Olivia winked and held up her arm.

Jack's face turned serious.

"Olivia, I never had a choice about what was going to happen to you. You need to know that I would have raised you. I held onto the thought that you needed me. I wanted to protect you, to know you were safe. I wanted everything for you I gave to my other children. When Bridgett moved away, I could only hope that she wouldn't follow through with her plan. And I prayed every day for that."

"I guess I'm living proof that God answered your prayers."

"Yes, indeed."

"Would you mind if I introduce you to my parents?"

"I would love that!"

Olivia called for her parents to come in. They stood behind her where her dad rested his hands on her shoulders.

"Hi, I'm Brad and this is Nicole."

"It's so wonderful to meet you. I have to say, I am so grateful to you for raising my daughter."

"Well, she's a peach. And it's worked out great for us."

Olivia squeezed Brad's hand.

"We've talked it over," Nicole began, "And think it would be great for you two to meet each other."

"I would be honored. We're having a family reunion over spring break—if that wouldn't be too overwhelming for you, Olivia. I'm happy to pay for your flight."

"I would love that!" Just the possibility sent tingles down her arms.

"Okay then, we'll keep in touch."

"Can I ask you one more thing?"

He nodded.

"Would it be okay if I called you Papa Jack?"

His deep chuckle warmed her. "More than okay."

Jack signed off and Olivia leaned back in her chair, crossed her arms, and just stared at the screen. She found her Papa.

Chapter Thirty-Five

Ross checked the attachment of the trailer hitch connection to the pickup.

"Be careful with this thing going around curves. It tends to yank on the truck because of the added weight. I've already paid for the baler repairs, so don't worry about that."

Peter nodded.

Ross put his hand on Peter's shoulder.

"And Peter, thanks. I really appreciate your help and allowing me to stay close to your mom."

Peter heard the unspoken—read between the lines. Mom wasn't getting any better despite the changed medications and strict adherence to the doctor's orders. He pinched the bridge of his nose, and his lips grew thin and firm.

"Yeah, okay. Happy to be here for you."

He drove to the end of his road where he picked up Olivia, dressed in jeans and a navy hooded sweatshirt.

"Hey—"

"Hey back." Her beautiful teeth flashed in her face.

"Get settled and tell me all about your conversation with your dad."

She buckled her seatbelt, and her lips drew into a wide smile reaching to her bright eyes.

"It was amazing. I still can hardly believe it. Not only did I find him, but I got to see him. We talked for over an hour."

"What did he say?"

"First, I still can't get over the letter he sent."

"Yeah, I bet he had no idea you would be the one to receive what he had written thirty years ago. Or that he'd be able to give it to anyone."

"I know. And he was so excited to have another daughter. He said his daughter Ondrea was really excited at the thought of having a sister."

She looked out the window at the passing fields, the newly plowed dirt a deep brown, waiting for seeds and new life.

"I had been so sure when he denied the possibility that I was his daughter that it would be the end of our communication."

Peter nodded, put on his blinker, and carefully passed a freight truck on the two-lane highway.

"Papa Jack was scared that Dad would be disappointed in him for giving him up and being an absent father. But he thanked my dad, Brad, for raising me."

She turned to Peter.

"This is so confusing—who's who in the zoo." She laughed.

"Papa Jack. I like that."

Peter pulled into the dirt parking lot of the equipment repair shop and shut off the engine.

"Anyway, he invited me to visit over spring break. They have a family reunion. Peter—I'll get to meet everyone!"

"I bet you're a little nervous."

"I am, but really excited too!"

Peter offloaded the bucket and got things squared away with the repairman. He pulled Olivia away from the aisle of vet supplies.

"Ready to go?"

"Yeah, I guess. This place feels like a candy store. There's spray for navel care, and vitamins for newborn pigs. And look at this—did you know there an indicator patch to help pinpoint when cows and heifers are ready to breed? Who knew?"

Peter laughed. He'd never have to wonder what to give her for gifts. There would be no end to the possibilities.

"Ready?" He tugged on her elbow.

"So many gadgets. I guess I'll have to tuck them in my mind for later."

PETER SHOULDN'T FEEL this good. Sitting beside Olivia, driving down the road with the sun peeking out intermittently between the clouds. It felt so right. So natural. Almost like this is how it was always supposed to be. He could imagine living this life forever. Her by his side, doing ordinary things, living life together. Maybe have a few kids and raise them on the farm where they could know their grandparents. He clamped down on a grin.

"What are you thinking?"

Olivia slid him that crooked smile—the one that grabbed him every time.

Peter slid his left hand to the top of the steering wheel.

"About you. About us. About being best friends forever."

He glanced at her. He didn't want to scare her off again. They were in foreign territory here and now that he had given in to his shifting feelings for her, he wasn't sure if she was in the same place.

Her hand slid to his and squeezed.

"I think I was wrong to push you away."

She looked out the window for a beat.

"It just scared me. I thought it would be okay to see you with someone else. But it wasn't. And I thought we could still be what we were before. But we couldn't. I couldn't. I don't know, it was all so confusing."

Peter laughed.

"Yes. Yes, it was. So, are we all right then? I mean, like in, all right to have a serious relationship? To cross that line?"

Did he really want to know?

Olivia leaned across the console and rested her head on his shoulder.

"I love you, Peter Gunderson. I always have."

"As a friend? Or as the man of your dreams? I just want to clarify."

One side of his lips quirked.

"As in, if you asked me to marry you again, the answer would be a resounding yes."

Peter could feel his Adam's apple virtually leap out of his throat as his eyes drifted to Olivia. He pulled the pickup over, vehicles passing, the swoosh of passing semi flying over him, he opened Olivia's door and pulled her out into a hug—his arms wrapped tightly around her.

"Ollie, would you consent to be my wife?"

Olivia giggled. "Yes. Yes, I would."

He lowered his head and let his lips fall on hers, enveloping her with a built-up intensity and passion that had filled him for eons. Water for a parched soul.

BACK ON THE ROAD, Peter's phone chimed.

"Can you get that for me?"

His dad's truck didn't have hands free ability.

"It's your dad."

Olivia glanced at him.

"Hello— She switched it to speaker.

"Olivia?"

"Yep—Peter's driving."

"Uh, could you tell him I'm at the hospital again with his mom? Just tell him he should come here before going home."

Olivia clicked end and put down the phone. She turned her gaze on Peter, who white-knuckled the steering wheel.

"You okay?"

Peter nodded and glanced out the side window. He pressed on the accelerator. This had to be serious if Dad wanted him there directly. But maybe this would just be like before—a few days in the hospital, lots of fluids and forced rest. She'd probably be fine.

Arriving, he found a place to park, and they walked hand-in-hand. He felt strength and courage in her touch.

The Willowbrook hospital was so small compared to Mercy. Their staff had increased over the years to a separate oncology department, specialist surgeons and an overflowing physical therapy department. And many of them worked in conjunction with Mercy so they had the knowledge backing for most care.

Still, he wished she were at Mercy, where he knew his pals would be looking in on her and would keep him appraised of any changes. On the other hand, having her close by gave him the opportunity to serve that role. He glanced at Olivia.

"Hey—I just prayed. She's gonna be okay." She squeezed his hand.

But would she? Peter's experience told him that praying didn't always equal the answer you desired.

They checked in and walked down the wood floor, passing the x-ray center, the pharmacy, gift shop and finally to room 43. The door was slightly ajar. Peter rapped on the doorframe and peeked in.

"You're here. Come on in."

His dad's voice was gravelly, and he looked exhausted—his eyes puffy and his salt and pepper hair mussed. He nodded towards Evelyn.

She lay sleeping on the slightly tilted bed, a thin sheet covering her frail body. A bandage covered her hand where an IV had been inserted and the slow drip of healing fluids flowed into her.

Peter took her hand. It was limp and she made no move to awaken. Peter shifted his glance to Ross.

"What happened?"

"I came in from the barn expecting to see her in the kitchen fixing lunch for me like she always does, but she wasn't there. I called for her, and she didn't answer. I found her unconscious on the bathroom floor."

His eyes began to well up.

"Doctor Hansen is very concerned. He isn't sure she's gonna make it."

Peter straightened. He had to talk to the doctor—find out what was going on. This wasn't going to be it. It couldn't be. She was still young. She had a lot to live for.

"I'm going to find the doctor."

Peter's voice was thick and unsteady.

"I'll go too."

Olivia reached for his arm.

"No, I need to go alone. Stay and keep Dad company."

He raced to the nurse's station and leaned on the counter. He read the name tag hanging in front of the nurse's blue patterned scrubs. Becky held up a finger as she nodded into the phone. Peter paced, his shoulder muscles tight. The long minute she talked on the phone was like watching grass grow. She finally hung up.

"Becky, I'm Peter Gunderson. What can you tell me about my mom, Evelyn Gunderson? Can I talk to Dr. Hansen? Is he available?"

She scrolled through her computer, looking for his chart.

The seconds ticked by, and Peter drummed his fingers on his thigh.

She looked up.

"Let me try paging the doctor to see if he's available. It would be best if you talked to him."

That wasn't a good sign. Or maybe it was. The doctor could tell him what the prognosis was. What a plan of action would be.

"He's with another patient. I can let you know as soon as he's available."

Her smile was one that said *I wish I could ease your pain.*

Peter's insides crumbled. He put his hands on his head and plodded down the hall.

Chapter Thirty-Six

The fierce winds from the previous storm had scattered branches and debris over the once serene trails. Towering Spruce lay strewn, leaving massive, tangled roots upended. Black-capped chickadees flitted between the splintered limbs, their songs sounding *fee bee fee*.

The skies were clear with no trace of the fury the wind had left. Nicole tugged her jacket tighter and zipped it against the cold, moist air. The air was thick with the scent of soggy wood and decaying vegetation, and the earth beneath Nicole's boots was damp and unstable.

Bree drove the all-terrain, pulling a trailer, the broad wheels cracking the fallen branches and twigs, and they bumped over the trail.

"Mom, watch out! You'll run over that little chipmunk!"

Maddie reached her arm out towards the steering wheel, her blond pony careening, pulled through a hole at the top of her knit cap.

Bree slowed down and watched the striped rodent turn from the few steps it had taken towards the path.

"That was close."

She slowed to a stop in front of a long spruce branch which had landed in front of them.

"Maddie, get the chainsaw. You can start hacking away at it and Nicole can pile branches into the trailer."

Maddie jumped down, pulled the safety glasses from her coverall pocket, and slid them on. Her eyes swept the twenty-five-foot branch, mentally calculating where the cuts would go. Laying the chainsaw on the needle covered path, she pulled the string, her broad shoulders and muscular arms tensing, and the saw hummed to life.

"This is a nice sized branch. Cut it into five-foot chunks and we can use them later for a fence or border."

Maddie nodded.

Nicole watched Maddie move with skill. She admired the kind of mom Bree was—giving her daughter confidence and get-er-done capabilities. Much like what she had taught Olivia.

Nicole donned her gloves, picked up the cut pieces—heavier than they looked, and laid them into the trailer. She avoided stepping on the fresh green fiddle fern sprouts, bringing new life through the chaos surrounding her. Nicole liked the smell of new moss which clung to rotted wood, and the spruce sapling sprouting from a nurse log brought her hope.

Being out here was refreshing, a contrast to the nightmare Olivia must have experienced in the barn. She was a brave, determined girl—she'd give her that much. Nicole wasn't sure she could or would have put her life in danger for an animal. Made her see that being a vet was the right choice for her.

Bree wiped her brow with the back of her sleeve.

"Looks great Maddie. Let's continue down the path to the next obstacle. Nicole, do you want to ride or walk?"

"I'm fine walking."

Continue down the path to the next obstacle. What might the next obstacle be? Everything seemed to go well. Brad was thinking about retirement. Olivia was happy in both her career and bio dad pursuit. And now she was engaged to Peter. She smiled. Yes, God was good.

"Peter?"

Dr. Hansen held out his hand.

Peter stood and took his hand. His handshake was firm. Confident. Peter felt hopeful.

Dr. Hansen nodded his head to the door, and they moved to the hall.

"I didn't want to speak with you in front of Evelyn."

He held his hand out motioning to some chairs.

"Okaaay."

Peter stretched out the word and sat.

"Start at the beginning. You've been her doctor for a long time. You've watched her story unfold."

"True. As you know, she's been putting up with fibromyalgia for years. And as a nurse, you know there isn't a cure—only things we can try in order to ease the pain and fatigue."

Peter nodded. "But her being in the hospital now is something else entirely, isn't it?"

Dr. Hansen's face grew grim. He crossed his arms.

"We've been looking at the symptoms—her lungs are weak, and she's developed pneumonia. We've started her on antibiotics and are hoping this will get her over the hump."

Peter thought back to the previous week. There had been so much going on. And the fire. He had noticed her cough. And shortness of breath. He should have paid more attention. He could have brought her in for treatment earlier and perhaps avoided this. Once again, he had failed to be there for the ones he loved.

"Thank you, Dr. I know she's in expert hands with you."

Peter returned to his mom's room. Evelyn lay sleeping with her mouth partly open, and Olivia was playing a game of rummy with his dad. She laughed as she set down a full run which emptied her hand. His dad palmed his forehead, and he showed her the two aces remaining in his hand.

How could they be laughing when Mom was so ill? Was he the only one who knew the seriousness of her condition?

"Why don't you guys go down to the cafeteria and get some lunch? I'll stay here with her."

He needed some time alone—just him and his mom. And, he guessed, time to include a little conversation with God.

Olivia stood and slid her arm around Peter's waist.

"Are you okay?"

Her forehead creased.

"Yeah, I guess. I'm really worried. I just need some time alone with her. That's okay, right?"

"Yes, of course."

She looked at Ross.

"Come on. I saw a cute little coffee shop down the road. Let's go get a mocha and something to eat."

Ross nodded and patted Peter on the shoulder. Peter reached up and covered his hand and squeezed.

Peter watched them leave and plopped down in the chair beside Evelyn's bed. He checked her IV. It looked good, giving a steady drip of fluids. The monitor gave reassuring steady blips. A wrist blood pressure cuff was hung on the wall near the monitor. Peter took it and lifted his mom's frail hand to attach it. She moved, her eyelids slowly opening and shutting again.

"It's okay Mom. I just want to take your blood pressure. It'll only take a few minutes."

He watched until it beeped. 120/80. That wasn't bad. She tried to talk but began to cough. Peter slid both arms behind her back and pulled Evelyn into a better sitting position. A weak smile moved her mouth.

"Peter?"

Her voice was barely a whisper.

"I'm right here Mom."

She cleared her throat and motioned for the glass of water. Peter held it for her and pointed the straw towards her mouth. She sipped and swallowed.

"That's better," her voice more normal. "Where's Ross?"

"He and Olivia walked to the coffee shop for lunch."

Evelyn smiled. "How are you two doing?"

"We're fantastic."

Peter looked at the ceiling trying to hide the smile filling his soul.

"We're superb. She said she'd marry me."

A wide grin filled his face like a beam of sunshine. He still couldn't believe it was real. It didn't seem right to feel so good when his mom lay weak in front of him.

"So, I finally get a daughter-in-law. I can't think of a better woman for you than Olivia."

"Me neither. I think I've been in love with her since we were little kids."

"Yep, I think so too. You were always together and fit together like puzzle pieces. Until you went to college. Not sure what happened then. I guess you just went separate ways."

Peter put his hand on his chin.

"I don't think I was always cognizant of what her friendship meant to me. Just kinda thought she'd always be there."

"Well son, when things are meant to be, you can't stop them. Like two magnets."

She smiled and reached for his hand.

"Let's start planning that wedding of yours. Where will you have it?"

"At our church. But I want the reception at our farm."

"Yes! We could decorate the barn, and your dad could make his famous ribs. If I take it slowly ahead of time, I could make pies ahead and freeze them."

Peter loved her hopeful outlook. But a heaviness was building in his soul. The chances of that happening were slim.

The door opened and her nurse came in pushing a cart. Peter wanted to watch him to see if he was doing everything properly. Then he took a breath. Maybe she was right. It wasn't all his responsibility. He could trust their care. And ultimately who was in control? Not him. He looked up and nodded.

Chapter Thirty-Seven

Olivia tossed her empty coffee cup into the trash in the airport lounge, and logged into her YouTube channel, then started the camera.

She took a cleansing breath.

Hello my friends. I've got big news! First off, I'm engaged to Peter. We haven't set a date yet. We've been best friends since we were little kids. And, well, I was kinda worried at first because I didn't want a couple relationship to ruin our friendship. And then I realized, well, that was kinda silly. Why wouldn't you want to marry your best friend and be with him forever? So, I'll keep y'all posted.

And next—Dun ta da dun—Drum roll please—This is the day I get to meet Papa Jack! I am so nervous. Happy, but really, really nervous. I fly out soon. I'll take videos and keep you posted. Pray for me!

SHE SHUT down her laptop and slid it into her backpack.

What was it going to be like meeting him? And his family? She'd FaceTimed, so she knew she'd recognize them. They would all have some element of her history that she couldn't wait to find out about. And they had her same DNA. It was possible that she would recognize expressions, looks, or mannerisms of herself in them. That was hard to wrap her mind around.

Would they love each other at first sight? Or would they resent having her in their lives? They would probably have as many questions as she did.

"Calling all passengers for flight 265 to Denver."

Olivia breathed in and held her breath, looked at the ceiling and smiled. She blew out her breath through pursed lips and walked down the ramp.

THE AIRPLANE WHEELS bumped the runway and Olivia held onto the armrests as the brakes pushed her back. She pushed down the jitters, turned her phone off airplane mode, and texted Papa Jack.

> Just landed—I have to get my luggage 🧳

> Perfect! I'll meet you outside in front of Area 11 ✈️ 😄

Olivia reached up to the overhead bin and retrieved her backpack.

"Here, let me help you."

A tall, handsome guy with dimples and a little scruff on his face, pulled it out. She held his gaze a moment longer than she should have.

"Thanks."

"Let me help you put it on."

Not one of those guys.

"Thanks, I've got it."

Hopefully he didn't notice her face scrunch up into the *I don't need your help or pity* look. If she didn't have Peter who knew her through and through, and she were looking for someone, she might try to make a connection. Maybe he was trainable. But, he would be someone else's project, not hers.

Her body screamed to jump and skip down the aisle, willing her to push those in front of her out of the way. Just be patient. Take a breath. The line finally moved, and she sped to baggage claim. As luggage slid down the shoot onto the carousel, her eyes darted around the lobby. She'd recognize him, right? He might be standing out there now. Probably was. Was he as nervous as she? Did he bring anyone with him?

Her new blue Samsonite bag slid to the carousel, and she hoisted it to the floor, pulled the handle up and forced herself to keep from skipping to the revolving doors. Her heart was pounding as she waited behind a couple, trying to manipulate a stroller through the rhythm of the glass, and tapped her foot. Finally, she slid through and scanned the sidewalk. Cars were pulling over, picking up passengers, men kissing their women, kids running to their grandpa, grown children linking elbows with aging parents. No sign of him. She looked up at the number posted on the pole. Five. Wrong place. *Come on—*

Her eyes welled up with tears as she sped around those blocking her way, those who were oblivious to this girl dying to finally meet the dad she'd been dreaming about her whole life.

And then—if this were a movie, it would show in slow motion —there he was. He jumped over a bench and ran to her, his arms spread wide and a smile that made her feel she had come home.

Chapter Thirty-Eight

Jack pulled Olivia into a powerful embrace. He smelled like cedar. And what? Sage? Olivia hiccuped a laugh and pulled back with her arms around his shoulders. His gaze was so deep it was as if he was seeing right through her pupils and tumbling thoughts. He pulled her into another hug and kissed her on the forehead.

"I can't believe this! A few months ago, I didn't know I had another child. And now, here you are."

Jack's blue eyes twinkled like a kid with a new bike.

"Here I am." Her shoulders bounced.

"Let me take your bag. The car's at the curb."

He nodded with his chin. They walked a few steps and a woman wearing jeans and a sky-blue loose pullover and jeans jumped out of the car and smiled.

"That's my wife, Lisa."

Lisa held her arms out to Olivia.

"Do you accept hugs?"

A quick glance at Olivia's arm and then back to her face.

Olivia smiled and walked into her arms, her thoughts turning inward. Did her arm have to define her? No, she needed to stuff that thought back into a safe place where it belonged.

"We are absolutely over-the-moon excited to meet you. The kids are at home. They wanted to come, but we thought it might be overwhelming for you to begin with."

Jack lifted her suitcase into the trunk and opened the back door of the Rav 4 for Olivia. He ran to the other side and scooted into the seat beside her.

Lisa pulled out, taking the exit to the freeway.

"How was your trip?"

"It was great. I tried to take a nap, but I was too jittery."

Olivia stuffed her arms between her knees.

"Well, we're glad you're here. We thought we'd stop at The Bindery before we head home. They have great ribs. Or are you vegetarian?"

"No, ribs are my favorite. My dad has an amazing recipe for them."

"Or salmon or oysters."

"Sounds yummy."

Could they hear her stomach rumble? She hadn't eaten since breakfast and the pretzels on the plane hadn't done much for her.

Lisa pulled into the center lane.

"You'll be sharing the bedroom with Ondrea. Then tomorrow the rest of the family will drift in. They should all be here by noon and the par-tay will begin."

"How many and could you tell me their names and relationships? I probably won't remember them all, but it will help me to hear them ahead of time."

"My brother Kurt and his wife, their son Marty and daughter Maria. And our sister Sandra who you already talked to on the phone."

"And Lisa, her sister Belinda and her four kids—they're all grown. Cindy has two little girls and Brian has a toddler. And your grandparents, Olivia. You'll get to meet Rhonda and Mike."

"My grandparents? I never would have thought."

This was a lot to take in. Coming from no kids to a bunch of cousins? God had really blessed her.

Lisa pulled into the restaurant parking lot.

Inside, heavenly aromas filled the air. Rich spices, onions, garlic, fresh bread. They found a table near a window where Papa Jack pulled the chair out for her. She glanced up and smiled at him, feeling as if she'd just won the lottery. Treated like royalty. She unfolded the cloth napkin and laid it on her lap.

"I want to hear everything about you."

Olivia pulled in her lips and looked at the corner of the ceiling.

"Like what?" Where should she start?

"Like, what do you like to do? What are you involved in? Do you have a boyfriend? What's he like?"

Jack took a menu from the server and set it down.

Lisa picked up her menu. "Do we want to figure out what to eat first? Then we can be undistracted."

Olivia scrolled through the offerings. Then noticed the prices. Maybe she should just have an appetizer.

"Order whatever you like. This is a day of celebration." Jack grinned.

The server returned, and she ordered grilled salmon and rice, a safe bet since she wouldn't have to cut meat. She wasn't ready to ask them to do her the favor.

She took a sip of water.

"Well, I've been working on my veterinarian degree. I still have a year to go, and I am absolutely loving it. Last week, I delivered lambs—one was breach, so I had to reach in and turn the little one."

She purposefully left out the details of the fire.

Lisa's eyes widened. "I'm a city girl. That is something totally out of my realm."

Olivia laughed. "I grew up around my neighbor's farm. I can't tell you how exciting it is to see something born. I spent the summer helping my neighbor Evelyn with her flower business. She has rows and rows of beautiful blooms that she sells at the farm and to local florists. People come from all around to take photos and buy from her. She also has a pumpkin patch—it's kind of a big deal—hayrides, catapults, photo booths, a maze. There's a lot to do."

She thought about Evelyn in the hospital. And about Peter. This was not good timing to leave him, but she'd waited her whole life for this. It took priority and he understood.

"That must be lovely. Do you have photos?"

Jack took his plate from the server and nodded a thanks.

Olivia opened her Instagram, and handed her phone to Jack who positioned it so Lisa could see.

"Wow! That *is* something."

They laughed at the video of Nate landing in the mud when he catapulted the pumpkin. "Who's the guy on the tractor?"

"That's Peter." Heat rose to her cheeks. "We've been best friends since we were little. He's been a nurse at Mercy Hospital in Portland but moved back home to help and care for his mom. She has fibromyalgia. She's actually in the hospital now. They're not sure what's going on." She reached for a roll. "Anyway, we're engaged."

Olivia couldn't miss Jack's eyes traveling to where he thought he should see a ring. His cheeks held a blush. May as well remove the elephant in the living room. She laughed.

"We haven't gone ring shopping yet."

She held up her arm.

"And obviously, I'll need to wear it on my right hand."

Lisa put her hand on Jack's arm.

"We're sorry. We didn't intend to create an uncomfortable situation."

"Oh, it's fine. This is new to you, but I've never known anything different." Olivia shrugged. "It's just who I am."

She let a bit of salmon melt in her mouth, a look of heaven drifted over her face.

"What else did you ask me?"

"What are your earliest memories? I missed being there for them."

Olivia had to think about that for a minute.

"Well, I remember sitting on the riding lawn mower with my dad. He let me steer."

She made air quotes and smiled. "I'm sure I wasn't much help, but I remember how comfortable it was to be near him and have his arms keeping me safe. And my mom would set me on the kitchen counter to put ingredients into the mixer for cookies. She'd urge me to sing silly songs with her and make up words."

Olivia took the last bite from her plate and looked at Jack. He was quiet. Reflective. Had she said too much?

JACK'S FOREHEAD wrinkled in thought. A lot of things had happened in her life that he never knew. That he missed out on. The first time riding a bike. First words, haircut, first booboo he should have kissed. But still, God knew that, right? And He had placed her in a home with loving parents. He had to rest in that. Maybe on some level it had been God's grace that Bridgett hadn't raised her. Still, he would have taken her in a hot second.

This is where trust came in. Believing that Creator God had us all in his hands.

Chapter Thirty-Nine

Papa Jack's great room was spacious enough to hold all thirty-seven relatives—Olivia's relatives. Glasses in hand, filled with punch or wine, laughter exploding, exhilarating chatter. They all knew each other. They all had a life outside of hers. Had built memories together. Memories that she hadn't been a part of.

But all that was changing as of this week, days that would forever etch themselves into her mind. She pulled out her phone and scanned a video of the room. Of the people. Her people. She hadn't talked to her mom since her flight. No doubt she was wondering how things were going. She sent it to her mom and ended with a selfie—a huge grin spread across her face. Then she typed *I love you!*

LAST NIGHT she had spent hours sitting on the bed talking to Ondrea after Owen had given her a fist bump and leaped over the stairs to go down and play video games—normal, she expected, for a middle schooler. Otis had just returned from basketball practice dressed in shorts and a sweaty T, orange ball under his arm. His hair was the color of Evelyn's golden zinnias. He'd smiled and wrapped a long arm around her shoulders to welcome her. Olivia had looked up at him, not sure whether to enjoy the moment, or gag from the overpowering odor of one who had put his all into a testosterone filled gym. Ondrea had slapped the back of her hand on his arm.

"Don't overwhelm her, you goof."

He grinned. "She's my sister. I should welcome her like one."

She and Ondrea had clicked from the start.

"I can't believe I have a sister. I always hoped my mom would have another baby and it would be a girl. Being surrounded by boys can be a bit much."

"I can only imagine. I never had siblings. It's always just been my dad and mom. And my grandparents don't live close."

The only guys she was around were her dad and Peter. What would it have been like to grow up with brothers?

"Cousins?"

"Yeah, I have one cousin on my mom's side. He lives in Kentucky, and I've only met him once."

"Holy moly, that would be so weird. Well, now you've got more relatives than you could possibly want. They're fun, but sometimes it can be a bit much." Ondrea smiled. "Tell me about yourself."

"I guess I should tell you that I don't really know what happened to my hand. My mom said it was wrapped in a bandage when they picked me up from the hospital and they were never told them what really happened."

Olivia held up her arm. "This has been a part of my life since before I can remember. Anyway, my parents just treated me like any ordinary kid. I played soccer, won swim meets, was valedictorian." She shrugged.

Ondrea's eyes grew large. "Those are no small accomplishments. You must be a strong woman."

Was she? She didn't always feel that way.

"I guess in some senses I am. I'm working on finishing my veterinarian degree. I love working with animals."

"I've never been on a farm. That must be cool."

"You'll have to come visit sometime." Olivia's eyes roamed the room and settled on a photo. "Do you have a boyfriend?"

Ondrea picked up a photo frame next to her bed.

"Yes—and he's the best thing since peanut butter ice cream. His name is Trevor. We've been dating for over a year. How about you?"

"Cute! Yes. Yes, I do. Peter. We've been friends since we were little. He lives next door. We just got engaged. I think you'd like him. He'd love you guys, for sure." The corners of her lips turned up into a ray of sunshine.

Olivia repositioned the pillows and leaned back.

"What was it like for you, finding out about me?"

"I'm not gonna lie. I was in shock. It was like, it made me realize that Dad had another life before us. And once he found out about you, he's been grinning ear to ear. It had to be a God thing."

Had it? Had what Olivia put into motion not just been trying to fulfill her desire to know? But rather, God had orchestrated it and set things in motion behind the scenes? If that was so, there was hope that she'd find her mom as well and the results would be just a satisfying.

Olivia had filled her plate with potato salad, macaroni salad, greens topped with grilled chicken strips and roasted veggies. She balanced it on her left arm and filled a glass with lemon water. She found a place to sit at the counter near where Papa Jack was talking with Kurt— Uncle Kurt his brother, their backs to her.

"This has been truly remarkable. Just a blessing. I'm so glad I didn't deny or deflect. This has ignited a joy and love that's been multiplied over and over. I know it's just the beginning."

"You look truly happy, bro. It had to have been a surprise."

"I can't even tell you! I had to shake it off and think, really think of the ramifications. I mean, I could have ignored it. But," he spread his arm around the room, "Look at all we'd have missed out on. She's our family, we're connected. Just knowing that I'm part of someone's puzzle and that I was that empty piece, ready to put into place." He shook his head.

"Unbelievable. Well, she's a delight, no doubt about that."

"She's engaged. I don't want to butt into their family, but part of me hopes she'll let me, and her dad of course, both walk her down the aisle."

Olivia hid a smile as Papa Jack turned and saw her. He cleared his throat and stood.

"Olivia, come meet your grandparents."

Papa Jack held her elbow and guided her to the couch where a woman with short white hair was deep in conversation with a man dressed in corduroys and polo shirt.

"Mom, Dad? This is Olivia. Olivia, Grandma Rhonda, and Grandpa Mike."

He started to stand, and Olivia waved her hand for him to sit.

"Glad to meet you."

Rhonda motioned to the empty chair beside her.

"My stars, you look just like the rest of Jack's kids, don't you think so Mike?"

"Same eyes. Your nose is like his. Maybe not your mouth. His is smaller."

"Hey, are you saying I have a big mouth?"

Jack's eyes squinted, then he laughed.

Rhonda put her hand on Mike's.

"She's got *my* mouth, honey. Surely you can see that."

Mike looked from Olivia to Rhonda and nodded.

"That she does."

"Well, we are so glad you're here. As you can see," her eyes took in the room. "The more the merrier."

The sound of someone tapping a spoon on a glass got everyone's attention.

"The talent show will be in ten minutes. Everyone get prepared."

A look of panic crossed Olivia's face.

"Don't worry, you get to be an observer. This time." Papa Jack winked.

Chapter Forty

The past few days had whizzed by. Olivia rolled up her clothes and placed them into her suitcase. She took one more look around the room—her sister's room. They had taken a selfie of both of them and had printed it. Now it sat on her desk in a treasured spot. She hoped Ondrea would continue to be a friend. They had clicked like they had known each other forever. Maybe in some small way they had. Olivia felt like the luckiest girl alive. She never could have imagined how much meeting her bio family would fill the gap she never realized she had. Maybe it was true—God had a plan for her and was working in the background with all the details of her life.

"Are you ready to go?" Papa Jack called from the bottom of the stairs.

"Be right down."

Olivia shoved her phone in her back pocket. It had dozens of photos and videos, and she couldn't wait to share them with Peter and her parents. Peter—she put her hand to her mouth.

She'd been so busy with her new family that she hadn't really asked him about his mom. Well, she'd be there in a few hours, and they could catch up then. He'd understand. He always did.

At the airport, Papa Jack jumped out of the car and put his hands on Olivia's shoulders.

"I can't even describe the joy of having you in my life. All those years I lost." He swallowed. "I feel so blessed. I'm glad you've had the opportunity to have parents who love and care for you. I never want to take their place, but I'd love to meet them and tell them thank you."

That so familiar sensation of tears moving their way from Olivia's heart up to her eyes. She let the droplets roll down her cheeks.

"Thank you. This has truly changed my life. I'll text when I get home."

PETER PACED, watching the empty conveyor belt turn. His eyes drifted to the escalator where everyone, but Olivia descended. This week had been painful. He hadn't wanted to let Olivia into the dozens of thoughts swirling around his brain, knowing it would interrupt the precious moments she had been waiting so long for.

Suitcases slid down the shoot, the sound jogging his attention back. Seconds later, Olivia ran behind him and slid her hands around his waist. Her musical laugh filled the room.

"You're here. Praise God."

Peter removed his hat and ran his hands through his hair.

"I'm here."

Her smile dimmed.

"Peter, are you okay?"

"Not really."

Olivia's baggage rounding the corner, interrupting them, and she grabbed it and lugged it off. Peter took the handle and slid it up into position to roll it. Olivia slid her arm through his.

"How was it? Everything you dreamed of?"

His voice was uncharacteristically flat.

"Yes. And so much more."

As Peter popped the trunk and hoisted her bag in, she prattled on about Papa Jack and Lisa, her grandparents, Ondrea, and her brothers. He opened the door for Olivia, and they rolled out onto the highway. He wanted to be excited for her as he listened to all the details. Wanted to enter into her world. But he couldn't muster the strength.

She stilled and directed her gaze on him.

"I'm sorry, Peter. I haven't even asked you about your week. Something's bothering you—is your mom okay."

He took a deep breath and whooshed it out.

"Mom died. Yesterday."

He could feel her questioning gaze without even looking at her. He heard the intake of her breath.

"What? How? Why didn't you call me?"

His breathing had gone tight and rapid, his lungs heaving with each painful sentence.

"I didn't want to ruin your time. Knowing yesterday wouldn't have changed anything."

"But I could have been there for you. I would have taken an earlier flight."

"I didn't want you to." He stared at the road.

"Do you want me to drive?" Olivia said.

"No, I'm okay." He sighed. "We had taken her home from the hospital. She was on the mend. At least that's what we thought. And the next morning we found that she died in her sleep. She looked so peaceful. But Olivia," he slid her a glance, "I'm not. I can't reckon with God taking her so soon. She's not, she wasn't, that old. I just feel like I could have done more, been there more, fixed it somehow."

His voice was thick and unsteady. He had rehearsed every move of the nurses, each word from the doctor. They had done everything right.

Olivia put her arm on his. Tears trickled down her face.

"Peter, pull over at that rest area. This isn't a conversation to have on the freeway."

They got out and Peter clicked the lock button on his fob. Olivia circled her arms around him and pulled him close. As she rested her head on his heaving chest, he let the tears he had been holding in course down his cheeks.

"It's not just the grief of her being gone," he said again. "It's knowing I couldn't save her."

His voice didn't just crack then, it broke. All of him broke. Hot tears and pain as deep as the cedars were high, rising to drown him even as Olivia wove her arms around him.

"It's okay, Peter. I'm here. I'm here."

Time stood still, and then he pulled back. She took his hand and kissed his palm, then placed it gently on his cheek. She wiped tears from his cheeks with her thumb and gently kissed him. Olivia was the only one he wanted right now. The one who could see the way to his heart.

They found a trail and walked under the towering cedars, new fiddle ferns sprouting and buds beginning on bare huckleberry branches.

"Peter, you had no control of when God decided to take her home. She loved you. She told me one day while I was working beside her how much she appreciated you and all you did. You made her smile. You brought joy to her life."

I could have done more. The words echoed in his mind, like a racquet ball hitting the wall, back and forth, back and forth, never stopping.

Sun shone through rain drops which still lingered on the tips of cedar boughs, with an earthy aroma infusing the air which was rich and somehow comforting. Peter cast his gaze through the branches and to the sky, where blue filled the space between puffy white clouds.

Peter, you don't have to be the hero. Just be yourself. You're not responsible for everything.

Mom was up there. At peace. And he imagined, the happiest she had ever been, wrapped in the arms of Jesus.

Olivia took his hand.

"I'm here. I will always be here for you."

Peter nabbed her palm. He lifted his eyes from their connected hands to her face and held it there. His look penetrated through her pupils he hoped down to her soul. Knowing she would marry him held the conviction that what she had just said was entirely true.

Chapter Forty-One

Peter held Olivia's hand as they walked down the aisle of the church to the front pew where the family sat. He hadn't known what to wear to his mom's memorial service, and finally settled on a blue and white plaid cotton button down shirt and jeans. Olivia looked pretty in her floral print dress. She said it reminded her of Evelyn's garden. Locks of hair dangled from under her brimmed felt hat.

Peter leaned over, his elbows on his knees and his fisted hands on his cheeks. Olivia slowly rubbed his back. His mom should have been here at the church bustling around for their wedding. Not this. Not contained in an alabaster box.

Olivia had helped him look through hundreds of photos to choose one to put up front. Evelyn's radiant smile and bright eyes showed what everyone loved about her. Always eager to help out, donate flowers for nonprofit events, make her delicious pies for potlucks. And best of all, give gentle words of wisdom.

Peter looked up when Ross sat beside him and patted him on the back.

"Nice photo you picked out. I remember that day. She had

brought me out to see her blooming iris. They were gorgeous. And she was radiant."

Peter rolled his shoulders.

Alex, the pastor stood at the front of the church.

"Welcome everyone. It's so nice to see such a large crowd here to honor Evelyn. It's hard to realize she's gone. We are all going to miss her."

They were asked to stand as the worship team began to sing. Peter couldn't open his mouth, could only take in the words.

When all I see are the ashes you see the beauty.

Olivia reached for his hand and squeezed. Really God? How can there be beauty in this? She was young. She was capable. She was so much. And now she wouldn't be here for his wedding. Or to see her grandkids. Or for them to know her.

The tears streamed down his face.

Alex read the eulogy bringing up visions of the fullness of her life. She had done a lot. It was hard to imagine though, that there wasn't so much more she could have done.

After the service, Ross and Peter greeted people as they passed to the reception area.

"I'm so sorry Peter. I loved your mom. She always had a smile on her face."

"You're so lucky you had a mom like her. I wish that had been my story."

"After the fire, we would bring dinners to her house and help her out. She was so cheerful, even with that burn on her arm. It was like, I don't know, like it never phased her. She was a real inspiration to me."

Olivia filled a plate with pulled pork, potato salad, jello salad and blackberry pie. She set places for three on the long table and showed Peter where to sit.

Ross put his broad hand on the back of Peter's neck.

"We'll get through this, son. Chin up. Look at how many

people loved her. She may not have lived out long years, but she certainly made a huge impact on our community."

Peter nodded. He felt blessed to have had her in his life. And now, more than ever, was glad he had made the decision to return home.

"Hand me that hammer, will you, son?"

Peter raised it to his dad, who was standing on a ladder. The barn was nearly repaired from the nasty storm and fire, leaving just a scent of the charred timbers. The rafters had been replaced, a metal roof put on, and a new sliding door had been set in place. Ross pounded a final nail into place and started down the ladder.

"You doing okay?"

Ross stopped at the bottom and settled his eyes on Peter.

Peter shrugged. "I guess. You?"

"As well as any widower, I suppose."

He folded up the ladder and carried it to the wall, where he set it down.

"You were a tremendous help with your mom. And with me. I couldn't have done it without you. Having your help with her meds? I could never have done that. I was proud of you."

Peter couldn't remember his dad ever saying he was proud of him. Well, he wouldn't be proud when he heard what he had to say next.

"Save that thought." Peter leaned against the wall and crossed his arms. "I was the one responsible for the fire."

Ross looked at him, eyebrows meeting.

"You couldn't have been. That was a lightning fire."

Peter shook his head.

"Not that fire, Dad. *The* fire. The one that caused Mom's burns."

"I don't understand."

"I was in too big of a hurry to get to my nursing exams. I saw some frayed wires. I was going to tell you."

Peter's voice choked.

"But I was in too much of a hurry and then I forgot to let you know."

His chin fell to his chest, the guilt he'd been carrying all these years weighing him down. Yes, his mom had basically said he shouldn't carry the guilt. And he should accept that. But he not only let his mom down. He let God down. How could he forgive him for being so selfish? For putting his parents in danger?

Ross walked to his son, arms open wide and pulled him into a big bear hug where he held him long enough to heal his wounds.

Peter's shoulders shook and he let the tears flow down his cheeks and into the fleece collar of his dad's jean Carhartt. He closed his eyes and rested in his dad's embrace. Not just a pat on the back. Not just a quick hug. A total embrace that seeped into all the empty places in his soul.

Ross patted him on the back and pulled back, his arms resting on Peter's shoulders.

"That's all in the past now. What happened, happened. There's no changing the circumstance. There's only changing our hearts."

They walked towards the open door.

"I'm so sorry, Dad."

Peter risked a glance at him.

"Your forgiven. Mom never held anger or resentment in her heart. Of course, we didn't know that it might have been prevented. But then again, God gives us trials, so we'll look to him for strength. I have to admit, she was better at that than me. I'm kind of like you—always trying to make things right. Fix things. But there's only One who can really fix things, right?"

Peter nodded. A beam of sunshine shone over the roof of the house and through the doorway. Was this God? The open door to his heavenly father's embrace? Peter wanted to believe so.

"Maybe you can get that fiancé of yours to join us for dinner." Ross winked.

Peter quirked an eye.

"You mean possibly fix something other than tater tots and chicken nuggets?"

Chapter Forty-Two

Glasses and dinnerware clinked in the Pitcher's Peak Pub, where Bree and Nicole ordered cold beers and burgers with sweet potato fries after a long hot day of trail blazing.

"Considering how hot it was today, we got a lot accomplished."

Bree dipped a fry into the sauce.

Nicole set down her mug.

"Yeah, I was grateful for the shade of the cedars. It made it bearable. And when the breeze blew the mist from the stream—that was a God wink."

Bree raised her eyebrows. By now, Nicole had realized that they were on separate planes regarding faith. But that didn't stop Nicole from inserting bits of her perspective into conversation.

"You went to college, right?"

Bree nodded.

"Where?"

"In Colorado Springs. I started a major in forestry and finished in Oregon."

"Sounds like a story's in that."

Nicole bit into her burger.

Bree eyes lifted to the corner of the ceiling.

"I was dating a guy named Jack. We got a little too close and I ended up pregnant at eighteen."

Nicole slowly set her burger down and stared at Bree.

"Our relationship was rocky, and I knew it wasn't going to work out, so I moved as far west as I could to get away from him."

"That must have been hard. What about your parents. Did you tell them? Wouldn't they have been supportive?"

Bree shook her head and scowled.

"They didn't need to know. Neither of them were exactly active in my life. Mom was an inspirational speaker who travelled all the time. She wrote a bunch of books and did book tours."

"She sounds interesting."

Bree scrunched up one side of her face, like she'd just tasted mold in her food.

"I wouldn't call her interesting. She was pretty self-righteous. Lots of God talk. But I never saw her show the love of that God she always talked about." She took a fry and dipped it in sauce. "That stuff's just not for me."

Nicole was silent, absorbing the revelation that Bree had a hole in her heart—one that needed some mama love. Maybe that was the root of the bitterness Nicole sensed in her.

"What about your dad?"

"He was never around. Too busy with his career."

Nicole did some quick calculations. Maddie was too young to have been born when Bree was eighteen.

"Were you able to find some support when you moved to Oregon?"

Bree nodded and smiled.

"I did. Yes. Planned Parenthood. They were there for me. There was no judgment. They took care of the situation. Best decision I ever made."

The burger in Nicole's stomach turned to a lump. Nicole brought her napkin to her lips. Tears formed behind her eyes.

"Can I ask when that was?"

"March of '93. Why?"

Nicole swallowed. Jack? Was this Olivia's Jack? Could she be Olivia's mom? No, that couldn't be. Bree had an abortion.

"Did you ever go by another name besides Bree?"

"Yeah, my real name is Bridgett. Why do you ask?"

Why did she ask? Because everything suddenly made sense. Maddie having features like Olivia. Jack. Colorado Springs. The timing of it all. Nicole stood, tipping her glass and spilling the remains onto her remaining burger and fries.

"I'm sorry, I need to leave."

Nicole ran to her car where she slid into the driver's seat, tears streaming down her face.

"Olivia. My baby. How am I ever going to tell you this?"

OLIVIA CLOSED HER LAPTOP. She had spent the better part of the day studying for her exams. She felt prepared, but there was always that test anxiety—something that had plagued her since she was in second grade when she got stuck on whether the word was t-h-e-i-r or t-h-e-r-e. She had frozen, her eyes stuck on the corner of the ceiling, her pencil eraser tapping her lip. She stood, raised her arms above her head and stretched. The spring sunshine seeped through the window, landing on Bella who lay at her feet soaking up the warmth. Bella cocked her head and licked Olivia's hand.

"What do you think? Shall we take a walk over to Peter's? See if they need any help?"

Bella's tail started a metronome of tapping and she let out a yip as she ran to the door. Olivia grabbed an apple from the bowl and headed out.

There had been so much going on. Her studies on the one hand, finding Papa Jack and her new family. And then there was

Evelyn. Olivia felt like she was a yoyo. Held in suspension like a cat's cradle with her studies. The high of her trip to California. The low of Evelyn. Her eyes drifted towards heaven.

Peter had been so broken. Not like losing Evelyn was a piece of cake for her. She was her mom's friend and had become hers as well. Olivia had worked along beside her for months and they had developed a close relationship. And she had looked forward to having her for a mother-in-law.

One thing she knew for sure—she would stick beside Peter as long as it took to work through the grief. Which could take till eternity. Which was okay with her because she wanted to be with him till eternity.

She took a bite of her apple. Bella grabbed a stick and brought it to Olivia who took it from him and threw it. Bella loped after it on her three good paws, held it in her jaws and retrieved it.

And what about finding her bio mom? Was she going to be satisfied with only finding Papa Jack? Not to belittle that miracle. She was still flying high from that. She had tried to accept that she might never know who her mom was. But somehow, she had a nagging need to find the last piece of the puzzle.

She bent down and rubbed Bella's head, running her hand through her soft golden fur and nuzzled her face into it.

"Olivia!" Peter had just left the barn—his long legs strode towards her. His hair was tousled and held the faint smell of hay and lanolin. The olive-green shirt he wore brought out the matching color of his eyes. He shoved his sleeves up and brushed his hands together to remove some of the dirt.

"Hi!" Olivia stood on tiptoes and gave him a kiss. "My head was exploding with knowledge, and I needed a break. Is there anything you need help with?"

"Are you sure you don't want me to quiz you on things for your exam?"

"Thanks for asking, but right now I need to be outside doing something fun."

"Dad and I were just talking about what to do with Mom's flower field. Should we continue it? Or hire someone to take it over? It's an enormous job. And we don't thoroughly have a clue what to do."

"So many people would be disappointed if it weren't here anymore." Olivia put a finger to her lip. "Did you take a look in her office at her vision board? That would be the place to start."

Peter shook his head. "And this is why I love you." He kissed her forehead.

They walked hand in hand to the barn where Evelyn had had a small office.

Olivia stopped at a pen where a teen ewe lay in the hay.

"Hey Lily, you're getting big." She reached for the ewe and held out her apple core. Lily stood and curled her lips around it.

"Good thing you saved that little gal during the fire. Which I still can't believe you actually did." Peter shook his head.

"You'd have done the same thing." Hadn't he come in and saved her?

Olivia stopped and took in the office where Evelyn spent hours of her time. Her rubber garden clogs lay neatly by the door, dirt still packed in the soles. The sunhat she was rarely without hung by a string on a hook. Stacks of starter trays lay on top of a file cabinet. And the faint fragrance of her lotion still hung in the air.

It took Olivia a moment to settle herself. Evelyn was not coming back.

They stood in front of a large white board graphed out into months and seasons. Pictures of flower types were attached throughout. Seed catalog names were written on other months with types and amounts listed.

"Looks like you've got your plan right here." Olivia pointed. "I think your first thing is to plow the pumpkin field. I can search and see if she's already got seeds, and if not, make an order."

Peter's phone buzzed. He glanced at the screen and raised his eyebrows.

"Just a minute." He walked outside. Olivia watched his fingers bouncing off the screen. His feet seemed to drag as he returned.

"You okay? You look like you're not sure about something."

Peter sat on the swivel chair, hands on the rests and moved it back and forth with his feet.

"Um, I need to tell you something."

"Is it bad?"

"Well, uh, there's good and there's bad."

"Start with the bad."

Olivia frowned and hopped onto the desk. She stuck her hand under her thigh.

"Phoebe and I did," he cleared his throat, "something behind your back." He turned to look out the window where his dad sat on the tractor mowing the field.

"Recently?"

Should she be worried? What could they have done? Were they getting back together?

"No, no, no." He shook his head. "Way back."

Olivia let out a breath.

"Well?"

"We thought we could help you try and find your mom by sending a form to the Search Angel organization."

"Oh. And that's the bad news?"

"We did it behind your back."

"Were you worried I wouldn't want you to?"

"Yeah, I guess."

"Well, I guess it would have been nice to know."

"You're not mad?"

Olivia shrugged. "You were trying to help. That's what you do."

Peter sighed. "Okay, so here's the good news." He paused. "They think they've found your mom."

Chapter Forty-Three

Olivia took Peter's phone from him. It took a mere two seconds for her to read the text. Two seconds that could change the trajectory of her life.

Her jaw dropped and she drew in a breath. Her eyes slowly traveled to Peter's. She didn't say anything, but her shaky fingers laced through his.

"Should we call the number?" A grin formed on his lips.

"Are you kidding? Yes!"

Olivia tapped the link and put the phone on speaker. She paced as it rang. Her heart matched the repetitive sound of the woodpecker on the metal roof.

"Hello? Yes, I'm Olivia Olson."

"My name is Frank. We think we have good news for you."

Olivia took a breath and held it. "Okay."

"Would it be possible to meet with you? Would today be too soon?"

Olivia bounced on her tiptoes.

"Yes! Anytime would work."

She set the phone down and grabbed Peter's arm. He grabbed

her around the waist and twirled her around where her laughter reverberated off the walls.

NICOLE KNEW her blood pressure had peaked to a level her doctor would scold her about. But what would he expect? She had just found out the most devastating news any mother could learn. Brad kept up with her pace as they walked the trail around Crescent Mirror Lake. She had planned to tell him when she got home, but he had been out of town, and she couldn't lay that kind of information on him over the phone.

"You must have something big to tell me, judging by your pace and fumes coming from your ears." Brad ventured a slight smile.

"This is the worst thing I could ever have imagined."

She kicked a rock out of the path.

"I went out with Bree to Pitcher's Peak after we finished the trail. Everything started out fine. We were just talking about stuff. I asked if she'd gone to college, and she said she had. I asked where and she said Colorado Springs. Where she met her boyfriend, Jack. Got pregnant. Moved to Portland. Hooked up with Planned Parenthood. And you can imagine the rest."

Brad glanced at her. "Hadn't you already told me she had had an abortion?"

"Yes. But don't you see? The pieces line up. Colorado Springs. Jack. Pregnant. Portland. And—" She stretched the word like a rubber band. "It was March of '93."

Brad stopped and faced her.

"Olivia." His eyes held recognition. And pain.

Nicole nodded and she let go of the tears that had been pent up. Brad wrapped his long arms around her and pulled her to him.

Grey clouds slid in front of the sun. Nicole shivered and pulled back.

"What are we going to do?"

"I guess we have to tell her."

"But how? How do you tell your daughter that her mom tried to kill her, but wasn't successful? It's going to devastate her. And to make it worse, it's someone I'm friends with."

Brad shook his head and pulled her back into his embrace.

OLIVIA ALIGNED her camera and fluffed her hair. She checked her teeth for any obvious left-over lunch, then straightened her shoulders and pushed record.

"You are never going to believe this! Months ago, Peter had contacted Search Angel and yesterday they got back to him."

She took a breath.

"They've found my mom."

Like a sunrise, a slow grin spread over her face.
"I'm excited. And nervous."
She curled her fingers into her lips.

"Will meeting her, that is, if she wants to meet me, be anything like meeting Papa Jack? Wouldn't that be amazing? Then again, what if she doesn't want to meet me? There was obviously some reason she gave me up. My mom would tell me to offer it up to the Lord. And ya know, she's usually right. So, pray for me, friends. I'll keep you posted!"

No sooner had she pushed end and posted than a flood of

comments came in giving her hope and encouragement that things were going to be amazing.

Olivia ran her hand through Bella's fur and scratched the back of her ears.

"Well, Bella, I hope this all goes well."

Bella flapped her tail on the floor. The front door opened, and Peter called to her.

"Ready to go?"

"Yes, be right there." Olivia closed her laptop.

"Did you tell your parents yet?"

"No, they went for a hike. I'll tell them later. I didn't want to tell them in a text. I want to meet with the Search Angel first and have all the information."

Peter handed Olivia a helmet and they took off on his motorcycle. They pulled up to the park where geese strutted through the grass near the pond. Walking hand-in-hand they made their way through the newly mown grass to the gazebo where they were to meet Frank. Olivia's heartbeat rose with each step.

A man of medium height rose from the bench, his salt and pepper short beard and twinkly eyes made him appear friendly. Suspenders connected his black pants in place over a denim shirt covering his bulging middle.

"Olivia? Peter?" He held out his hand. "I'm Frank from Search Angels."

He motioned to the bench and set a briefcase on the table.

"I'm a volunteer who has spent a lot of time understanding genetic genealogy. There are hundreds of us all over the world and I was lucky enough to latch onto your search."

Frank opened his briefcase and pulled out a file. In it were several pages of forms.

"So, here's what I've found. Peter had given me your birth date and hospital name and city. And that's pretty much all I had to go on."

Olivia wrapped her arms around her stomach and held onto every word.

"I think you had already found out her name is Bridgett. Looking at DNA matches, I found that she has two other children, teens, a boy and a girl. And from what I've found, we know she still lives in Oregon."

Olivia looked at Peter. He took her hand and squeezed. A squirrel ran across the railing, stopped, and stared at them.

"Can I meet her?" Olivia whispered.

"First, I wanted to share what I know and ask if you want to try and meet her. The next step will be for me to contact her and see if she wants to meet you."

Olivia looked at Peter. Of course she wanted to meet her. She wouldn't be here if she didn't. Surely, Frank knew that.

"Yes. Yes, I do want to meet her."

"Okay then, I'll get in touch with her and let you know what I've found out. It may take a few days, so don't get anxious if I don't call back right away."

Frank stood and shook their hands, nodded and saluted.

"Other than the two kids, that's not much more than we already knew."

Olivia brushed a lock of hair from her eyes.

"But Peter, I have two more half siblings. That's exciting, right?"

"Almost makes me wish I were adopted—then I might have a sibling or two."

He knocked his shoulder into hers.

"Well, since we're in town, I thought you might want to go to the jewelry store. You haven't picked out a ring yet." He winked.

Olivia turned towards him, put her arms on his shoulders and jumped onto his waist wrapping her legs around him.

"So, I take it that's a yes?"

Chapter Forty-Four

After picking out a ring with a diamond and several small aquamarine birthstones circling it, Peter drove down a dirt road behind the hay field and slowed his motorcycle to a stop. He let Olivia dismount first and set the kick stand. They removed their helmets and hung them on the handlebars.

"What is this place? I never knew this was here."

Blackberries had overgrown what used to be a solid picket fence, their branches creating a mass of stringy vines with protective thorns and white flowers promising berries. Crows stepped lightly over the moss-covered roof of an old house, cawing to each other and claiming their territory.

A bald eagle soared over towering Spruce which leant shade to the east. Box hedges had overgrown along the west side and could clearly use a good trim.

"This," Peter unlatched the rusty gate and held it open, "used to be my parents' first home. It actually had been my grandparent's before them. My dad was born in this house."

"Really. Wow. It could use a coat or two of paint." Olivia laughed.

"I like those shutters around the windows. And look at this glass."

He touched a spot.

"See this bubble? These windows were hand blown. Cool, huh?"

"I've never seen that before. That's amazing."

There was no doubt it would take a bit of work to pull this place into some kind of shape to turn it into more than an old run-down house, but into a home for the two of them. Maybe a place where kids could roam and play with sticks and make mud pies. He reached under the broken front step and retrieved a key.

The doorknob squeaked as he turned it. They stood in the opening and let their eyes drift over the living room, where a floor to ceiling stone fireplace stood. Olivia jumped when a starling flew out of the firebox. She laughed and the flustered bird flew over their heads out the front door.

"It has potential. Pull up the gold shag carpet and put some laminate down."

"And clear out the bird nests." Peter put his hands on his hips and surveyed the room.

Peter took her elbow and led her to the kitchen. Sun streamed through the bits of dirty glass of the bay window where Olivia rested her hand on the dusty wood table. Her new ring sparkled and cast rainbows on the ceiling.

"Rainbows—that's a sign of hope, right?"

"Indeed."

Hope she'd find her mom and the hole in her heart would be filled. Hope that they could enjoy a long life together. Hope that the ache he felt with the loss of his mom would fade. That he could stop replaying her last days and could find peace.

"When I quit my job, I thought about this house. I wanted to have a home. A place with a wife and kids. Somewhere I'd want to settle down for many years."

"It would take some elbow grease."

She went to the old porcelain sink. Other than a few rust stains, it was in great shape. Nothing some Comet and scouring pads couldn't fix.

Peter pictured her with suds up to her elbows gazing out the picture window at the meadow and washing dishes. With one or two little kids sitting on stools helping her.

Olivia turned and wrapped her arms around his shoulders. He ran his fingers through her hair, removing her hair band and letting the blond strands fall over her shoulders. Peter cupped her head and let his thumb skim lightly over her chin and to her lips where he outlined them.

The warmth of her skin on his shoulders sent a dozen sensations through him. He slowly brushed his lips to hers and fell into a passion he had dreamt of for months. For years.

She was nothing short of perfection. Nothing could interfere with the happiness he felt in this moment.

NICOLE LOOKED out the window as Peter pulled up and kissed Olivia goodbye. She waved goodbye and pulled the front door open. Nicole moved back to the kitchen table where Brad sat, his hands wrapped around a glass of iced tea.

They spoke over each other, their words mingling with both joy and sorrow.

"Hi Mom and Dad. I have some exciting news!"

"Olivia, you're home. We need to talk about something."

Brad looked at Nicole. They stood and motioned her to the living room where the evening sun cast soft rays through the picture window. This was a setting that should have been peaceful. Comforting.

Olivia sat on the love seat and slid her legs under her.

"Me first. I have to tell you what happened. Peter had contacted Search Angels, and we met with a man this morning.

Frank thinks he's found my mom! We already knew her name was Bridgett, but he said she has two other kids. A boy and girl. And she lives here in Oregon. Isn't that cool? He's gonna contact her and see if we can meet."

Olivia's shoulders jiggled with excitement.

"Mom, you don't look excited. Should I not try to find her? Will it make you feel bad?"

Nicole shook her head.

"No, it's not that. It's just—"

Brad took over. "It's just that we know who your mom is."

"You do? And that's not exciting?"

Nicole swallowed.

"There's something you should know. First off, your mom is my friend Bree." *Was* she her friend? No. She was not her friend anymore. How could she be?

"Bree? Hmmm. That's cool. Isn't it? How did you figure that out?"

"I was asking her where she went to college. She said Colorado Springs. When she was eighteen, she had a boyfriend named Jack. They were having troubles and when she found out she was pregnant she moved to Portland."

"I don't get it. Why is this bad? Did she already know I was her daughter? When she came for my birthday, she did a double take. I wasn't sure what that was about at the time, but—" Olivia glanced out the window.

"Honey," Brad's Adams apple rose and fell. "This is really hard. Bree went to Planned Parenthood after she found out she was pregnant."

"Where they 'took care of the situation.'" Nicole finished. She swiped at her eyes.

Olivia frowned. Tilted her head.

"Wait. You mean she tried to abort me?" Her voice was barely a whisper.

Nicole walked to her and placed her hands on Olivia's arms.

She pulled her to her feet and embraced her. She ran her fingers through her hair and rubbed her back. How could there be any worse news than this to deliver to her precious daughter?

"I know, honey. This was news we weren't expecting either."

Olivia nodded her head.

"I just want to go for a run. I need time to think."

Chapter Forty-Five

Olivia's running shoes crunched on the gravel.

She had to get away.

How could her parents have told her that? But then again, they loved her. They had to tell her. But it was possible they were wrong, right? Maybe it just seemed like the pieces lined up, but it wasn't actually true. Anyway, how could she have been aborted and survived? Was that even possible?

And if it was, that had to be the answer to her missing hand. Olivia shuddered at the thought. Did Bridgett, Bree, even know that her baby had survived? She must not have. Hadn't she told her mom that her pregnancy had been 'taken care of'? And why, oh why, did she wait so long? Couldn't she have waited two more months and had me and then given me up for adoption? God could have still chosen Nicole and Brad for my parents.

Olivia came to the mini mart, crossed the street and turned back.

And then I wouldn't have lived life without a hand. I could have been normal. God never answered all my prayers to restore it. He could have looked so good if miraculously he had regrown my hand. Think of all the glory for Him. But no. Does God even care about me? It sure doesn't feel like it.

Peter waved at her from the mailbox. Olivia slowed to a walk. "No kiss?"

She shook her head. "I need to tell you something."

She relayed what her parents had hit her with.

"Wow. I never saw that coming." He raked his hand through his hair. "How are you holding up?"

"I'm angry. Confused. I don't know."

Olivia leaned her forehead into Peter's chest. He wrapped his arms around her.

"Do you think your mom could be wrong?"

"I don't know. I thought of that. But there are a lot of matching pieces."

"So, wait, is this the same Bree that your mom volunteers with? And she and her kids were at your birthday party, right?"

Olivia nodded and pulled back. "And remember, Frank was going to set up a visit if he could?"

Peter nodded slowly. "That might be a shocker for her. To find out that you're alive."

"I know. But Peter, how could I talk to her now? She tried to kill me!"

Tears sprung to her eyes.

Peter took her hand and began to walk with her to his house. Zip ran to them, his black tail wagging and white border collie face begging to be petted. Olivia absently ran her hand through his face and ears, then stood.

"Maybe it was for this moment that I'm here. I think I want to talk to Bree. I've searched this long and now that I know who she is, I want to have a heart to heart with her. Let her realize what she did. I mean, I'm not out to make her feel guilty, but I want to understand her perspective. Maybe she had a really good reason."

"You're a better person than me. All I want to do is strangle the woman."

"I can't say I hadn't thought of that. I need to get home. My parents are probably having anxiety fits over me."

PETER WASHED his hands and searched his phone for a pizza recipe. His mom used to make it from scratch, and right now he was missing his mom. All this stuff with Olivia and finding her mom was overwhelming. What he wouldn't give to be able to discuss this with her.

He had thought it would be such a great idea to help speed the process along. Hadn't she had the best ending to her story when she found Papa Jack? He had been sure that this search would end well.

Obviously, that was not going to be the case. At least, he couldn't figure a way that it would be. Then again, maybe Bree would be delighted to have found her, to have found out she lived. Maybe over the years she felt guilty and wished she had never done that. He knew there were women who had changed—who had felt guilty afterwards. And frankly, he hoped she would feel guilty.

He read the recipe and poured warm water into a bowl and added a package of yeast and salt. The recipe said to let it sit until it bubbled. He found the bag of flour and checked the fridge for mozzarella and pepperoni. Oh, and sauce.

"Hey son. What are you up to?"

Ross entered the kitchen and looked over his shoulder.

"This isn't exactly your territory. You're more the bowl-of-cold-cereal kind of guy."

"I don't know. I was missing Mom and thought I'd try making pizza like she used to. Want to help?"

"I don't know how good I'll be."

Ross stuck an envelope in his back pocket and washed his hands.

"Measure two cups of flour and pour it into the liquid. You can turn the mixer on low."

Ross frowned and looked at the KitchenAid. He plugged it in and set the knob on low. The beater started clanking around the sides of the bowl.

"Something doesn't sound right. Take a look at this, Peter."

"You must have to line up the holes with the pegs and press it tight. Try this."

The machine started to whirl.

"Dad, I just want to tell you how much I love you. I know I don't say it much, but I truly appreciate you."

"Same."

Peter filled him in on the long sordid details about Olivia and Bree and Nicole and Brad. The whole darn mess.

"Well, now that is a muddled mess. What is she going to do?"

"I think she's going to try to meet her. She wants to talk to her and find out what really happened and motivated her. Dad, she's really hurting right now."

"She may wish she had let this alone."

Peter turned off the mixer and pulled out the dough. He kneaded it a few times and set it on the counter to rise.

"I know. I really miss Mom. I wish she were here to give her insight. She always knew what to say."

"Well, actually, that's why I came in to find you. Will that dough be okay for a while?"

"Yeah, I think so."

"Come on, let's sit."

Ross pulled the sealed envelope from his pocket.

"I was going through Evelyn's desk and found this letter."

He handed it to Peter.

"It's written to you."

Peter traced his finger over his name and looked up. He felt the emotion rise in his chest and slid his finger under the flap.

"I'll let you be. I need to feed the dogs. I'll be back in a bit."

Peter listened as the door clicked shut.

Dear Peter,

I don't know how long I have left to live. This disease is taking its toll on me. But even if I have much more time than I believe, I want to write this now while I still can.

I was so proud of you when you got your RN degree. I know that was a challenge. And I'm so glad you found such good friends to bond with. They are truly remarkable and fun humans.

But I have to admit, I wasn't totally surprised when you quit your job. Med surge takes some patience, precision and informed decision making. And I've gotta say, those aren't always your finest qualities.

Peter looked up and smiled. She had that right.

However, the same qualities it took to be a nurse—compassion, caring, sense of humor—are the same qualities that brought you home to your dad and me. And no matter what you choose to do, I am most proud of the characteristics you possess which you will carry with you wherever you go.

I know you don't want to talk about the end, but after I'm gone, Ross is going to need some looking after. He's got the farm all figured out, but the house has always been my domain. And he's also going to need you as a friend. And don't underestimate his wisdom. Talk to him. Ask him for advice. It will enrich your relationship.

I'm so glad you've come home. God must have known what he was doing. Ha ha.

Now about that young lady. Your dad and I couldn't be more pleased to see you and Olivia together. We've known since you were little that you were made for each other. She's spunky, fun, smart, ingenious, and confident. But she's also tender, and I think she could use your wisdom and support. I'm hoping I'll make it to your wedding, but only God knows the day and the hour. If not, I'll be there in spirit.

I love you, son. You're one of the best things that ever happened to me. Hold on to your faith. And I'll see you on the other side.

Xoxoxo

Mom

The front door closed, and Ross removed his boots and hung up his hat. He looked at Peter who nodded his chin at him. Ross sat down across from him. Peter pinched the bridge of his nose, holding back the tears that had begun to form at the corners of his eyes.

"You okay?"

Peter nodded and scooted the letter towards his dad. Peter excused himself to the bathroom.

He ran water over his face and looked at himself in the mirror. His eyes were puffy, and a lump was forming in his throat again.

"Mom."

It was all he could utter. He wiped his eyes with the back of his hand.

"Thank you. You always knew what I needed."

Peter toweled his face and returned to his dad whose face was visibly moved.

"Well now. That was nice. Real nice."

"I know. I miss her so much."

"Same." Ross patted Peter on the back.

Chapter Forty-Six

Olivia walked into the living room as Nicole held her phone to her ear.

"I'm sorry I ran out on you, Bree. Something you said hit me really hard. I would really like to talk to you. And bring my daughter."Nicole nodded.

"Can we meet at the park? Go for a hike?"

She nodded again. "Tomorrow at ten?"

Nicole raised her eyebrows in question to Olivia.

Olivia nodded slowly.

"Okay, see you then."

Olivia locked eyes with her mom as she pushed end. She wasn't sure who was more nervous—her or her mom. Her mom was motivated by anger. Olivia, by pain and curiosity.

"Should we take anything with us?"

"Like what? Your birth certificate? Pictures?"

Olivia shrugged.

"Yeah, maybe. I think I should bring the DNA results. I mean, that's the clincher, right?" Nicole nodded.

IT WAS perfect weather for shorts and a tank top. A few puffy clouds drifted lazily in the sky. Olivia's body tingled with nerves. But this time, meeting her mom, was way different from meeting Papa Jack. She wasn't sure what she was going to say. But she was sure she wanted to find out the details from Bree's point of view.

Nicole pulled up the parking lot and Olivia locked eyes with her.

"Ready Freddy?"

Olivia's lips turned in a twisted smile. She nodded. Bree was standing, hands on hips as she looked at something on the needle strewn path.

"Hey Bree." She turned and Nicole gave a flat smile.

"Oh, hi." Bree quirked an eyebrow.

Olivia nodded at her. This was one of those moments she knew she'd look back on years from now. And, good or bad, it would be life changing.

As they strolled down the path, Nicole pointed out places and things they had done to fix it up.

Olivia's heart beat like the wings of a hummingbird. It was now or never.

"Bree, I'm pretty sure that you're my bio mom."

Bree glanced her way and frowned.

"What would possess you to think that? I'm pretty sure you're not."

"I just met my bio dad—Jack Murphy. He lives in Colorado Springs. He dated you and you became pregnant when you were in college."

Bree didn't respond.

Olivia pulled the DNA results from her back pocket and showed them to Bree. She stopped and looked at them and shook her head. Then looked up.

"Okay, but this doesn't make sense. I did date Jack—for a few weeks. Then I found out I was pregnant. Our relationship was rocky. I was only eighteen and there was no way I was going to have this baby. I told him I was going to have an abortion, but he resisted. So, I moved to Oregon to get away from him. Anyway, just because your DNA matches his doesn't mean I was the mom. It could easily be some other female."

"But there was a gap of seven months between finding out you were pregnant and actually having the abortion," Nicole said. She crossed her arms.

"How do you know all this?"

"Because Olivia has been researching for months, trying to find you. It would have saved her a lot of grief if she had known you were right here in the vicinity." Her whole body was tense.

Olivia put her hand on Nicole's arm. She had to calm down. How was Olivia ever going to have the conversation she needed to have if her mom was all worked up?

"Okay, you're right. I was three months when I found out. When I got to Oregon, it took a while to find a job and housing and time slipped by. But then I found Planned Parenthood, which was the best thing that could ever have happened to me. They took me in, supported me, lined me up with friends and set an appointment date. And I walked out of there, end of story."

Bree straightened her shoulders, turned and started walking back down the trail.

"Oh, but it wasn't, Bree." Nicole chimed in. "Your baby lived. She survived. And she's standing right here."

Bree turned and looked at Olivia then her eyes traveled down to her arm.

"I suppose you're going to blame me because you don't have a hand."

"Don't you see? I lost it during the abortion procedure," Olivia said.

"Oh, well then. It would have been better if the abortion had been successful. You wouldn't have had to live with a disability."

Nicole's mouth dropped.

"Listen, supposing what you're saying is true, which I still don't believe, I don't really want to develop a relationship with you, if that's what you're thinking. It'll just mess things up with my kids and husband for them to know."

A single tear formed in the corner of Olivia's eye. It spilled over and down her cheek. Her heart was a puddle of confusion.

"I'm sorry about your arm, Olivia, but I did the right thing. It's what I needed to do."

OLIVIA PULLED into their driveway and let Nicole out of the car.

"Mom, I need some space."

Nicole put her hand on Olivia's arm and started to say something but pulled back.

Olivia backed out and sped down the driveway leaving gravel flying in her wake. Her fingers wrapped around the steering wheel like it was a lifeline. She gripped it in desperation, her white knuckles up to her tight shoulder muscles.

She hadn't allowed herself to cry, she was too angry. Why would Bree have chosen to abort her? She was seven and a half months for pity's sake. Woof. Olivia slammed her palm against the steering wheel. And apparently, she didn't even know I lived? God, what in the world are you doing?

She turned onto what they called the highway, which was really just a two-lane road that traveled between Willowbrook and Salem. There wasn't much traffic and she sped well past the 55 mph limit. She didn't see the orchards, small peaches forming, nor the fields of hops. Her eyes blurred and she let the tears fall.

My mom tried to kill me. And I find this out simply because I wanted to find her and thank her? The irony. She remembered Peter telling her this was the chance she had to take—with the possibility that she would be rejected. Guess he was right. Still, it didn't make it any easier. The tears fell fast, and her tongue reached out tasting the saltiness.

She rounded the corner where a slow-moving tractor dawdled.

Her white knuckles pulled the wheel and turned into the oncoming lane where she was met face to face with a freight truck. A violent crunch of metal colliding with metal, a grating noise as the car's body crumpled. Sharp shards of glass shattered and flew through the now empty space, landing on the dash.

"Call an ambulance!"

PETER'S PAGER SOUNDED.

"Medic 104. Priority traffic collision."

Peter ran to his motorcycle and sped to the fire station where he and Vinny shared the cab of the ambulance. They arrived at the scene and Peter choked. That was Olivia's car. No, it couldn't be. It had to just be a car like hers.

He jumped out and ran to the driver's side where the airbag had deployed, where he realized it *was* Olivia who was draped unconscious behind it. Peter held his fingers to her neck. He breathed a sigh of relief when he felt a pulse.

"Olivia, can you hear me?"

He turned and said, "She's out, Vinny. The airbag has deactivated. Bring a gurney."

"Olivia, babe, you're gonna be okay. You have to be okay. I'm here. We'll take care of you."

Peter sounded like a babbling idiot. He had to focus. She was breathing and had a heartbeat. Two good things.

"Vinny let's get her out of here. I think she needs a neck brace."

They strapped on the brace and carefully extracted her, laying her on the gurney. Peter checked her over for other injuries. Lacerations on her face. What appeared to be a broken rib. No apparent bleeding. Hopefully no internal injuries.

Cars ahead, their back lights blurred in the dusk, pulled to the side as the siren wailed and Peter hit the pedal and pulled in front of them. His heartbeat pumped a staccato that prevented him from taking a deep breath. That same dread in his stomach, happening again. Was he too late?

He had to get Olivia to the hospital soon. He couldn't lose her too. He shook the thought from his head. No, this wasn't Mom. This was Olivia. She wasn't going to die. She couldn't die. Not like Mom. It was going to be alright. It had to be.

He pulled under the eaves of the emergency room where they wheeled her in.

Chapter Forty-Seven

Olivia had made it through surgery hours ago, but she was still unconscious. Two broken ribs, internal bleeding, a slight concussion. Nicole and Brad had sat vigil for nearly sixteen hours and now stared vacantly at the wall. The only sound in the room was the steady, reassuring beep of the monitor. Unfinished sandwiches dried out on the forgotten hospital tray.

"I'm going to get some coffee. Can I get you anything?" Peter stood.

They shook their heads. Peter knew they hadn't slept. Their shoulders were bent and eyes red and bleary. He knew exactly how they felt. In fact, he probably looked the same.

Daniel met him in the hall.

"How are you holding up, Peter?"

Daniel led him to the staff room where he poured a cup of strong coffee and handed it to him.

"Your hands are jittery. You look wiped."

Peter lifted his cap and ran his fingers through his hair.

"Olivia and I just got engaged. I can't even imagine life without her."

"She has quite extensive injuries. But bro, she'll survive. She'll do more than survive. She's a fighter."

He put his arm around Peter's shoulders.

"It'll take some time, but you know she's got the best nurses in the state." Daniel smirked.

Peter paced the floor.

"Can you take some cups to her parents? I have somewhere I need to be."

Peter's clipped steps echoed in the vacant corridor where he found himself in the chapel and plopped down in a pew. He leaned back and crossed his arms. How could this be? Nicole had filled him in on their conversation with Bree. Sure, he would expect Olivia to be upset. Who wouldn't be? But why couldn't she have come to him? He would have been there for her. And then this wouldn't have happened. He could have talked her through it.

This was all his fault. He should never have started with the Search Angel. *I'm such a failure, God. First my part in the fire. Now this.* His mind was all afuddle. The anxiety, the grief, the worry had his insides crawling all over. He closed his eyes.

It had been twenty-four hours since he found her at the accident. So much blood. The panic. So much yelling that had come out his own mouth. The slow motion.

Only twenty-five hours ago he thought his life was coming around. He had started to see a future. One with a bride. And now? He placed his hands on either side of his head. God, where are you?

OLIVIA HEARD FAINT VOICES. She tried to open her eyes, but they fluttered shut. Was that her mom? A soft hand was cupped around her own.

"Olivia? It's Mom and Dad."

She turned her head towards the voice and blinked. Why was it so hard to keep her eyes open? For a moment she drifted back to dreamland. More like a nightmare. Sounds of crunching, shattering glass. Why couldn't she wake up?

"Olivia?"

She worked her eyelids up and tried to turn her body, but a dull pain overtook her.

Blinking, she whispered, "W-where am I?"

Her voice was scratchy. She couldn't lift her arms—they were so heavy. And what was that pain in her chest? What was wrong?

"You're in Mercy hospital, honey."

Her dad hovered over her.

"We've been waiting for you to wake up from your surgery."

"You were in an accident," her mom said.

Nicole rubbed her thumb over Olivia's hand.

An accident. The tractor. The oncoming freight truck. The crash and splintered windshield.

"Peter was at the scene."

Olivia gave a slight nod of understanding.

"Where is he?" Her voice was thick, and her tongue swollen. Her eyes roamed the room.

PETER STARTED. Orange and purple shadows fell over his feet, the sun making its way through the stained glass. He must have fallen asleep. Must have relaxed enough to give up—not just his physical self. But his heart. Unclenching the stranglehold, the unthinkable agony that he might lose her too. He saw himself holding his hand out towards Jesus. Peter had opened his fist, the same one he shook at God not so long ago., felt the anger, the heartbreak, his fear, slip through his fingers like cleansing water. And in its place, there was peace.

OLIVIA DIDN'T KNOW how many days she'd been laying in that hospital bed. There was no doubt she felt better. She could actually slide out of bed and take slow steps to the bathroom by herself. One day at a time.

She studied her mom for a moment—this mom who had taken her in as her own. She, a girl with only one hand. Rejected by the one who conceived her and carried her in her womb.

God knew. He knew that what was meant for evil would turn to good.

"Mom. I love you."

"I love you too sweetheart. So very, very much."

"I want to talk about Bree. Is that okay?"

"Yes, of course."

Nicole set her knitting down.

"I was so angry. And hurt. I only wanted to tell her thank you for giving me life. For not aborting me. And then, I find out what really happened. I had a paradigm shift in my thinking. From thankful to astounded. I hated her, Mom. How could she have done that?"

"Olivia, what you went through? A billion emotions. Anger. Sadness. Grief. I know. Your dad and I felt all of them too. It's okay. We're human. And we're allowed to be weak. I was reading about something called prenatal trauma. Your heart and mind take on the abuse you suffered and can just now came to light. And there's no manual for how to navigate it."

Olivia took this in. "Maybe this was how God made a way for me to be in your lives. I mean, you prayed for a child for many years, right? And he's a big God. I guess he can orchestrate situations to answer prayers. And he knew the desires of your heart. And he must have known what the desires of my heart would be."

She was beginning to understand that this God, the one who had known her since before she was born, had really seen her all along.

Nicole leaned back into her chair. "Sometimes we have to listen to the stories we tell ourselves. For a long time, I thought God didn't love me because I couldn't carry a child. That I wasn't good enough to be a mom. That others were better than me. Fulfilled. And then I would look around and see women who got pregnant and didn't want their babies. Didn't have time for them in their careers. Were too busy. Too poor. I don't know, too selfish maybe. And then I found you and that hole in my heart was filled. It took a long time, but I finally understood that the one I thought didn't care, was the one who I needed to find my identity in. It wasn't in whether or not I could carry a baby. It was purely about knowing and believing what God says about me."

Nicole ran her hand through Olivia's hair. "Did you know he sings over us?" She laughed.

Olivia smiled. "I guess I told myself that I couldn't be whole until I knew my roots. There was a mom of my imagination out there who gave me up because she loved me and thought that was the best thing for her and for me. I thought that she just thought someone else could parent me better than her. And then I imagined throughout the years, she would have thought about me every year when my birthday came around and wondered about me. I even thought that if I found her, she would welcome me into her heart and be really happy. The truth is that it was really a horror story."

Nicole reached for her hand. "I hope you've never doubted that you were wanted. We loved you from the moment we first saw you. This is *your* story. Yours is the story that counts."

Olivia let the tears come, let them fall, spilling down her cheeks and onto her lap. Tears cleansing her heart. She let go of her hurt, saw God grabbing it and laying it onto his own heart. She opened her hands and let go of Bree where she saw God embrace Bree and hold her to his heart. Saw God smile down on her and Peter. On Brad and Nicole.

Nicole handed her a tissue. Olivia blew and took hiccuping breaths. She looked at Nicole and nodded her head. Nicole smiled. And Olivia smiled. Laughter bubbled up from her soul and spilled over the room.

Chapter Forty-Eight

P eter and Olivia hopped onto the kitchen counter and surveyed what they had accomplished in the past month. Through the dining room window, the outbuilding stood that would be turned into her veterinarian clinic. There would be no lack of patients—the beauty of living around farms. And though she had passed her exams and received her license, she was sure every day would be a learning experience. She still had her internship where she would still be under the tutelage of Dr. Hunter, there to check in and answer any questions. And Peter would be her left-hand man—a natural fit with his nursing skills. There was a lot of work to be done before they could practice, but the building bones were there, and meanwhile, she could build her dream alongside the man she loved.

Peter had helped rip up the filthy shag carpet and padding of the living room and pried the staples one by one with pliers. They rejoiced when they found hardwood floors beneath the carpet. Sanding had been a chore, but now that they had finished the floors with Varathane, they were stunning.

They had chosen different colors for each wall—burnt orange, lime green, teal and red. Then they stained wood slats and attached them to the orange wall, allowing the orange to peek through. Just having one room done made them smile.

"I think your mom would have loved this. She liked to be surrounded by color."

Peter nodded. "That reminds me. I have something to show you."

He pulled a letter from his back pocket and handed it to Olivia.

"Dad found it in Mom's office."

She began to read, and tears formed. She slipped her fingers through his and squeezed them. The letter slipped to her lap, and she turned to him.

"Peter."

Words wouldn't come and she leaned her head into his shoulder where he wrapped her in warmth.

"This is so beautiful."

Olivia could see Evelyn's bright eyes and the twinkle she had as she put words on the page. The same eyes as her son's.

"She knew you so well. It feels like she's right here with us. It must be healing to you."

Peter nodded. "I feel an odd peace—like Mom being in heaven was where she was supposed to be."

He kissed Olivia on the small residual scar on her cheek.

"And finally, I know that I know I'm free."

"That makes two of us!"

Olivia couldn't love him more.

TINA ADJUSTED a white magnolia comb into Olivia's chignon after Nicole had finished engaging the myriads of covered buttons of her wedding dress. Kaitlyn's daughter Claire twirled in her flower girl dress feeling like a princess from a Disney movie. And Tina and Nate's newly adopted son, Brody, who had become Claire's new best friend, would be the ring bearer.

"Ready?" Nicole looked her up and down, checking every detail.

Olivia laughed. "100%" Was she ever. She had never been happier.

She had found a man who loved her entirely for who she was. Who wasn't ashamed to be seen with a girl with a limb difference. Who embraced the challenges and gifts it brought.

Life was complicated. But that's what made it interesting. And who would she rather spend her future with besides her best friend who had known her since forever? She looked up. Yes, she was known and loved through and through and she was beginning to understand how all things could work together for good. No doubt there would be other bumps along the road, but she knew she and Peter would navigate them together and come out better at the end. A cord of three could never be broken.

Review

Reviews are so important
for authors.
They help others decide to buy this book.

Would you be so kind as to write one for me?

Acknowledgments

Before I began thinking about what Peter Gunderson's story would be for book three in the Mercy series, I first knew what his girlfriend's story was.

When I was in college, I thought I had fallen in love with a guy. He was beautiful. Blonde curly hair, blue eyes. We both worked at an amusement park and he'd come by my food booth each day and buy a grape soda.

Then one day, he brought me a bouquet of flowers and I was totally smitten. It didn't take long before I became pregnant. And before I realized that fact he had moved back to Chicago.

When I called on the pay phone to tell him the news, he refused to believe it was his kid.

Fast forward five years. I met Dick and Nancy Magathan and played a small part in their fertility walk. They adopted a baby girl, Amy, who they later found had some physical challenges.

Years later, as an adult, Amy asked about finding her bio mom so that she could tell her thank you for having her.

Her true story is what motivated The Way to My Heart.

I could not have written this without her input and for that I am eternally grateful.

I would also like to thank Angie Clayton and Jackie Baker for sharing their experiences with me—Angie's as an adopted child who met her bio mom, and Jackie who chose to allow others to parent her two daughters. Their perspectives were essential to my understanding.

Afterword

Dear Readers,

I was honored when Jan reached out to me when she was in the beginning processes of writing this book for ideas and for my input. I am equally as honored to write this afterword for *The Way to My Heart*. Thank you Jan, for this opportunity to share some of my truths about the topic of abortion for you readers. So glad you are here!

You see, like Olivia, I am an abortion survivor. That is a term I think is hard for many to understand; but it is something that happens more often than the general public realizes. The United States does not do a good job of tracking abortion survival rates (babies that survive when their birth mother's abortion procedure fails). In fact, there are only a handful of states in our nation that keeps track of babies who survive. Canada does track this information. Based on correlated data from Canada; the lack of effective failed abortion reporting requirements in the United States caused an average overlook of approximately 1,734 born-alive abortions every year (Shamo, A. (2022, n.d). *Estimated Number of Born-*

Alive Abortion Survivors Extrapolated Canadian Data. abortion-suvrviorsnetwork.org). Some of those survivors live only for a few seconds, a few hours, and some like me; are blessed to thrive. I now feel led to share my story with others so that the truth of the impact of abortion can be known. Abortion impacts not only survivors like myself but it impacts mothers, fathers, siblings, aunts, uncles, cousins, and grandparents. Abortion impacts generations.

I didn't always know about my birth beginnings. A handful of years ago, I, like Olivia, wanted to find my birth mother and father. I am so blessed to have had the opportunity to be adopted to a loving husband and wife who desperately wanted a child of their own but couldn't when I was only a month old. My mom and dad are simply the best (and they are good friends of Jan and her family). My journey to discover my birth story and some time later, bio parents/relatives has been one that has taken me up, down, and all around as far as feelings and emotions are concerned. I spent some time in shock, followed by grief, shame, and disbelief. I thought I was the only one. My (adoptive) mom and dad have also shared a mix of emotions with this process right along with me.

Thankfully, through this process I also connected with the Abortion Survivors Network. The CEO, Melissa is a good friend of mine and also a survivor. Last time I checked this network has connected with over 750 survivors of abortions worldwide. Being able to walk through this journey alongside others with stories similar to my own has been life changing for me. Reaching out to my bio mother and father has led to some openings of doors and closing of others. I have a tremendous amount of respect and empathy for how my birth parents think and feel about abortion. I have been fortunate to be in contact with my birth mother and I see her as an incredibly brave individual. I'm thankful for her and I pray for her and my birth father often. I have forgiven them which has grown my heart and my faith in ways I can't express properly on paper. I'm hoping that my start to communicate with them will grow into something that is healing all the way around.

I'm so glad you chose to read *The Way to My Heart* and I hope and pray it inspires you to do your own research about the abortion industry and the thousands and thousands of others out there just like Olivia and I. I really hadn't paid attention to this topic or knew much about abortion before it was providentially placed in my path. Now I consider it an honor to speak for the millions of babies who lost their lives to abortion and could not speak for themselves. I also speak up for their mothers, fathers, and families and *anyone* who has been impacted by abortion.

Your stories matter.

Sincerely,
    Amy Miles

P.S. Discover more about abortion survivors and their families on Abortion Survivor's Network's website: abortionsurvivors.org

Nuns with Guns

A holiday caper

An encounter ensues when a man wearing bunny slippers steals the van from the Sisters of Mercy, thrusting them into pandemonium with a group of ex-cons.

Chapter 1

The only thought invading his head the week Bernardo was released from his two-year stint in the clink, was to see his daughter Amelia. She had been three when he was convicted of stealing an assault rifle from an FBI car. He remembered those irresistible dimples he liked to kiss, and the smell of her soft curly brown hair that he combed after her bath.

His wife wasn't too happy about his jail time and didn't come to visit him or let him see their daughter. Not that he blamed her. Marie hadn't met him outside when he was released, and he wasn't looking forward to seeing her reaction to him showing up at their door. Maybe he'd be able to convince her that he'd changed. And he had, hadn't he? He had gone through counseling and was going to start fresh. Get a job. A real job with a real paycheck. Be able to support Marie and their daughter. He could do this. She was a good woman and deserved his best.

He knocked on the door and was surprised to hear little footsteps and then laid eyes on his daughter. She stopped still and looked up at him, expressionless. Her deep dark chocolate eyes stared at him; her curly hair pulled into a long pony. She looked just like her mama. Marie came up behind her, wrapped her arm protectively around Amelia's waist and pulled her in.

"What are *you* doing here?" Marie's eyes narrowed.

"I'm out. I wanted to see you and Amelia."

Marie rolled her deep brown eyes, the same ones he used to gaze into before...

"Two excruciating years without a word and now you want to waltz in here and disrupt our lives? I don't think that's a good idea." She released Amelia. "Go sit on the couch and finish watching your show, baby."

"I just want to talk to you. I don't expect you to welcome me, but could you just hear me out?"

Marie reluctantly moved aside and motioned her head to the kitchen table. The room was spotless. Dishes were put away and the table was wiped. The floor was swept, and the shine reflected the overhead light.

"You never came to visit me." Bernardo's shoulders slumped.

"I thought it would be better for Amelia not to see the inside of a jail."

"But *you* could have come."

She shook her head. She set the kettle on the stove and turned up the gas.

"Listen, I'm sorry. What I did was really stupid. But that was two years ago. I've changed. I'm not the same man."

"And how am I supposed to know that? You're gonna have to build some trust here, you know."

"I know." He started to reach for her hand, and she pulled it away.

"Tell me about Amelia. Is she in school?"

"Yeah. Kindergarten."

"Does she like her teacher? Does she have friends?"

"She does." The tea kettle whistled, and she shut off the gas. "Tea?"

"Sure."

"You still like that licorice flavor?" She opened a drawer with several boxes in it.

"You remember that?" He watched her pour the water over the bag and hand him the cup, the one that said *I love my dad*. His eyes grew misty.

"Babe, I'd do anything to repair the damage I've caused. Leaving you a single mom and not helping with the bills." He lowered his head.

She set the tea before him. He wrapped his hands around the mug and let the fragrant steam warm his face. He wished the steam could melt the ice between them.

"Bernardo, there's something you need to know. Amelia has a medical condition. The doctors performed extensive tests. She needs expensive medication that I can't afford, and state health insurance isn't going to cover it." A tear slipped down her cheek. "She's gonna die, Bernardo."

That had been two weeks ago. Marie had allowed him to spend some time with Amelia. He'd spent a day with her at school, took her for ice cream, and a movie—not all on one day. She wore out easily. Marie hadn't been ready to let him move back in, so he'd resorted to couch hopping. Not ideal, but better than living in his jeep, or worse yet, sleeping on the sidewalk.

Joey Lagratto swiped a hand down his tattooed face, his eyes closed, and let it rest there as he whooshed a long breath. Getting caught was one of the risks of pulling a heist. He just had to figure out the next step. He reached for his phone and tapped in a few numbers.

"Bernardo, I need you to take care of an item for me while we're out of commission. Meet me at four."

"What's in it for me?"

"Don't worry, you'll get your fair share." Bernardo's shoulders tensed. He didn't like being in a position to let Joey get the upper hand. But for now, he felt like he had no choice. He'd been couch surfing at his house more than anywhere else along with the five others who had been in jail with Joey. There was always a price to pay.

Bernardo nervously tossed a Rubik's cube up and down. He slid into his navy green jeep, the paint faded and worn through to the base and coughed the engine to life, leaving a trail of exhaust fumes in its wake. Weaving between cars on the D.C. highway, he thought of how his reward would be enough to get him on his feet. No more couch hopping. Or digging in the garbage cans for his next meal. His hands tightened on the steering wheel.

A glance at the mirror showed someone tailing him. He tested it out, turning at the next exit and into an old neighborhood, swerving into the left lane, and passing a semi-truck. No doubt about it—he was being pursued.

Bernardo parked the jeep in a one-way alley and jumped out. He slid the Rubik's cube into his sweatshirt pocket and exited the other side. He walked nonchalantly along the sidewalk wearing the bunny slippers he had run out of the house with. He slid a glance back. No one was going to keep him from this job. It had to end in success. He had to save his daughter.

About the Author

Jan Johnson has been writing since fourth grade when she wrote and her dad published The Little Red Man, a space story. That was back in the day when we were all sure aliens lived on Mars.

Jan lives on a sheep farm in Brownsmead, Oregon a mile from the Columbia River with her husband Ed. Don't mistake living on a farm as meaning she likes animals. Well, she actually does—from a distance.

She's passionate about building relationships, meeting new people and hearing their stories. You know what they say—Love God, Love People.

When she isn't writing, starting something new, or podcasting, she catches up with her ten children who are scattered hither and yon.

Connect with her at jan-johnson.com where you'll find links to her books and can listen to both podcasts—Women of the Northwest and Just Talkin' About Jesus

Amazon for all books

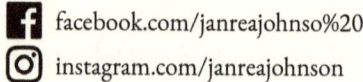
facebook.com/janreajohnso%20

instagram.com/janreajohnson